Halvar let the boy go.

He started again for the Rabat, mulling over what he had learned in his conversation with Devallon. He was certain Milord Henry Summersby was connected with the smuggled muskets somehow. If only he could prove it! Then he could arrest this so-called milord… He bent forward, trying to ease the effects of the biting wind that blew across the island.

"Capitán! Capitán!"

His head jerked up as a sharp cry brought him out of his thoughts.

"There's trouble in the souk!" Musa, one of the guardsmen who had accompanied him to the Yehudit quarter, grabbed his arm.

"What now?" Halvar grumbled as he followed the guardsman across the Broad Way, past the posts that marked the boundaries of the souk and into the tangled maze of stalls and stands.

A crowd had gathered in front of Yussif the Tailor's shop. Halvat shoved through to the center of the action.

On the ground in front of the tailor's shop lay the body of a Town Guardsman; Halvar guessed at his identity by the size and shape of him. Guardsman Zoltan had not heeded the warnings, and had come to a violent end.

Also By Roberta Rogow

Murders In Manatas
Mischief In Manatas
Mayhem In Manatas
Menace In Manatas
Malice In Manatas

MADNESS IN MANATAS

The Saga Of Halvar
The Hireling
Book 6

Roberta Rogow

ZUMAYA OTHERWORLDS   AUSTIN TX

2018

MADNESS IN MANATAS

© 2018 by Roberta Rogow

ISBN 978-1-61271-386-1

Cover art and design © William Neagle

"Zumaya Otherworlds" and the griffon colophon are trademarks of Zumaya Publications LLC, Austin TX, http://www.zumayapublications.com

Library Of Congress Cataloging-In-Publication Data

Names: Rogow, Roberta, 1942- author.
Title: Madness in Manatas / Roberta Rogow.
Description: Austin, TX : Zumaya Otherworlds, 2018. | Series: The saga of
 Halvar the Hireling ; book 6
Identifiers: LCCN 2018013972| ISBN 9781612713861 (trade paperback : alk.
    paper) | ISBN 9781612713878 (Kindle) | ISBN 9781612713885 (epub)
Subjects: | GSAFD: Alternative histories (Fiction) | Mystery fiction.
Classification: LCC PS3568.O492 M33 2018 | DDC 813/.54--dc23
LC record available at https://lccn.loc.gov/2018013972

To

Debby Buchanan

and

Eileen Watkins

My Sisters In Crime

Acknowledging...

Lynn Holdom and Rachel Kadushin were present when I first invented the world of Manatas.

Liz Burton has stuck by me and encouraged me to continue to write the Saga of Halvar the Hireling.

Thanks to Debby Buchanan, who read the manuscript and made suggestions for improving the story, and Eileen Watkins, who insisted that I give the horse a name..

And thanks to the many people who gave me nuggets of information that found their way into this story.

Manatas Town
And Environs

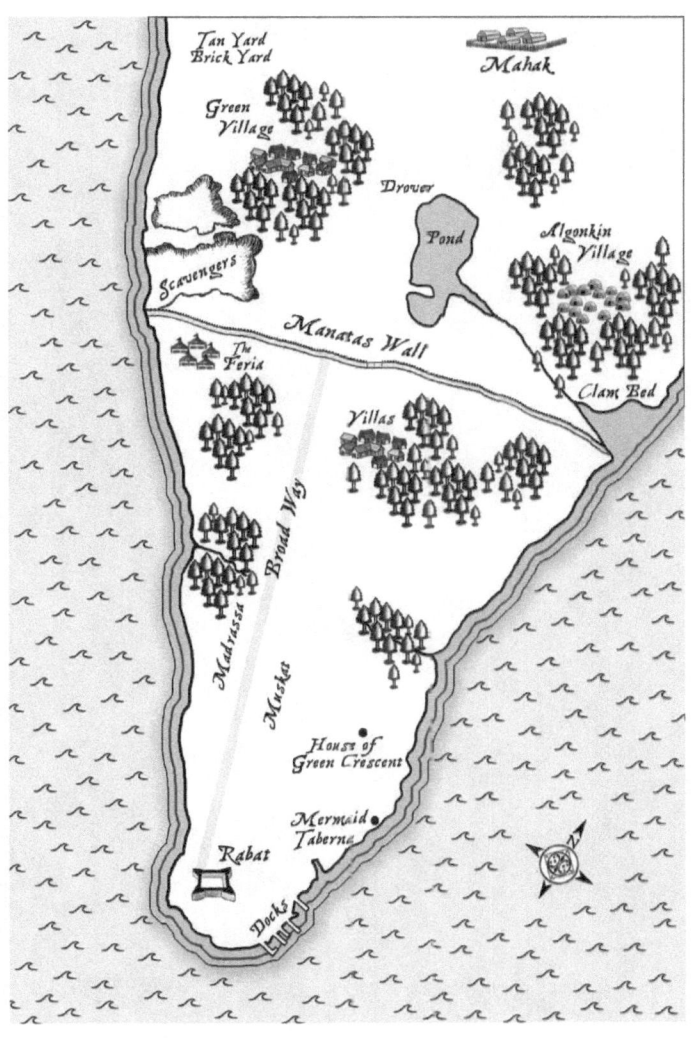

Tan Yard
Brick Yard

Mahak

Green
Village

Drover

Pond

Algonkin
Village

Scavengers

Manatas Wall

Clam Bed

The
Feria

Villas

Broad Way

Madrassa

Mustra

House of
Green Crescent

Mermaid
Taberna

Rabat

Docks

Chapter 1

HALVAR DID NOT WANT ANY MORE EXCITEMENT.
He'd had a whole week of it, and he was ready to be bored.

Instead of rejoicing at Yule, thanking Thor and the All-Father for returning the sun to the Earth, he had been dealing with the death of Captain Franz Girard. He had faced down fierce beggars, battled enraged chickens, and fought a duel on the docks. He had watched helplessly as the ship *Belle Fleur* was wrecked on the rocks across the bay.

Then came the death of the messenger boy Snake, and the complications that arose when muskets were found in the ballast of the wrecked ship. When he should have been praising the Redeemer and Mother Mara in chapel, he had spent Nativity Day chasing up and down Manatas Island—dealing with fanatic Purist Kristos in Green Village, devious Afrikans in Manatas Town, and a furious wild cat in the hills north of the settlement. Two more deaths, two more bodies, and still no answers!

1

And, as an added distraction, there was the matter of the poisoned professor at the Manatas Madrassa, which might (or might not) have been linked to the musket-smuggling, since the confessed killer was an alchemist known for his experiments with gunpowder.

Finally, just to make his life complete, Halvar had to cope with Milord Henry Summersby and his servant, Edgar Norris, who had taken over a cottage on Pearl Street, in the very shadow of the Rabat, along with Andres Devallon the ex-musketman, an unwelcome reminder of Halvar's early life as a mercenary in Oropa. Milady Summersby and her foul-mouthed companion had tried to get away from Manatas; but Dame Brigitte had fallen into the bay, and Milady was stranded on the Long Island when the ship foundered on the rocks.

All this in the space of ten days!

He had had enough! This morning he sat at the table in his small office at the Rabat. The stone fortress dominated the southern tip of the island between two rivers—the Great River flowing north, and the East Channel that separated the island called Manatas from the Long Island to the east. There were times when the closeness of the walls, and the dim light provided by the high window and the two lanterns oppressed him. Even so, he reveled in its coziness, the way the brazier in the corner let off just enough heat so he could undo the frogs that held his green wool coat closed against the winter chill.

He shifted in his wooden chair and stretched his long legs under the table, trying to find a comfortable position, one that would ease the pain in his shoulder where a stray bullet had nicked him. He still wasn't sure who had shot at him, and whether it had been deliberate or if the shooter had been aiming at the mountain cat ravaging the settlement. Halvar had killed the cat the following day, to the acclaim of onlookers, but his shoulder still hurt.

He yawned mightily, and tried to focus on the reports being read aloud by his self-appointed adjutant, the willful daughter of Sultan Petrus. Salomey preferred to be called Selim, just as she preferred the padded jacket and trousers of a young man to the filmy skirts and veils considered suitable dress for a marriageable Islim girl. She had assumed the post of Halvar's amanuensis, taking notes on his observations and organizing his meetings, and would not be deflected from this office, no matter what her father said, or for that matter, what Halvar wanted.

She continued to read aloud from the papers collected on his desk over the past week.

"Item: The butcher Gavril wants payment for the sausages consumed by the dog during the fight in the souk yesterday."

"I thought we did that."

"Gavril says five white wumpum wasn't enough."

"Let him take it to the sultan at the next Grand Divan," Halvar groused.

"This is the sort of thing Tenente Gomez used to handle," Selim pointed out.

"Tenente Gomez did a lot of things he wasn't supposed to do." He *was making himself the ruler of Manatas in the stead of the sultan appointed by the calif,* Halvar added silently. *He killed at least one innocent that I know of, and very nearly killed me!*

"He said he was taking the burden from my father," Selim said.

"And how would he have taken care of the butcher? Paid him off?"

"Oh, the butcher wouldn't have bothered to ask for payment, because if he had, the Guards would have made sure he didn't get any business at all."

"What else is there?" Halvar grimaced at the papers neatly piled on the table, all written in characters completely beyond his reading ability. He could barely make sense of the angular characters of Rune. The curves of Ogham and swirls of Arabi baffled him.

"A letter from Rav Nahum, from the madrassa, about detaining one of their learned colleagues on a charge of murder. The Yehudit want him to be released, since the Rabat is no place for an esteemed teacher of alchemy."

"Albrecht LaPierre, the esteemed teacher of alchemy, gave one of the other esteemed teachers a cake he knew could poison him. That makes him a murderer, in my eyes. He stays where he is. What's next?"

Selim picked up another paper. "Rav Shimon Layzar regrets to inform the Capitán that one of his guardsmen has been making improper advances to Yehudit women shopping in the souk, and begs that he will restrain this guardsman from such offensive behavior. Tenente Flores told you it was a bad idea to take Zoltan and Fergus off the waterfront and put them into the souk."

"Zoltan was taking bribes from the women on Maiden Lane and their, um, protectors," Halvar said. "He was even running a few of them himself. It sets a bad example. The Town Guard should be honest, brave, trustworthy."

"Whereas Zoltan is large and strong, but not very trustworthy." Selim frowned at him, her heavy eyebrows nearly meeting over her nose. "You don't look well, Capitán. You should get some rest."

"So say all my physicians." Halvar grinned ruefully. Dr. Moise, the official surgeon of the Manatas Town Guard, had dressed his shoulder with a combination of salves from his store of medications. Eva Hakim, the nizim of the Sisters of Fatima, had told him to spend a day in complete repose to allow his humors to balance. Frater Iosip, the apothecary at the Green Village Fratery, had recommended bed rest after his fight with the mountain cat. "I tried last night. I went to my quarters…"

"But…?" Selim's heavy eyebrows rose above her snub nose in silent question.

"I had to deal with…a situation. Milady Summersby was waiting at the taberna."

"Oh." Selim packed a world of meaning into one syllable. "How did she get off the Long Island?"

"I suppose she bribed someone to sail or row her across the bay. She's here on Manatas Island again, and she's not happy about it." He closed his eyes, recalling the evening's activities.

Devallon had joined him as he headed for his quarters at the Mermaid Taberna. intent on having a simple meal, a game of tables, and a long night's rest in his very own, very large, very comfortable bed.

Instead, they had been accosted in front of the taberna by Milady Summersby. As soon as she saw them, Charlotte had launched into shrill recriminations in Franchen, translated into Franchen-accented Erse by Devallon.

They had taken her into the taberna, where the host, Hannes Zilberstam, made it clear the only woman welcome in his establishment was the Danic cook, Fru Marta, and she remained in the kitchen. He sneered at Milady Summersby, and announced loudly that if she wanted to find shelter, she could go to one of the hostels on Maiden Lane.

Halvar had consumed his gobbler-giblet soup and stale bread with Charlotte on one side and Devallon on the other, each demanding his attention, trying to outdo each other in volume. As far as he could tell, Charlotte needed somewhere to stay, and Devallon wasn't sure where he could put her. The lodgings for whores on Maiden Lane were clearly unacceptable for Milady Summersby, who claimed she was now a respectable married woman, no matter what she had done in the past. On the other hand, the cottage on Pearl Street where Milord Summersby had taken residence was full with men, with no room for Milady.

Selim's voice brought him out of his reverie.

5

"What did you do about the Franchen woman?"

"Fru Marta, the cook at the Mermaid Taberna, took her in. She's got the cottage on Pearl Street next to the one Milord and Edgar are using. Her daughter's the girl who milks the goat and collects the eggs from the chickens in the yard across from the cottages. "

Selim sniggered. "At least she'll get fresh cheese and baked eggs."

Halvar stretched again. "Is that the end of it?"

A bang on the door ended the session. A guardsman poked his head in.

"Someone from Green Village to see you, Capitán!"

The guardsman was shoved aside by a lanky youngster incongruously clad in the green coat of the Manatas Town Guard, worn over the multi-colored trews favored by Bretains.

"Capitán Don Alvaro! Message from Tenente Donal. They've found the body of Ned the Cooper. He's dead, and Frater Iosip says it's murder."

Chapter 2

HALVAR STIFLED THE IMPULSE TO SNARL AT THE eager youngster. Ordinarily, he would have bounded out of the Rabat, eager to get away from the confinement of the office. Not today. He eyed the messenger and asked, "Who is this Ned Cooper, and why should anyone want to kill him? And why am I supposed to run to Green Village to look at him?"

The young man stood straight, at attention, and stared somewhere over Halvar's head.

"Tenente Donal told me to remind the Capitán Don Alvaro Dánico that all such deaths are to be referred to the Capitán. By his own orders."

"True enough," Halvar groaned. "I don't supposed Tenente Donal is mistaken? That this Ned died naturally?"

"He didn't," the constable said firmly. "And Tenente Donal insisted that you come, in person, to look at him, before they take him to the fratery to be made ready for burial."

Selim added, "After the fuss you made about the messenger boy being moved, if this man Ned *was* killed, you really ought to go and look at him."

The constable grinned gratefully at her, then snapped back to attention.

"Tenente Donal told me to say that he has already summoned Frater Iosip and Frater Leonidas from the fratery to examine the body, so you don't have to bother Dr. Moise to come."

Halvar lifted himself from his chair with some effort.

"Very well, Constable..."

"Bertram." The youngster salaamed clumsily. "They also call me Bouncer, because I bounce the drunkards out of the Gardens of Paradise."

"Constable Bertram, go to the gate and summon Avaram the Donkey-man. We'll need a cart to take us to Green Village. Selim, bring your notebook and pen-case. Let's get this done."

Bertram bolted from the room. Halvar fastened the frogs on his coat, adjusted his fur cap, and prepared to face the freezing wind that swept across the tip of Manatas Island from the cliffs across the Great River to the Long Island on the other side of the bay.

The cold air hit him like a fist in the face when he opened the door to the courtyard, after the warmth of the office. He braced himself against the wind and nearly ran into the bulky person coming in.

"Capitán!" The Andalusian guardsman Flores, whose scarred face and crushed nose belied his fragrant name, stepped aside, to let Halvar pass. "You're going somewhere?"

"They've found another body," Halvar explained. "Tenente Donal's sent for me to go to Green Village."

"That's too bad, but I've just come from the sultan's rooms. He wants to see you."

8

Halvar hesitated. This was a breach of chain of command. Usually, Sultan Petrus gave *him* the orders to be directed to his underlings, not the other way around.

"Tell him I'm called away to Green Village. One of the Bretains has been murdered."

"Which one?" Flores looked almost cheerful at the news.

"Someone called Ned the Cooper."

"That one? A judgment upon an infidel, preaching against the Prophet's Word!" Flores spat on the cobbles.

"That is not for us to decide... not yet," Halvar warned him. "And Tenente Flores, a word in your ear. Tell Zoltan to keep his tongue in his head, and his hands on his cudgel, not on Islim or Yehudit women doing their daily business in the souk."

"I've already told him, but Zoltan is Zoltan, and it was your orders, not mine, put him in the souk," Flores said.

"Tenente, you are his commanding officer, and you are responsible for seeing that he behaves himself. And I want a muster, all the men who are on duty, this afternoon between mid-afternoon and evening prayers. Drill, with halberd! Here in the courtyard."

"In this perishing cold?" Flores's scowl deepened into a frown. "The men won't like that."

"They'll like it even less if one of those rascally Scavengers gets near them with a knife," Halvar retorted. "Tenente, you have your orders!"

Flores salaamed and stamped away, muttering angrily in Arabi.

Halvar gritted his teeth and reminded himself these people lived far from the tightly regulated towns of Al-Andalus. Donal had acted as keeper of the peace in Green Village, more or less on his own, and Flores had been a mere guardsman until chance and the elimination of two seniors had elevated him to his present rank. Both were used to

9

going their own way, doing what they thought needed to be done without notifying Sultan Petrus.. Not for the first time, Halvar wished that Old Sergeant Olaf were alive to take these rebellious soldiers in hand, as he had once done with a certain Danic recruit so many years ago.

A cry from the Rabat gate brought him back to reality. Constable Bertram called "Donkey cart's here!"

Avaram had attached a yellow banner to the back of his cart to indicate he was now on official duty for the Manatas Town Guard. Halvar, Selim, and Bertram climbed on board, and the donkey jogged off northward on the Broad Way.

The cold wind had sent most of the usual passers-by indoors. There were no vendors on the street hawking small trinkets or pamphlets opposite the rambling buildings of the Manatas Madrassa. Students were either at their classes or huddled inside the mokka-shops that catered to them. With most of the holy days done, merchants were safely in their offices, adding profits and losses for the past year and calculating how much they would make or lose in the next one. The Spring Feria was three months away, but it was not too soon to start making arrangements for the next crop of kutton and tabac from the south.

Halvar turned to Bertram.

"Tell me about this Ned Cooper. Who was he, and why would anyone want to kill him?"

"He was one of the Pure Sect," Bertram replied. "You may have seen him with Andrew MacAlan, when he tried to stop people from going to the festivities at the Gardens of Paradise on the Watch-night of Nativity.."

"The big fellow next to MacAlan?"

"One of them. The other was Angus MacKay, the cloth merchant from Bos-Town. MacAlan and MacKay were staying with Ned at the cooperage, along with Angus's son, Seth, and the trapper Kevin MacFergus."

"And none of these people noticed their host was missing all night?"

"I can't say, Capitán. Tenente Donal sent me to fetch you when I got finished cleaning out the taproom at the Gardens of Paradise."

Halvar grunted, partly from the twinges in his shoulder as the cart jolted along, partly at the confirmation of his suspicion that Donal's men were largely recruited from his team of bully-boys who kept order at Manatas's chief center of entertainment.

"Was it Ned the Purist who got in the way of the good folk trying to enter the fratery chapel on Nativity Watchnight, too? Just how fervent was this cooper?"

"Very," Bertram said as the cart approached the wall and the gate that set Manatas Town apart from the rest of the island. "He'd stand in the middle of the common green and call out verses from the Holy Book. He'd rail against the Gardens of Paradise, said it was a hotbed of sin and vice."

"And it is!" Selim agreed, with a grin. "I hear they allow women to eat and drink there, with their menfolk, and there are women performers who sing aloud, and tell bawdy tales."

"And they dance in scanty clothing, and there is hemp as well as alcohol." Halvar added, recalling the pleasures offered on his past visits to the Gardens of Paradise. "And gambling and, um, other activities." He glanced at Selim, and hoped the girl did not understand quite what that entailed. "But Mullah Abadul preaches against the same vices, and no one has stuck a knife into him."

Not yet! he added to himself.

"Ned would get fits when the Spirit of the Lord God moved him," Bertram went on. "He'd yell out that we were all doomed to Sheol, that the Pit yawned beneath our feet..."

"I'd yawn, too, if I had to listen to a lot of that jabber," Selim sniped.

"But it still doesn't merit a knife in the back," Bertram retorted.

"Is that how he died?" Halvar asked.

"So I heard Frater Iosip say."

Avaram guided the donkey across the field where, in a few months, the Spring Feria would be set up. Now it was barren, only patches of stubble remaining, with a flock of geese pecking and squabbling here and there. They scattered as the cart went through common ground, hissing and flapping their wings in outrage at being disturbed in their search for food. The donkey protested loudly, the geese squawked back; but the cart proceeded unimpeded across the field towards the cluster of houses on the other side.

They crossed a little stream, now frozen over, and plodded along the path around the common ground past the three-story building surrounded by an iron fence that dominated the settlement. The Gardens of Paradise never quite ceased business, but today its windows were shuttered against the wind, and the door was shut. Only the smoke from the chimney indicated there was life within.

"Where is this body?" Halvar asked,

"In a room in the cooperage," Bertram said, pointing to a rambling wooden building at the northern end of the green, just past the palisade that separated the fratery from the rest of Green Village. "Stiff and cold, like I said."

Avaram pulled his donkey cart to the door of the cooperage. Two Mahak watchmen stood to the right of the door, glaring at an Oropan constable who guarded the left. Tenente Donal, the burly Bretain bouncer from the Gardens of Paradise, greeted them in Erse, while Firebrand, the leader of the Local watchmen, regarded Halvar impassively.

Both had adapted their usual garb to the brutal cold. Donal's green coat covered his red-and-blue-checkered trews, while Firebrand had added a cape of fox fur to his deerskin hunting shirt and leggings. Donal wore the red tarboosh of the Guards, whereas Firebrand insisted on keeping his head bare, displaying his Mahak warrior's scalplock in defiance of the cold.

Halvar clambered out of the cart.

"Tenente Donal, Tenente Firebrand...show me this body. I hope you haven't dragged me all this way on a fool's errand, chasing a wild goose."

"Not at all," Donal said. "It's a puzzle. Here's a man, dead in his own house, and no one seems to know how or why."

"Don Alvaro is known for solving puzzles," Selim stated, with a glance at her idol.

Halvar grimaced under his mustache. He only hoped he could live up to the girl's expectations.

Chapter 3

THE COOPERAGE WAS A LARGE BARN-LIKE STRUC-
ture, built in the Bretain style of sawed boards fastened together with wooden pegs, covered with a sharply-pitched
thatched roof. Donal and Firebrand led Halvar into the main
workspace, an open area that ran the length of the building.
The air was fragrant with the scent of freshly-cut wood.

Tools hung neatly on pegs over the worktable where
Ned had shaped the smaller barrels, kegs and firkins. Heat
came from a small forge in the middle of the room, where
Ned could shape the copper bands that held the wooden staves
in place. A small table near the forge held sharp instruments
whose function Halvar could only guess at, and some small
copper circles with toothed outer rims..

Waiting inside were a large man and larger youth in typi-
cal Purist dress—long woolen coats of fine gray wool, wool
breeches, and the distinctive high-crowned, broad-brimmed
hats favored by the sect. The third man could have been a

Mahak, except for his heavy black beard, being dressed in a leather hunting shirt that mimicked the one Firebrand wore. Like his countrymen, he wore woolen breeches; like Halvar, he wore an araghoun fur cap; and like Firebrand, he preferred macassin to heavy boots.

Donal made the introductions in Erse.

"These are the men who have been living with Ned Cooper since the Fall Feria. The big fellow is Angus MacKay; the stripling is his son, Seth. And this is Kevin MacFergus—he's one of those who goes up-country, into Mahak territory, to bargain for furs."

Halvar nodded. "Where's this body you want me to see?"

"Up the stairs. There's a loft with a small room where Ned did his business accounts." Donal pointed to the narrow staircase, not much more than a ladder, that led to the storage space. Halvar followed him up, with Selim close behind them.

Ned Cooper was not one for elegance. His office was little more than an enlarged cabinet holding a table with writing materials, a shelf for his accounting-books, and a neatly-made wooden chair. Ned had sat down in that chair and apparently died in that chair.

Frater Iosip, the rotund frater whose bulbous nose was adorned with a set of spectacles, and Frater Leonidas, tall and graceful, stood over the body. Halvar edged into what little space was left; Donal and Selim hovered just outside the opening. There was no door as such, just a heavy leather panel attached to a rod that separated the private office from the storeroom. Clearly, Ned Cooper had thought he had nothing to hide from his fellow Villagers, and had no fear of thieves.

"Have you moved him?" Halvar demanded.

"Only to ascertain that he was dead, and that the cause was not natural," Frater Iosip stated.

"When was he found? By whom?"

"Young Seth came to the Gardens of Paradise to fetch me at dawn, just before morning prayers," Donal said. "I came,

I saw what you see, I called on the fraters, They came, took a look, saw he was dead. Frater Leonidas tried to move him to see if he'd had some kind of attack of the heart, or a sudden brain-stroke."

"It was neither of those," Frater Iosip stated firmly. "I am all too familiar with the symptoms of both. I am also familiar with Ned Cooper. A misguided soul, but ardent in his beliefs. Not a drinker of alcohol, nor a smoker of tabac or hemp. Quite robust, with a good set of lungs to proclaim his views on everything from the Redeemer's words to the evil state of affairs that has led Green Village to unite itself with Manatas Town."

"Any ideas as to what killed him? Or who?""

"It's clear enough what killed him." Frater Leonidas turned the chair so the back of the body could be seen through the wooden rods set into the seat. "He was stabbed, right between the ribs. Neatly done, with a very thin, sharp blade. Not a rapier, nor a short sword, not a Franchen poignard, which leaves a triangular mark. This was a flat knife, more like a Bretain dirk. Do you agree, Frater Iosip?"

The older man peered at the wound through his lenses and nodded.

"We will have to examine it further, but I expect we will find the wound was made by a Bretain dirk. Quite a long one, to penetrate his coat and waistcoat."

Frater Leonidas opened the cord that kept the dead man's shirt closed around his neck.

"Woolen undershirt as well."

"And when do you think he died?" Halvar edged out of the room so Selim could squeeze inside to make a sketch of the wound in Ned's back.

"By the stiffness of the limbs, and the color of the flesh, I would say at least twelve hours before he was found," Frater Leonidas drawled. "Agreed, Frater?"

"I concur. And I'm sure your Islim bone-setter would, too."

Frater Iosip couldn't resist getting in a dig at his rival at the Rabat.

"That would be, perhaps, sundown yesterday?" Halvar frowned. "And no one missed him? No one looked for him? Not even those three downstairs, who lived with him?"

"They say they were upset by what happened to Mac-Alan," Donal said.

"As well they should be." Halvar paused to let Selim out of the room, "An assassin's blade, you think? I thought we'd got rid of them when we killed off the Franchen at the Mermaid Taberna."

"This one's not Franchen. I'm sure of it," Frater Leonidas pronounced. "Of course, we will have to make a more detailed examination, with your permission, Capitán."

Halvar descended the stairs carefully, trying not to strain his wounded shoulder. He could see a crowd forming outside the cooperage. Word had already got out that Ned Cooper was dead, in his own chair, slain by a mysterious enemy.

"Tenente Donal, get some of those men to bring the... Ned...to the fratery, so that Frater Iosip and Frater Leonidas can get a better look at him. And I want to have a word with those friends of his, the Purists who were staying at his cottage. There must be somewhere warmer to question these three witnesses."

The three Purists were huddled over the glowing forge, absorbing what warmth they could from its coals.

"There's always the Gardens of Paradise," Donal suggested.

"That place of filth? Never! I will not step over that cursed threshold!" MacKay protested. "Nor will I expose my son to its vices. We can go to the cottage next to the cooperage, where we have been staying these last two months."

Halvar gave a flurry of orders. "Constable Bertram, take these witnesses to their cottage, and make sure they don't leave until I get there. Tenente Firebrand, your men can assist

17

Frater Iosip in taking this poor fellow to the fratery. Tenente Donal, inform the Green Village council that I will meet with them at the Gardens of Paradise after I have questioned these Purists. I want to know more about Ned Cooper, and whether or not he was tied into whatever Andrew MacAlan was doing with Albrecht LaPierre.

"Leon...that is, Frater Leonidas...will you come with me and Selim? I want a better look at that cabin where Master LaPierre worked. I want to see for myself what went on there. And Selim, take Ned Cooper's business papers with you. If he made barrels for Andrew MacAlan, I want to know how many, what size, and what they were going to hold."

He strode back out into the freezing wind. He wasn't sure what good any of this would do, but at least he was doing something!

Chapter 4

HALVAR STOPPED OUTSIDE THE COOPERAGE TO take a brief survey of his surroundings. The houses, barns, businesses, and workshops of Green Village had been erected around the common green, with the three-story Gardens of Paradise towering over all of them. The fratery palisade was to the northwest, the cooperage to the northeast of the common.

Between them, the path straggled northward through the trees toward the rocky outcrops that gave the island its unique shape. Halvar knew it forked about half a mile north of the settlement. One path led east past the Algonkin and Mahak villages to where Leon di Vicenza was planning his bridge. The other went west on a ridge skirting the Great River, past the brickyard and tannery to the hilly outcrops where wild cats, bears, and wolves were rumored to roam.

The woods beyond the settlement had lost their leaves. Spindly branches of birch, aspen, and willow waved in the wind, a lacy web across a sky that was turning from a clear blue to a misty gray, indicating an impending storm.

The crowd outside the cooperage parted to allow Firebrand's watchmen to carry the contorted body of Ned Cooper from the cooperage to the fratery, a matter of a few steps. Firebrand joined Halvar and Selim, while Frater Leonidas consulted with Frater Iosip.

Halvar looked towards the woods north of the settlement.

"Has anyone been near that cabin since the lion hunt?"

Firebrand frowned. "The dead ones—the Afrikan and the Bretain—were gone from there. Their ghosts will not disturb us. We took the dead cougar away to be skinned. You may take the hide as a trophy, and use the teeth for a talisman. Not everyone can say they fought the cougar at his lair and won.

"As for the rest of these people, they came back with us to Green Village. I did not see anyone staying behind. Why would they?"

"There might have been something of value in that cabin. "

"Gunpowder," Selim put in. "Or the notes he was making on how to make it. That was what the cabin was for, wasn't it?"

"I want to see that cabin," Halvar decided. "Frater Leonidas! Leon!"

The erstwhile frater stopped in mid-stride.

"Capitán?"

"Come with me." Halvar set out on the path northward, through the trees. "Frater Iosip, tell Abbas Mikhail that Frater Leonidas is assisting in the investigation into the death of Ned Cooper, and will be back in the fratery before noon prayers."

Frater Leonidas smiled at his colleague. "I promise I will not run off," he assured him. "I prefer the comforts of the fratery, bleak as they are, to the perils of the forest in winter."

Firebrand led the way through the woods. Bare trees and prickly shrubs lined the path that had been trampled by many feet over the last two days. Frozen puddles crunched underfoot, their crackling the only sound besides the ever-present whine of the wind.

Halvar knew when they passed the brickyard by the smell of burning wood, and the tannery by the foul reek of urine and rotting flesh. Then they reached the outcrop where he had fought the mountain cat the Locals called a *cougar*.

The cabin had been built against the rocky slope to take advantage of what little shelter it could give, a square structure made of logs, cut and shaped in the Scanian style, topped with a peaked roof of Andalusian tiles. A brick chimney protruded from one side wall, evidence of a fireplace within. A small wooden shed a few feet away from the cabin was apparently the necessary.

Halvar circled the cabin, checking for exits. There was only the one—the wooden door, with its wrought-iron hinges and latch. He scanned the ground around the cabin and the attendant woodpile.

"Ground's frozen," he muttered. "No footprints. Anyone could have come here since the lion hunt."

"Could have, but didn't," Firebrand stated. "My men would have seen anyone on the path."

"There was quite a crowd," Halvar reminded him. "The students from the madrassa, the layabouts from Manatas that Milord Summersby called out to help find the mountain cat, most of Green Village, even a few of the Local women who stayed behind to sell maiz and trinkets for the holy days."

"None of them stayed here after the sun set," Firebrand insisted. "There are no lanterns or torches here to light the path. The moon is narrow, and rises late at this time of the month. The only folk this far away from Green Village are the Afrikans at the tannery and the brickyards, and they don't go out after dark. There are worse things than cougars in these woods."

Halvar tried the door. The hasp on the large lock that was supposed to deter intruders had not been fully engaged. The door opened with a squeal from the iron hinges.

The only light inside the cabin came from the open door. Selim slithered around Halvar, poked around, and found a small oil lamp of the sort used by scholars at the madrassa. She used the fire-starter in her pen-case to light the wick and held it up so that Halvar, Firebrand, and Leon could see the rest of the room.

Halvar and Leon followed her into the cabin. Firebrand remained in the shelter of the doorway, unwilling to trespass on the property of someone recently deceased.

A large lantern hung from the ceiling; Halvar lit it from the feeble flame of the lamp and took a harder look at the interior of Albrecht LaPierre's experimental gunpowder manufactory.

There was a lot to see, but little of it made sense to him. A table had been placed against one wall, with shelves above it containing copper and brass vessels of various sizes. Baskets lined another wall, two filled with yellow stones that gave off the odor of bad eggs. Another basket held chunks of half-burned wood. On either side of the door were more shelves, with crockery jars that reeked of urine.

Halvar watched Leon poke his elegant nose into the odoriferous jars. Selim was checking the elaborate apparatus next to the fireplace, a weird construct of copper tubes and glass beakers, ending with a small stand with a sieve propped into the top of a wide pan.

"What do you make of this?" he asked as Leon and Selim continued to search the cabin.

"The rocks are sulfur," Leon explained. "Charcoal, sulfur…"

"Piss?" Halvar pointed to the jars near the door.

"Not quite," Leon said. "Saltpeter. Made from urine, distilled and purified. What you see here, Halvar Danske, are the ingredients for gunpowder."

"But not the black powder itself?" Halvar said, a note of hope in his voice.

Selim had been investigating the tightly-woven baskets on the worktable.

"A little, here, but nothing worth killing over."

"Barrels, kegs," Halvar muttered, looking around the cabin again. "Andrew MacAlan wanted kegs of gunpowder, not a few grains in a basket. But there are no kegs here."

Leon smirked. "I'm sure Master LaPierre promised him enough black powder to fill many kegs. Anything to keep the ingredients coming in. LaPierre is one of those scholars who are willing to promise the moon, whether they can deliver it or not, just to get the wherewithal to continue their studies."

"Not like you, Leon," Halvar jibed. "You charm your way into the halls of power. All you promise is a good time."

"That was in the past," Leon said. "I have given all that up. I am Frater Leonidas, a good Kristo. Leon di Vicenza is no more."

"Perhaps," Halvar said. "Selim! Have you found anything else?"

"It's what I didn't find that I don't understand," Selim said. "Didn't you once tell me that it's not just what's there, but what isn't there that's important? Well, if this is where Master LaPierre was doing his work, where are his notes? Where did he write? There's no paper, no ink, no record of what he did here. And the fireplace is bare—there's no ash or even soot."

"Wood's been chopped for a fire." Halvar waved toward the stack of logs outside the door.

"Chopped, to be sure, and logs stacked, but not used. I don't think Master LaPierre has done any work in this cabin at all. He might have been making ready to do it, but hasn't done it—not yet, anyway."

"Could all this be a scheme to get money out of Mac-Alan?" Halvar tugged at his mustache. "Just an elaborate swindle?"

"That doesn't sound like Albrecht LaPierre to me," Leon said. "I don't like the man—he's far too much of a fanatic and narrow-minded, and he was far too taken with that scrubby messenger-boy, the ugly one—"

"Snake," Selim put in. "He even killed Master Kupernik for Snake's sake."

"Not knowing that the lad was already dead," Halvar concluded. "But all this makes no sense. Why go to all this trouble, and then not use the cabin…unless it's a part of something else?"

Leon sniffed loudly. "That's up to you to find out, Capitán. I am needed at the fratery. They appreciate my voice at prayers, and I have a painting to complete."

"And the journal of the late Captain Franz Girard to translate. Have you finished that?"

"As much of it as I can. I've finished my transcription and sent it to the Rabat. Selim will find it…interesting reading. Unfortunately, it doesn't say much about Girard's business dealings, and most of that is in his private code. Not a very forthcoming man, Captain Girard, except about his romantic exploits."

"You *have* been busy, Leon. And you still had time to organize the building of the bridge. How are you doing with that?"

"We've shut down for the winter," Leon said. "I've secured the scow that carries supplies back and forth, and notified the foreman across the river that we're not going to risk building again until the ice breaks in the spring. Until then, we can stockpile bricks, and take measurements of the water levels."

24

Leon grew more animated, forgetting to be blasé and superior in his enthusiasm for this new project.

"I've had the brick pylons banked with reeds to divert the ice from the bricks. The wooden pier has been reinforced, made into a jetty, so that barges can land with more bricks from either bank. There's a ferry towline, and the path down to the East Channel has been widened and straightened. We should be able to get to West Caster easily once the spring thaw sets in."

"And you can make your escape from Manatas," Halvar finished for him.

"Now, why would I want to do that?" Leon asked innocently. "Everything I ever wanted is right here. Food, clothing, shelter, meaningful work, good company…"

"Everything but the freedom to go your own way," Halvar said. "To do as you please, when it pleases you, with whomever you like to do it with. You don't have that."

"Oh, that. Yes." Leon's innocent smile vanished.

Halvar headed down the path back to Green Village, mulling over what he'd seen in the cabin. None of it seemed to make any sense. Perhaps a chat with Master LaPierre was in order. He considered the next steps in this investigation.

What was it Old Sergeant Olaf had told him, when he complained about standing night guard while the officers slept? *You don't send an officer to do what a soldier can do. We stand guard so they can think,* he'd told the young men under his command.

Very well, Halvar told himself. *I'm an officer now. I'll do the first questioning, then Donal can take over in Green Village while I finish the job on Master LaPierre. Making gunpowder is more important than the murder of an artisan, no matter how mysterious the manner of his death.*

They passed the tannery and the brickyard and came to the edge of the woods that marked the boundary between Green Village and the rest of Manatas Island. Firebrand and

Leon stopped for a moment with Halvar, to breathe and wait for Selim to catch up with them.

"What did you think of Ned Cooper?" Halvar asked the two.

Leon smirked. "I didn't think of him at all. Why should I? He didn't come to the fratery chapel for prayers. He led the Purists in singing their hymns—doggerel verses set to banal tunes. He howled sermons on the green. I don't know whether he made good barrels. I have no use for them.

"On the other hand, this Mahak may have another opinion. He was the target of some of Ned's wrath."

Halvar regarded the Mahak with raised eyebrows.

"What did he have against you?"

Firebrand grimaced. "He was fanatic about his Lord God. He called Manitou a demon and a false god. He called for fire to come down and remove the Mahak and Algonkin."

"Sounds like a good reason to hate him," Halvar observed.

"He was not worth hating," Firebrand declared.

"For once, I agree with you, Mahak," Leon said. "Ned Cooper was a ranting bigot. But he was also a good craftsman, which counts for something in this world."

"I suppose, along with his other rants, he might have singled *you* out for some attention," Halvar persisted.

"If you mean concerning my personal life, that was nothing. He accused me of the Sin of Sodom, and I have never denied my taste for young men. He was quite annoying, but I tell you again, not to the point where I would try to silence him with a knife in the back.

"And now, with your permission, Capitán Halvar Danske, I have several things to do at the fratery, not the least of them joining Frater Iosip in examining the body of Ned Cooper. I think I know how he was killed."

"No ideas as to who did the deed?"

"Oh, that's your business, my dear Halvar, not mine. I will send word as soon as Frater Iosip finishes his examination. May the Redeemer send you a good year!"

With that, Leon strode toward the palisade of the fratery, leaving Halvar to seethe with frustration.

"What now?" Selim asked.

"Let's have a word with Ned's companions," Halvar decided. "Living in close quarters, folk get testy with each other. It could be one of them found Ned Cooper's preaching unbearable and decided to end it."

Chapter 5

THE THREE MALE PURISTS HAD BEEN JOINED BY two women and three more men, all Bretains The men had removed their high-crowned broad-brimmed hats, but the women retained the plain white caps that covered their severely braided and coiled hair..

Donal had herded them into the main room of the cottage attached to the cooperage. They huddled near the fireplace, the main source of heat in the chilly room. Selim looked around for somewhere to place her notebook and pen-case, found a small table near the door, pulled the three-legged stool from under it, and sat down, ready to record what was said.

Halvar pushed through the crowd to the fireplace and eyed the group sourly.

"Is this the lot?"

"We are the Pure Sect," MacKay stepped forward. "We harm no one. We ask only to worship the Lord God and the Redeemer, as was set forth in the Holy Book."

"No one's stopping you," Halvar pointed to the leader. "Angus MacKay? That's you?"

"It is."

"And you speak for all of your people?"

Angus sighed. "In the absence of our brothers Andrew MacAlan and Ned the Cooper, I must."

Halvar looked around the sparsely furnished cottage.

"Is there anywhere to sit down?"

Donal indicated a large chair beside of the fireplace, a carved masterpiece with a leather cushion on the seat that dominated the room. Halvar plopped down into it, suppressing a grunt of pain as his shoulder jolted, and eyed the group sourly.

"Angus MacKay, when and how did you find out that Ned Cooper was dead?"

The Bretain cleared his throat nervously. "Hem! I did not find him."

"It was me found him." The youngest of the group, Seth, stepped forward. "It was when he didn't come for evening meeting."

"And you didn't miss him before then?" Halvar's eyebrows went up in amazement. "So small a group as you are, and you didn't wonder where he was?"

"Oh, we knew where he was." Kevin, the jaunty trapper, spoke up. "It was his way to go to his place in the cooperage before evening meeting to read the Holy Book and consider what text would be the sermon for the day. And what he thought of the Redeemer's words, and what they meant for us. And how we should behave, in light of those words."

"No one liked to disturb Ned," Seth put in. "Especially not when he was communing with the Lord God."

"Hard man, was he? The sort to make enemies?" Halvar hinted.

"Not enemies…" Angus said hastily. "Disagreements we had, but we were not enemies. None of us could have done

29

such a thing! We are like a family, sons and daughters of the Lord God Almighty, worshiping together in the manner of the Redeemer and his Followers. We have our disputes, to be sure, but to slay one another? This is against everything the Redeemer said. 'Love thine enemies', the Redeemer said."

"But did he mean for us to embrace the idolaters?" one of the other men asked. "Brother Andrew said that we must not allow idolaters to rule us."

"The tale of the Samaritan shows that he meant all enemies," the oldest woman responded. "So said Ned. We live among the Islim. We may not like them, but we must not kill them. They must be convinced of their error, we must remove them from their wickedness."

"The mountain cat—the cougar—was it a sign from the Lord God that Brother Andrew was in error?" the younger woman quavered. "It was as the Holy Book predicted—a fearsome beast!"

"Surely, a sign of the Lord God's displeasure, at Brother Andrew's sin of killing the Afrikan." Angus nodded. "I have had dealings with Samuel Igbo. He was an honest man, even if he was Islim."

"He killed a messenger lad, too," Halvar reminded them. "I would have taken him alive, but he ran from the cat and fell over the cliff."

"A demon in disguise!" the younger woman gasped. "The Lord God's vengeance upon the sinner!"

"Just an animal, defending its home," Halvar assured her. "But your Brother Andrew was observed killing the messenger, and the messenger was most definitely Kristo."

"Roumi Rite, but still—Kristo," Selim added from her place at the table.

"And we think he was plotting something, using that cabin in the woods to make gunpowder, which is forbidden under the laws of Al-Andalus," Halvar went on. "Do you know anything about that?"

No one spoke. Then Angus said, "The cabin was no business of ours. Brother Andrew had an arrangement with one of the masters at the madrassa in Manatas Town. That was all he told us."

"So, none of you ever went there?" Halvar looked them over. "Seth, you knew where the place was. You led us to it. Surely, you must have had some thoughts as to what went on there."

Seth turned red. "I thought...perhaps, if Master LaPierre needed an apprentice, he would take me on," he sputtered. "I know—I wasn't a student at the madrassa. I wanted to go to madrassa, like Owen, but my father wouldn't have it, said I'd do better to learn a trade, so he apprenticed me to Ned Cooper. When Brother Andrew called for someone to take things to the cabin, I did the fetching and carrying. I didn't hear anything about what the cabin was for, or who was supposed to go into it.

"I saw Master LaPierre once, when I was bringing some small kegs from the cooperage. I wanted to speak to him, ask him if I could work with him, but Brother Andrew stopped me before I could say anything, and I had to leave them. I didn't hear what they said to each other.

"I never was allowed into the cabin itself. All I did was chop the wood and bring the water." He ended with a resentful sniff. "I could have done what Master LaPierre wanted. I'd have learned something. It would be better than stoking Brother Ned's forge and sharpening tools for him, and sweeping the shavings off the floor."

Halvar thought this over. So far, everything seemed quite logical. Albrecht LaPierre had wanted a quiet place to do his experiments. He got permission to build the cabin, he stocked it with all the tools and ingredients an alchemist needed to make gunpowder. And then...what?

"When was the last time any of you saw Ned Cooper alive?" he asked.

There was a muttered hubbub as each of the Purists consulted with the others. Kevin, the trapper, spoke first.

"I saw him during the hunt, when that fat fellow—"

"Milord Summersby," Donal identified him.

"Yes, him. He was trying to control that horse of his. Ned laughed, said he couldn't sit his horse, and never could sit his horse. Said he was more fit to snare rabbits than to kill a great cat."

"Never could?" Halvar picked up on the phrase. "Then, he knew Milord Summersby?"

"I suppose he did," Kevin said, with some surprise. "He was laughing too hard at Milord, and to tell the truth, I was more interested in what you were doing, Capitán. That was quite a battle!"

"Ned knew Milord in Bretain, before he came to Manatas? Did he say how, or where he'd met him?" Halvar was not be be deterred by flattery.

"I didn't hear any more, and truth to tell, it's not done in Nova Mundum, to ask what anyone was or did before coming across the Storm Sea. If someone wants to tell you, they will. Otherwise, best not to ask." Kevin grinned. "You might not like the answer."

"We live new lives in a new land." The older woman spoke fervently. "Whatever our sins were, they have been washed clean. We are reborn in our faith."

"Amen!" the younger woman agreed with her. "We sat down to our evening meal. Brother Angus noticed that Brother Ned was not with us. He sent young Seth to fetch him. Seth said that Brother Ned was still reading his Holy Book, and would come presently. But he did not come, so Seth went again, and came back with the news that Brother Ned had left for a better world than this."

"And you didn't think to call anyone? Tenente Donal of the Guards, or Frater Iosip, for medical assistance" Halvar regarded the Purists with growing anger. "You just left Ned Cooper sitting there?"

"There was nothing we could do for him," Angus protested. "It was after nightfall, the beasts are about. For all we knew, the mountain cat had a mate, eager to avenge him. We sent for Tenente Donal at first light," he added.

"So you did." Halvar admitted.

There was awkward silence as Halvar tried to organize his thoughts.

"Heer Angus, what do you know of that cabin, and its purpose? If, as I suspect, Andrew MacAlan had it in mind to set up a manufactory for making gunpowder, with Master Albrecht LaPierre providing the alchemy and Locals providing the materials, what was he planning to do with the stuff?. Was he thinking to sell it at the feria, to whoever would buy? Perhaps use it to foment a rebellion against the calif and take this land for Bretain? Or sell it to the Mahak, to use against the Huron?"

"Not that, not at all!" Angus blurted. After an inward struggle, he said, "It was Brother Andrew's scheme for us to leave this sinful island and go elsewhere."

"Where?" Halvar frowned. "Across the Great River? That's Mahak territory."

"To be sure, but Brother Andrew was certain the Lord God meant for us to go forth from here to spread the light of the True Faith. He and Brother Ned were of two minds on this matter, and they argued over it. Ned was for building up our congregation here, in the lands of Al-Andalus. Brother Andrew was intent on going inland, to establish another place, not tainted by Islim, where we can worship the Lord God as we are instructed to do by the Holy Book."

"He'll have to deal with the Locals and their shamans," Donal reminded the Purist leader, glancing at Firebrand. "They don't take kindly to folk who blaspheme against their forest spirits and demons."

Halvar brushed aside the theological debate.

"When, exactly did you last see Ned Cooper alive? Before or after the call for sunset prayers?"

"I thought I heard the fratery bell ringing," Kevin offered. "It was after the lion hunt, when everyone had come back to Green Village. We gathered in this cottage to talk over what had happened at the lion hunt. "

"The fight with the mountain cat!" Seth enthused. "What a battle! And then you slew the beast! With one blow!"

"It wasn't my idea," Halvar said modestly. "All I wanted to do was get Andrew MacAlan out of that cave, to take him back to Manatas Town to question him about the death of the messenger."

"The Evil One must have entered Brother Andrew," Angus declared. "Why else would he have done what he did?"

"He wanted to hide what he was up to in that cabin," Halvar stated. "He killed the messenger and the Afrikan because they could link him to a Franchen sea captain who had a shipment of muskets to dispose of and needed gunpowder to complete his deal."

The collected Purists gasped in shock and dismay at the news.

"I cannot believe Brother Andrew would collude with a Franchen!" Angus burst out. "Madness! It must have been madness!"

"Or greed," Halvar amended.

"But he did not kill our Brother Ned," the gaunt older woman pointed out. "For Ned was alive and boasting well after Brother Andrew was taken down and brought to the village. I saw him talking to one of the folk from Manatas just as the bells were ringing for sunset prayers."

"Indeed, Sister Lucy," Angus agreed. "Now that you mention it, I saw him with the fellow who attended the milord."

"That long drink of water with the fancy Erse?" Kevin chimed in. "He wanted to take the skin and head of the cat for himself. Tried to get me to skin the beast. Offered silver for it, too."

"That was wrong!" Firebrand spoke up from his position at the door. "The skin and the teeth belong to the one who killed the cougar, not to some merchant bargaining for them."

"I told that black-coated swine what he could do with his silver," Kevin said fiercely. "A man who kills a cougar with a spear deserves the skin and teeth as his reward. Of course, if you want to sell, I can give you a good price..."

"I'm thinking about having the skin made into a coat," Halvar told him. "But thank you for the offer." He looked about the room and tugged at his mustache, taking in this fresh information. "So, Edgar Norris, Milord's servant, talked with Ned Cooper? Did any of you hear what they said?"

"The servant pulled Brother Ned aside," the younger woman said. "I could not tell what was said, but Brother Ned was smiling, as he often did when he thought he was right and the other was wrong."

"As was his way," Lucy, the older woman, chimed in. "He was so certain he was right he would not hear any opposing views."

"And then what?"

"Sister Lucy and Sister Anne went into their own cottage to prepare our evening meal," Angus explained. "Then, we met here, in this cottage, for our evening prayers, and I sent Seth to fetch Brother Ned."

"And I went to the cooperage, and up the stairs, and pulled aside the leather door, and he was sitting there, stiff and cold—dead!" Seth said, with a shudder. "I ran to tell the others, but it was dark, and Ned was already dead, so we did not call Tenente Donal until it was light. And that is all I can tell you. I don't know who killed him! *I* didn't do it!"

"I never said you did," Halvar assured him. "I'm not even sure how it was done. But if none of you went near the man after sunset prayers..."

"None of us did," Angus stated. "Every one of our small community was praying for the soul of Brother Andrew."

"Not to mention the Afrikan, Samuel Igbo," Halvar added. He heaved himself out of the chair. "Selim, have you written all this down?"

"I have!"

"Then I will trouble you people no longer. If anyone recalls anything else about Ned Cooper, who he might have annoyed or injured, tell Tenente Donal and he will tell me. For the rest, I wish you a good day."

He pushed through the group to find a larger crowd gathered on the common in front of the Gardens of Paradise.

"So much for Ned's friends," he told Selim. "Let's hear what his foes have to say."

Chapter 6

THE CROWD OF GREEN VILLAGERS HAD INCREASED
when Halvar emerged from the cooper's cottage. Men in work-
men's leather aprons, women in long skirts with kerchiefs
over their heads and shawls around their shoulders had been
joined by youngsters of both sexes,. All of them looked ex-
pectantly at him, waiting for him to announce that he had
already solved this baffling mystery.

Halvar could not oblige them.

Instead, he marched across the green to the iron fence
that enclosed the Gardens of Paradise, where Dani Glick
waited for him, Tenente Donal at her side.

"A good day to you, Fru Dani Glick," he greeted the
proprietress of the establishment, who was dressed in her
most respectable Yehudit Widow outfit of embroidered jacket and skirt over multiple petticoats, her head covered with
a bright scarf.

"Do you think you own this place, Capitán?" Dani dis-
pensed with frivolous greetings. "You commandeer my rooms,

you order people to gather here as if it was your own office at the Rabat. By what right—"

Halvar broke into the tirade. "The Gardens of Paradise is the largest space here in Green Village," he pointed out. "It's also the warmest, since you're the one who got the first stove Leon di Vicenza built. So, it only makes sense for me to use your back room for this business of Ned Cooper's murder. Besides," he added with a grin, "think of the prestige!"

"I can't make money on prestige," Dani said sourly. "All these folk will want food and drink, and won't pay for it."

"You can send the bill to the Manatas Town Council," Halvar pointed out. He turned to Avaram, who was waiting with the donkey cart.

"I don't know how long this will take. You'd best step into the taproom, out of the wind, until I'm ready to go."

The driver gladly followed Halvar and Donal into the central room of the main building., where he found a seat at one of the tables.

Halvar and Donal went through the main room to the small private chamber where a round iron stove had been placed in one corner, giving off a welcome warmth. Seated around the square table in the middle of the room were the leading citizens of Green Village. Cormack MacCormack, the ironmonger from West Caster, was the loudest and largest of them, representing the merchants who came to the Spring and Fall ferias. His son Padraig sat beside his master and mentor, the lanky printer Simon Singer, whose *Gazetta* was rapidly replacing Daoud the Newscrier and his minions as the principal source for news in Manatas.

Opposite Simon sat two more men, one in the striped trousers and red coat favored by Franchen merchants, the other in a Danic jacket and baggy breeches much like Halvar's. The Franchen's hands were stained with ink, the Dane's scarred with burns and cuts.

All of them stood when Halvar entered with Donal at his heels. Selim slipped in behind them, found a space at the table, elbowed herself into it, and took out her notebook and pens. Clearly, this was an official meeting, to be recorded.

Two more men edged into the room behind Selim. One, in the canvas trousers and jacket of a seaman, nodded to Cormack.

"Hallo, Captain Gibson!" Cormack greeted him. "When did you get in?"

"I just landed this morning with my catch. What's this about Ned Cooper? He was supposed to fit me with new barrels for the next run."

"Dead, in his own chair," Cormack reported, before Halvar could speak. "What news from the south?"

"Only that the Afrikans met with the young calif in Bell' Mar'." The fisherman eyed the group warily.

"Which Afrikans?" Halvar asked.

"Ahsanti, Yoruba, Igbo—all of them met with Sultan Calvera and the Calif. Quite a show it was, too!"

"And what was said?"

"I don't know—they went into the meeting-rooms and shut us common folk out. I suppose the matter's in the letters I gave the sultan when I got in. What's this about Ned Cooper being dead? I need more barrels for the next catch. Who's in charge of the cooperage, if Ned's gone?"

"A good question, which won't be solved until we learn who killed him," Cormack said. He frowned at the man behind the fisherman, a short, stout figure in the brown robes of the fraters of the Order of Poverty. "Frater Paulus? What has the fratery to do with this business of Ned Cooper's death?"

"Abbas Mikhail sent me, his prior and assistant, to assure all Green Village that he had nothing to do with the woeful death of Ned the Cooper, but will pray for the deliverance of his soul."

39

"He had good reason to want the man dead," Simon said. "Ned had no good words for the Order or the fraters."

"That may be so," Frater Paulus replied. "But we of the Order of Poverty do not take a knife to those who disagree with us and slay them in their own homes.. We leave that sort of thing to the heretics and freethinkers who infest the Roumi Rite, and particularly those who follow the evil one who calls himself Papa of all Kristos!"

He fairly spat out the last phrase.

"Episcopus Innocente claims he received his revelation directly from the Redeemer, in a vision," Simon countered. "I have it from Prester Nicodemus himself."

"Both Episcopus Innocente and Prester Nicodemus are in error!" Frater Paulus declared. "There is nothing in the Holy Book, other than a brief statement from the Redeemer to one of his Followers, that would place the Episcopus of Rouma over every other Kristo in the entire world. And that authenticity of statement is also debatable."

Halvar put an end to yet another theological dispute.

"I didn't call you all here to talk religion. It's this business of the murder of Ned Cooper."

"Killed, you say?" Simon said.

"He was found dead, in his own chair, in his own cooperage office," Halvar told the group.

"How? Poison?" Simon's very nose quivered at the idea of a juicy scandal to fill the pages of the *Gazetta*.

"As Frater Paulus said, a knife in the back. I assume you got that piece of information from Frater Iosip."

Gasps of outrage and astonishment went around the table.

Simon nudged his apprentice. "We must put out a quick edition of the *Gazetta*!"

Padraig rose to leave.

"Not so fast," Halvar stopped him. "At this time, we don't know who did it, or even how. Only that Ned Cooper was seen, alive and well, at the lion hunt yesterday afternoon. Did any of you see him after that?"

"I saw him at the lion hunt," the Franchen said hesitantly.

"I heard much the same from his friends, the Purists," Halvar said.

"He didn't think much of Milord Summersby," Padraig put in. "I heard him say the man never could sit a horse."

"As did the trapper, Kevin." Selim flipped through her notebook.

"He was loud enough," Donal sneered. "Everyone within earshot could hear him."

"Including Milord?" Halvar inquired. That was an intriguing thought.

"Milord was on the horse," Padraig said. "His man, the one called Edgar, he was nearby. He might have heard."

"And probably didn't like having his master shamed by a loudmouthed working man," Donal commented. "But he left soon after Milord Summersby. I saw him pass the cooperage myself."

"So, then, who was left? And why creep into the cooperage to stick a knife into poor Ned?" the other Dane objected.

Halvar tugged at his mustache. "By what I hear, Ned Cooper wasn't one to let politeness or policy get in the way of his opinions. How many of your friends and neighbors did he offend with his preaching?"

Cormack let out a guffaw. "He accused me of shady business practices! Told me to my face that I would burn in the fires of Sheol for charging five wumpum for a knife that cost me two. I told him business is business, that if he didn't want the knife he could go to the souk and get one for less, but it would go dull and probably break on the next stave he cut with it."

"No way he would do that," the other Dane sneered.

"Never went into Manatas Town. Hated the place. Said it was full of Islim infidels, that the Evil One ruled in the Rabat. Hated the idea of sending money to help the calif in his wars against the Kristo Franchen, didn't even take a stall at the feria, only sent his small kegs and firkins to be sold by others," the Franchen added.

"He also accused me of printing lies and blasphemy," Simon said.

"Lies in the *Gazetta*?" Selim's head went up. "But you only print the truth. It says so, right on the front of the page.."

"Blasphemy in some of the books I set in print for the madrassa," Simon explained. "One of the professors, a foreign name, like Cooper…"

"Kupernik?" Now he had Halvar's attention.

"That was it. He came to me with some papers, a tract he wanted published, regarding his observations on the movements of the planets. Ned got wind of it, for all I know from that Purist from Bos-Town, the one who put his lad into the madrassa. Next thing I know, he's howling outside the Gardens of Paradise, claiming it's not only a den of vice but a place where the Evil One lurks to lure the Faithful from the True Path through the tracts and books I print, and through the *Gazetta*. I told him I'd print up his speeches, if he would write them down, but he wouldn't take my offer."

Halvar looked across the room at Dani Glick.

"I don't expect your business suffered from this fellow's preaching."

"Hardly!" Dani laughed. "If anything, he was an advertisement for the delights within these gates. I didn't like the man, but if he was killed as you said, I didn't do it. I didn't order it done, either. And none of the folk in this room had any reason to kill Ned Cooper, however much we disliked him."

"What about you, Frater?" Simon turned to the robed figure, who had sat silent during the discussion. "Ned Cooper

42

was the leader of the Purists. He had some hard words about Abbas Mikhail and the Order of Poverty."

"It is true that Ned Cooper and his sect were most critical of Abbas Mikhail and the fraters of our order. He stood outside our gates and accused us of betraying the Redeemer, mocking him by living in luxury while taking money from the poor and spending it on frivolity. He was particularly unpleasant about our allowing the painter, Frater Leonidas, to decorate our chapel.

"He called our good Abbas Mikhail an apostate! Said he was installing the Roumi Rite in Green Village!" Frater Pulus sniffed scornfully. "I do not approve of such images myself, but our revered abbas pointed out that the decorations were useful in instructing those who could not read the lessons of the Holy Book."

"All over a few pictures on a wall?" Halvar shook his head in disbelief. "And what did your abbas do?"

"Abbas Mikhail is a forbearing man," Frater Paulus said. "Ned Cooper was not of our flock. He placed himself and his followers outside the palisade, would not allow worshipers to come to chapel. He was an annoyance, with his ranting…but he was Kristo, nonetheless. Abbas Mikhail prayed for him to come to his senses."

"The man was mad with religion," Cormack agreed. "He was incensed that we should ally ourselves with Manatas Town. He didn't care what the Islim did, so long as they did it apart from Kristos, but when we became one settlement, he started preaching that we were on the path to Sheol."

"It only makes sense to have one law for a place as small as this island," Halvar said. "And if that law is Sharia in Manatas Town, it should be Sharia here in Green Village. And in the Mahak and Algonkin villages as well. No one can escape justice by running to one or another."

Cormack shrugged. "We did manage to convince your calif to make a few small concessions to Bretain law and custom."

"Like that rigmarole about warrants and searches?" Halvar grumbled. "If I didn't have to waste time getting the sultan to sign one, Samuel Igbo would not have gone to Andrew MacAlan, and might well still be alive."

"And if you want someone with a grudge, how about the Mahak?" Donal interrupted the argument before it got too personal.

"Firebrand?" Halvar's eyebrows went up another notch. "What did Ned Cooper have against *him*?"

"Not just him, but all the Locals," Cormack said. "When we had our Harvest Feast at the end of the Fall Feria, the Mahak shaman came to bless us. Ned accused me to my face of apostasy, allowing a pagan to attend our festival. It was no good telling him it was a courtesy, a gesture of good will toward the Mahak for allowing us to use their land for our own crops. He just kept spouting texts from the Holy Book until the leader of the watchmen told him to be quiet, or Manitou himself would shut him up."

"Firebrand?" Halvar called out.

The Mahak, who preferred not to enter Oropan houses, had reluctantly come into the building, and now stepped into the doorway of the back room.

"Did you quarrel with Ned Cooper?"

"I did not quarrel with him. He quarreled with me." The Mahak regarded the group with his usual stoic calm. "He was offensive. He insulted our sachem, Gray Goosefeather, and our shaman, Sees-in-the-Clouds. He insisted that all lands belonged to him and his Purists as a gift from their god."

"And what did you do about it?" Halvar asked.

"Nothing. I do not regard the bellowing of fools. Ned Cooper was a fool, and I did not have any reason to kill him. What is more, if I had, I would not do it by sneaking into his house and putting a knife into his back. When I fight, it is in the open, and I use my tomahawk."

"So much for that," Halvar murmured as Firebrand stalked back to his position outside the room. "To tell you the truth, I am as puzzled by this as you are."

"It's a puzzle, to be sure," Cormack agreed. "Not only who did it, but how was it done?"

Selim summed it up. "Everyone is sure that Ned Cooper walked into his office at sundown. No one came near the place *after* sundown, so how was he killed? And why?"

"I don't know, not yet," Halvar said. "But I intend to find out. Ned Cooper was an unpleasant man—a bigot and a braggart—but he was a citizen of Manatas, and it is my duty to protect all the citizens of Manatas, even the unpleasant ones. I will find out who killed him, how, and why. And when I do, I promise you, that person will be punished."

He stood, squared his shoulders, and marched out. He had no idea how he was going to make good on his promise, but he had given his word, and that meant a great deal.

"Where to now?" Selim asked, ever at his side.

"Back to Manatas Town," Halvar decided, waving to Avaram to bring the donkey cart as he went through the main room. "I want you to take a good look at those business papers you got from Ned Cooper's office. And then, I have to report to Sultan Petrus. He's not going to like this, not at all."

Chapter 7

AVARAM TOOK HIS PLACE ON THE THE DONKEY cart at the gates of the Gardens of Paradise while Halvar faced the Green Villagers who had gathered on the green.

"Regarding the death of Ned Cooper," he announced. "At this time, I cannot say with any certainty who killed him. Be assured that I will find out, and the guilty one will be punished."

"Was it a Mahak?" someone yelled from the back of the crowd.

"As far as I know, it was not." Halvar clambered into the cart. "If anyone can recall anything about Ned Cooper, anything at all—where he came from, what he did before he came to Manatas—tell Tenente Donal, and he will tell me."

"What does it matter now that he's dead?" the same raucous voice called out.

"Sometimes the past comes back to bite us," Halvar retorted. "Anything you remember about Ned Cooper may be important, even if you don't think it is." He nodded to Donal, who stood proudly at the gate. "Tenente Donal, Tenente Firebrand, take your men and look carefully around the cooperage and the house where Ned and the Purists are living. Try to find some indication of exactly where Ned was stabbed, whether it was inside the cooperage or somewhere outside. Look for bloodstains, or some place where someone wiped a bloody knife on the ground or on a bush. Send word by messenger when you've finished your examination."

"I will send my best runner," Firebrand promised. "But I do not want to take my men away from their post at the bridge. There is something happening there—too many people for this time of year."

"I thought Leon shut that down." Halvar frowned.

"On our side, yes. On the Bretain side, not yet. We keep watch." Firebrand nodded firmly.

Halvar nodded back, and salaamed to Donal.

"You and your constables check with the people who were at the lion hunt. Find out exactly who heard Ned mocking Milord Summersby, what was said, and to whom. It may mean something different in their kind of Erse."

He and Selim took seats in the cart. Avaram prodded the donkey, who brayed loudly but plodded obediently back toward Manatas Town across the feria field, to the great annoyance of the geese. A large gander flapped his wings and squawked his displeasure at being disturbed at his feeding.

"What do we do next?" Selim asked.

Halvar tugged at his mustache.

"There's something about this murder. It reminds me of one that happened when I was first taken into the calif's service in Corduva. One of the loose-livers who hung about the court was found dead in his bed, a knife wound in his back, but no one had come near him all night. He'd been drinking and gambling, was a known womanizer, but had no really bad enemies."

"No one ever found out who killed him? Or how?"

"There were suggestions, hints. He was said to be involved in some of the harem schemes—to put one of the concubines' sons into the calif's chair instead of Don Felipe—but that led nowhere. And he was supposed to have won a large bet, but no one could remember whether it was ever paid or not." Halvar opened his eyes, stared ahead at the walls of Manatas Town. "There was even talk of Leon di Vicenza being involved, but this happened after he'd been sent away to Nova Mundum, so that came to nothing, too."

"And how he was killed? Did anyone ever figure that out?"

"It didn't seem likely that a man could be stabbed and not know it, go all the way up the stairs and into his own bed, with no blood showing..." Halvar tugged at his mustache again. "I only hope Frater Iosip isn't one of those who refuse to open the body of a dead man. At least Dr. Moise performs a proper examination."

They reached the town wall. Halvar greeted the guard on duty, and the cart plodded on until Avaram stopped.

"What's the matter?" Halvar looked up and realized there was a crowd on the Broad Way, blocking the route to the Rabat. People, dogcarts, and donkeys had gathered in the street where the Grand Muskat and the Manatas Madrassa opposed each other, physically and metaphorically.

The donkey nodded as Avaram prodded him again, gently shoving people out of the way.

"What's going on up ahead?" Selim stood up to get a better look.

Halvar decided it would be faster to use his own long legs to get through the crowd. He thrust Afrikans, Danes, and Andalusians aside to reach the center of the throng.

The disturbance was centered on the space in front of the Grand Muskat, where three distinct groups had assembled, a mixed crowd filling the street behind them. Mullah

48

Abadul, magnificent in his ceremonial robe and turban, his beard streaming over his chest, stood in the doorway of the muskat, his imams behind him. Next to him, radiating righteous indignation, was Emir Achmet, the chief Scavenger, decked in his least shabby caftan and fur cape, his turban decorated with a glittering stone that might even have been a real ruby..

Leading the crowd in front of the muskat was a tall man in the long black coat and broad-brimmed, low-crowned hat used by Yehudit, wearing a bloodstained apron, the sure sign of a butcher. Next to the butcher stood Benyamin ben Mendel, one of Leon's erstwhile students who called themselves "Seekers of Truth".

He was a rotund young man whose chin sported the beginnings of a curly black beard. Behind him were three black-coated Ashkenat Yehudit, all furiously shouting in their Danic dialect.

Two men in striped caftans and neatly-wound turbans stood a little apart from the Yehudit, their burka-clad women between them, glaring angrily at the focus of the controversy, who stood defiantly in the middle of the street. They added their voices to the din in Arabi.

Between the two groups of angry men, Tenente Flores and Guardsmen Zoltan and Fergus held their ground.. Fergus and Zoltan were armed with cudgels, Flores with his halberd. At the edge of the crowd stood two more guardsmen with halberds at rest, but ready to lower the blades if necessary.

Halvar shoved into the middle of the confrontation.

"What's going on here?"

Mullah Abadul pointed to Zoltan.

"That man is a walking cesspool of corruption! He dares to accost Islim women in the souk!"

"The Town Guard is a disgrace to Al-Andalus," Emir Achmet echoed piously. "These men stand about, harassing honest folk who are simply going about their business."

49

"You mean those young pups who take fruit from the stands and bread from the bakeries?" Zoltan retorted. "I've got my eye on them, Achmet! You keep your little thieves out of my territory!"

"He's had his eyes on my sister, too!" the Yehudit butcher added.

"Who?" Zoltan looked confused. "Which of them is your sister?"

"Raquel, who sews for Yussif the Tailor," Benyamin reminded him. "You've been seen talking to her."

Zoltan smirked. "Oh, her. A seamstress, and nice piece of goods she is, too! But she won't talk to me."

"You see how shameless he is!" Mullah Abadul roared. "He admits his guilt! Remove him from his post!"

Halvar turned to Flores. "I thought I told you to rein him in," he muttered.

"I've tried, but Zoltan is Zoltan," Flores replied. "And he's the only one big enough to keep those young thieves away from the fruit and bread. Remember? Yesterday he caught that messenger boy for you."

Halvar didn't know which annoyed him more, the self-righteous mullah, the smug Emir of the Scavengers, or the unrepentent guardsman whose behavior had started the confrontation.

He became aware of a distraction, a flurry of activity at the edge of the crowd. One of the guardsmen at the edge of the crowd shouted, "Not so fast!" He hauled a squirming youngster in ragged trousers and tunic into the center of the street.

"What have we here?" Halvar grabbed the lad before he could run away. "Thor's Hammer, I do believe it's a thief! With a string of wumpum in his fist!"

"That's mine!" the boy whined. "Honest wages. Really!" He looked at Emir Achmet for support. The Scavenger leader had found some more interesting sight.

"This is why we set guards in the souk," Halvar declared. "To prevent thievery, and to keep Manatas safe. Take this boy to the Rabat," he ordered.

Before the guard could act, the boy twisted out of his grip and dived behind Emir Achmet. The Scavenger chief beckoned his second-in-command, Rachev, who grabbed the boy before one of the guardsmen could move.

Halvare glared at Achmet. "Was this your idea? To set up a crowd so your light-fingered lot could pick wumpum off belts?"

"You dare to question the actions of this godly Islim?" Mullah Abadul put in before Emir Achmet could speak. "He is one of the righteous, allowing the Faithful to perform deeds of charity."

"And helping himself to a goodly portion of the profits himself," Halvar retorted. "Revered Mullah, regarding this man Zoltan." He stopped to gather his thoughts and remind himself every word he spoke would be repeated in every house in Manatas by nightfall. In his most elegant Court Arabi, he went on. "If one of my men has offended, he will be dealt with as I see fit. It is for me to decide his punishment, as Sultan Petrus and the Calif Don Felipe have given me this responsibility. I will be guided by Islim law and the customs of Al-Andalus. Tenente Flores!"

The squat Andalusian stepped forward.

"Disperse this crowd!"

Flores lowered his halberd. Zoltan and Fergus unhooked the cudgels from their belts. The guards at the edges of the crowd did the same.

Mullah Abadul snorted angrily and stalked into the safety of the Grand Muskat. One by one, the men in the crowd took shelter in the mokka-shops, offices, or lecture-halls of the madrassa that lined that part of the Broad Way. The black-shrouded Andalusian women at the edge of the crowd drew back to let the men pass. Yehudit women, marked by their colorful headscarves, followed the crowd, chattering in the colloquial Arabi of Manatas. No one remained

Halvar faced Zoltan., the only man in Manatas to whom he had to raise his eyes.

"This won't do. Since you don't listen to your tenente, maybe you'll listen to me. See me at the Rabat, as soon as you get off your shift. For now, get back to your post, and keep those young thieves away from the stalls. And don't talk to any of the women in the souk!"

Zoltan said nothing, but glowered as he sketched a salaam.

As he strode towards the Rabat, Halvar heard Fergus's high whine.

"You should tell him! You've got to tell him!"

"What for? It won't put wumpum in our pockets. I know what I'm doing. We'll be better off—"

Avaram's donkey brayed, drowning the rest of the response.

Halvar continued towards the Rabat with Selim trotting behind. Whatever it was that Zoltan had to tell him would have to wait. He had a more important interview, and he was not looking forward to telling Sultan Petrus about the latest upset.

Murders in Green Village were bad enough, but there seemed to be a rebellion brewing in Manatas itself. That, alone, demanded the sultan's attention, and Halvar was the only one who could demand it.

Chapter 8

HALVAR STRODE SOUTHWARD TO THE VAST PILE
of the Rabat, the fortress that dominated the skyline of Manatas. Originally a wooden palisade, it was now a three-story
edifice built of brown stone blocks from the quarries just
across the East Channel in West Caster. Its three towers loomed
over the tip of the island, with a stone wall separating the
fortress from the Broad Way,

The guardsman at the gate salaamed and opened the
gate before Halvar could give the order. He proceeded to
the central tower, where Sultan Petrus had his large audience
room. The sultan's personal quarters were on the second
story, with the harem where his wife Lady Ayesha lived with
her servants and the brand-new nursery for Baby Zuzu on
the top floor.

The Afrikan doorkeeper grimaced as Halvar started up
the stairs to the second floor.

"Go easy, Capitán," the servant warned. "He's had a bad night. Too much rich food, the baby's been fretful, and now this!"

"The killing in Green Village?"

"Bad news from the south."

"What next?" Halvar muttered as he and Selim entered Sultan Petrus's domain.

It was a large room dominated by a round table in the center that was covered with maps, charts, scrolls, and books. Leon's stove lurked in one corner, radiating heat to counter the wind that found its way through the gaps in the frames of the glass windows set in the walls that overlooked Manatas Bay.

Selim scurried in and found her usual seat, a large cushion next to a low table under the one window whose glass panes let in enough light for her to see what she was writing.

Sultan Petrus sat in a large armchair that had been moved from its usual position in the middle of the room to near the stove. His back was supported by a pillow, his ivory limb propped up on a small footstool. The small ivory-inlaid ebony table beside him held his constantly re-filled brass pot of mokka and cups. He was reading one of a sheaf of papers when Halvar greeted him.

"Salaam aleikum, Excellent Sultan. I hope you are well this morning."

"I am not," Petrus snarled. "My head aches, my belly aches, and I've got the rheum in my nose. And what's this about Green Village? The news-crier says there's been a killing."

"A workman, found dead in his own cooperage. I'm looking into it." Halvar noted the papers in the sultan's hand. "What news from our honored calif, may he rule long?"

"He writes one thing, Roderigo writes something else." Sultan Petrus sniffled. "According to Don Felipe, all is well, the Afrikans are willing to resist any advances Imperator

54

Lovis might make, should he send his ships across the Storm Sea to menace their settlements.

"On the other hand, Roderigo tells me the Afrikans are a tetchy lot, each trying to gain power over the others, all of them hiring Oropans to serve in their armies, paying with land that isn't theirs taken by force from Local hunting grounds. The mountains served as a barrier to expansion, but advance scouts from one of the Oropan companies found a gap in the range, so now Afrikans and Oropans are able to get through the mountains to the river-lands beyond and settle in the Locals' territories."

Halvar thought this over. "If that's so, then it explains the musket-smuggling. Girard was probably planning to take the muskets south to the Afrikans, to sell them to whoever would buy. But he'd have to include gunpowder in the deal. It's possible that Purist, Andrew MacAlan, was negotiating with Girard to provide the gunpowder, with Samuel Igbo acting as middleman."

"Hmph," Sultan Petrus grunted. "What has this to do with your dead artisan?"

"I'm not sure," Halvar said. "He made barrels, which could hold the gunpowder. I had a look at the cabin where the stuff was supposed to be made."

"But there wasn't any gunpowder there," Selim put in.

Halvar nodded. "True. I want to have a word with that alchemist, Albrecht LaPierre. Is he behaving himself?"

"I suppose he is." Sultan Petrus sipped mokka.

"You suppose? Isn't he in the cells? Has he harmed himself?" Halvar's voice rose in alarm.

.Sultan Petrus wiped his nose on a cloth. "He's not here at the Rabat. I sent him to the Yehudit. As far as I know, he's being held in their study-house."

"You let him go?" Halvar exploded, forgetting to defer to the ruler of Manatas. "Why? He's a murderer! He belongs on the gallows, not in the study-house!"

"While you were off chasing murderers in Green Village, I had a delegation this morning," Sultan Petrus snapped back. "I sent for you because I wanted you here to meet with them. Rav Nahum from the Madrassah, Benyamin ibn Mendel, and some loud-mouthed butcher were here, all insisting the Yehudit had the right to keep their own prisoners. There was even a letter from Rav Shimon Layzar, pointing out the Rabat has no provision for heating the cells, so keeping a prisoner in them was inhumane."

"Tenente Flores gave me that message," Halvar said. "But the matter at Green Village seemed more important at the time. You turned Master LaPierre loose?"

"I did not! I told you he's under guard at the Yehudit study-house," the sultan stated. "He's not going anywhere. And I interviewed him myself. He swears he didn't know how badly the nguba beans would affect Master Kupernik, and it's not his fault the man died from eating them."

"He made sure Master Kupernik couldn't wash them out of his mouth, and he jammed the door so Kupernik couldn't fetch help. That makes him a murderer." Halvar frowned fiercely.

"That may be so, but I remind you that I am the one who is in charge of justice in Manatas, by the calif's command!" Sultan Petrus glared back.

Halvar bit back the retort bubbling on his tongue. "Of course, Honored Sultan. However, it is possible Albrecht LaPierre may have information that is relevant to the musket smuggling."

"Go and talk to him, if you like. I couldn't get any sense out of him, except that he swears he's innocent of murder." The sultan sniffled again. "There was more from the Yehudit delegation. What's this I hear about some guardsmen in the souk bothering the women? The butcher wants the big fellow dismissed. I told him that was your business, you're in charge of the guards."

"I've got that in hand," Halvar assured him. "But the Scavengers are getting more brazen, and Emir Achmet seems to have made some kind of bargain with Mullah Abadul, in the name of charity."

"Mullah Abadul takes too much on himself," the sultan groused. "Just because he was trained in Baghdad, he thinks himself more holy than anyone else in Manatas. Ever since he came from Al-Andalus, he's been trying to reform the muskat, forcing the strictest interpretation of the Prophet's words, pushing himself into things that are no concern of his."

Like the makeup of the sultan's household, and his child's upbringing, Halvar said to himself. It was at Mullah Abadul's insistence the loose-living Leon di Vicenza be dismissed from the sultan's staff that had led to the events resulting in Halvar's being sent to Manatas.

"He's fomenting riots against the Yehudit and Kristos," Selim asserted. "I've heard some of his sermons."

"And the Purists aren't much better," Halvar added. "I'm beginning to wonder if it was such a good idea to combine Green Village with Manatas Town."

"Don Felipe said it himself—we can't have three different codes of law on one small island. So, I suppose you'd best look into this matter of the dead cooper before those Bretains start yammering at us for more justice—and their own court—again." Sultan Petrus riffled the papers in his hands. "Is there anything else? I want to read what Roderigo has to say about the situation in Bella Mara. Sultan Calavera has invited yet more Bretains to settle there. According to Roderigo, it's become a staging-post for every unemployed mercenary who doesn't want to take service with Imperator Lovis or one of his sons."

"In his letters…does Don Felipe mention…me?" Halvar asked. He could not beg, he *would* not beg, for news of whether or not he would be hired for the coming year.

57

"Not particularly, except to praise the way we've kept Manatas quiet so he can proceed with his journey. Is there something you want me to say when I write to him?"

"No. Nothing. With your permission, Excellent Sultan, I will go to the Yehudit study-house and question Albrecht LaPierre. I want to get to the bottom of this matter of the smuggled muskets and the gunpowder manufactory. Once that's done, I can deal with the dead cooper."

"Do you think there's a connection?"

"I'm not sure," Halvar admitted. "But there's something going on, that's for certain."

"It's all mad," Sultan Petrus decided, with a loud sneeze. "Get out of here, and find out what's going on in Manatas!"

Halvar salaamed and made his way down the stairs to the courtyard, where he stood for a moment in the doorway, out of the wind. He stared at the surrounding walls and tried to gather his thoughts.

His shoulder itched where the wound was healing. His head ached from the cold, even with the fur cap over the leather-lined cloth one. He bit his lip in frustration. The year was turning, and he had not been paid for the next one. Would his hire continue? Or was he to be turned out, a servant who had ceased to have a purpose to serve?

He pulled his coat closer at the neck and tried to focus on what had to be done. The muezzin's cry alerted him to midday prayers. He reached under his coat and shirt to clutch the amulet that might have been the crux or Thor's hammer.

"Redeemer, Mother Mara, Thor…you've been good to me so far. Please intercede with the Three Old Women for me now!"

The last time he'd been cut loose from his livelihood had been seven years before, Then, he'd been left for dead on a battlefield. If he hadn't been put on the wrong transport, he probably would have been in Valhalla by now.

Instead, he'd been taken to Al-Andalus with the rest of the wounded. He'd been cared for by the Sisters of Fatima until they deemed him healthy enough to survive on his own. Then they gave him clothes, one dinar, and the blessings of Ilha.

He'd been alone, in a strange country whose language he did not know. If he hadn't interfered in that knife fight...

But he had, and whether it was the Redeemer and Mother Mara, or Thor and the Three Old Women who did it, his life had changed for the better.

Now he was facing a similar fate. He was in a strange place, whose language and customs he didn't understand. What would he do if the calif decided to throw the old dog out of his kennel and leave him to fend for himself?

Behind him, he heard the scuffling of booted feet. Selim hovered behind him, her round face creased in a worried frown. Her heavy eyebrows nearly met over her snub nose. There were several dark mustache hairs on her upper lip. She was not a pretty girl, but she made a strong, courageous lad, and she was devoted to his welfare.

Her father had hinted he would not look unkindly on Halvar if he approached him with an offer to marry the girl. Didn't every tale end with the poor soldier marrying the sultan's daughter? It was a way out of his dilemma...

"Are you all right, Don Alvaro? Capitán?" He could hear it in her voice—she was on the verge of falling in love with him. He could easily take the sultan's offer, marry the girl, and live the life of the sultan's son-in-law.

But he could not do it. He could not take advantage of a young girl's infatuation and an old man's plotting.

He turned and forced a smile. "Just hungry. Let's have a bite at the barracks, and then we can tackle the Yehudit."

Together, they crossed the courtyard. The gobble-bird stew was always ready, and Halvar needed sustenance. Once that was done, he would deal with Albrecht La Pierre, and then have that long-postponed talk with Guardsman Zoltan. Personal matters would have to wait.

Chapter 9

AFTER THEIR BRIEF MEAL, HALVAR AND SELIM
strolled across the Broad Way and entered the souk, the day-
to-day marketplace of Manatas. The twice-yearly ferias might
attract buyers and sellers from all over Nova Mundum, but
for ordinary shopping, the people of Manatas patronized the
shops and stalls of the souk.

Vendors offered fish from the waterfront, vegetables
from Green Village, even bread made with rye and wheat
flour from West Caster, a change from the ever-present maiz.
Mendel the Bookseller had shielded his wares with boards,
making a small hut out of what had been a tent. Yussif the
Tailor's shop was also boarded up, but a sample of his craft
hung from a bracket over the door, advertising the coats and
jackets available within.

On this day, the market was less crowded than it had
been only days before. A few women shrouded in black
burkas strolled along Market Street, the main east-west thor-

oughfare that led across Manatas Island through the marketplace to the Yehudit study-house and the tangle of houses clustered near it. A knot of black-clad Yehudit scurried from the river toward the Broad Way, their long coats flapping around their legs while they held their hats firmly on their heads lest the wind send them flying. A party of students in long cloaks, their heads hidden in hoods, had gathered in the gap between Mendel the Bookseller's and the path to the madrassa.

Vendors in long striped caftans and turbans who were accustomed to stand beside open stalls to shout their wares to passers-by now huddled inside the doors to their shacks, whose shutters were drawn against the blasts of wind coming off the Great River.

Instead of the usual stream of donkey carts and dog-pulls loaded with produce, only one lonely cart and its driver plodded along, carrying wood to heat the homes of the people of Manatas. No Afrikan women in colorful draperies and wrapped head-scarves strolled along the street offering cooked nguba beans and popped maiz kernels.

One brave Local woman had set up her small brazier in a sheltered corner between two wooden shanties, trying to persuade the few customers who hurried past to spend a white wumpum for her roasted ears of maiz. Beside her, the large dog who pulled her three-cornered rack sat, eyes alert for anyone who might snatch something from the leather bag next to her.

Halvar trudged along with Selim in his wake, taking in the scene.

"Not too many folk about," he noted.

"The Holy Days are over," Selim reminded him. "The Yehudit are finished with their Festival of Lights, and Fasting Month ended two days ago. Yule, Nativity—all done."

"Not all done," Halvar objected. "There's still the Turning Day. And the Kings' Visiting Day. Until then, for Kristos, the holy days aren't over"

"Maybe so," Selim said, "but as far as Islim is concerned, once Fasting Month is done, there's nothing left but winter. And that's coming, and coming hard." She glanced upward, and shivered. "More snow on the way, I think."

Halvar regarded the shuttered stalls.

"Where are the vegetable sellers? The butchers? The bakers?"

"The bakers' ovens are indoors, the butchers slaughter close to the river, where they can rinse the blood away. The farmers are mostly gone back to Round Island—there are a few from Green Village who have small plots where they grow things like turnips. The Local women who stay at the Algonkin settlement have the beans and maiz and escouash they harvested. It's too cold here for anything else to grow in the winter."

"Just like the Dane-March," Halvar said. "Thor's Hammer, how tired I got of pickled cabbage by spring!"

He stepped aside to let two Yehudit in broad-brimmed hats trimmed with fur pass by.

"Someone's in a hurry," he muttered.

"Short day for Yehudit prayers," Selim reminded him. "Aha! There's Zoltan and Fergus! Salaam, Guardsmen!"

"Salaam, young Selim. Salaam, Capitán." Zoltan sketched a salute.

"Salaam, Guardsman Zoltan. Good to see you're back at your post." He tilted his head to look the guardsman in the eye. "Anything new to report?"

"All quiet now the mullah's gone back to his lair," Zoltan told him. "All this wind has sent folks indoors."

"Including the thieves," Halvar said. He looked around the street. There were two men wheeling a cart loaded with dripping carcasses towards them. "Not easy to take something off a butcher's cart, but someone's bound to try. Keep your eyes open, Guardsman."

"I always do, Capitán."

"Don't forget to see me when you get off shift." Halvar added as he resumed his slog through the muck.

Fergus, usually a step behind his friend, called out, "One more thing, Capitán. There's something you should know—"

Zoltan cut him short. "Can't you see the Capitán is in a hurry? It can wait."

Before Halvar could respond, a black-clad Bretain draped in a dark-blue cape accosted them, greeting Halvar in passable Arabi.

"Salaam aleikum, Capitán Don Alvaro Danske. How do you fare this morning? It is, indeed, a cold day."

Halvar grinned under his mustache. "Aleikum salaam, Heer Edgar Norris. You seem to be making progress in the local tongue."

Edgar switched to Erse. "I do what I can, but it is not easy to provide for Milord Summersby in a place where one does not know the common language. I have been buying supplies, such as they are, for our cook. There doesn't seem to be much here, but I assume she will manage some kind of meal fit for Milord. She insists on cooking in the Yehudit style, adhering to their dietary rulings. And she is most particular about her utensils. She has mislaid one of her knives, which makes her cross."

"Cooks tend to be temperamental," Halvar said. "And Milady Summersby? How is she faring at the cheesemaker's cottage?"

"Well enough, considering the cheesemaker's daughter was never trained to be a lady's maid. Milady Charlotte is not pleased with the garb she brought with her from Brookline. However, she found some of the garments left by Dame Brigitte, which are more suitable, if not particularly fashionable. I am looking for a seamstress to adapt some those to Milady's figure, being she is somewhat shorter and narrower than the unfortunate maidservant."

Halvar pointed to the shop behind them.

"You've come to the right place. There is Yussif the Tailor. He makes all my coats. And next to him is Oscar, who sells used clothing for both women and children. Between them, they can find you the best sewing-woman in Manatas."

"I shall certainly do that. I only hope that my Arabi is equal to the task."

"It's not an easy language to grasp. It took me a while to get the hang of it, and I was in a: court in Al-Andalus. What they speak here in Manatas isn't what they do in Corduva. But Yussif understands Erse well enough. And silver talks in any language. Good luck to you, Heer Edgar."

Halvar looked around, trying to spot the rest of the Town Guard. Tenente Flores was helping himself to an apple from a basket in front of one of the stalls. Suppressing the urge to chide his underling for committing the same petty theft as the Scavenger brats, Halvar called, "Tenente Flores! With me!"

Flores hastily swallowed a bite of apple and thrust the remains under his coat.

"Capitán!"

"You and your men, come with me. I want to question Albrecht LaPierre again. I think I can get him away from the Yehudit and back into the Rabat where he belongs."

"Good luck with that!" Flores sneered. "Those Yehudit, they're a clannish lot. They'll never let the alchemist go, no matter how well you talk."

"I may not know much fancy Arabi, but I can make sense in good Danic and Erse," Halvar stated. "If that doesn't work, I may have to use another way of getting that killer behind the walls. I hope I don't have to do that, but I want you and your men with me, just in case someone objects to parting with Master LaPierre."

"Zoltan!" Flores called., trying to distract the tall guardsman from his conversation with the Local woman at the brazier.

"Not Zoltan," Halvar told him. "He's caused enough trouble for one day. Let Guardsman Zoltan finish his shift here in the souk. I'll have a word with him when he goes to the Rabat for his dinner. Those two, over there—who are they?" He pointed to guardsmen standing next to Mendel the Bookseller's stall.

"That's Isa and Musa. Good lads, been with us since Gomez's time."

Halvar recognized the taller of the two, a dark-skinned Andalusian who might well have had an Afrikan ancestor lurking in his past.

"That fellow is the one caught the Scavenger lad nicking wumpum off belts while Emir Achmet had his say at the Grand Muskat."

"That's Musa." Flores waved the two guardsmen over. "The one with the scar on his face is Isa."

The two guardsmen approached their superiors warily. Flores wasted no time with pleasantries.

"Come with us," he ordered. "The Capitán is going to reclaim a prisoner!"

They fell into line behind him.

The brick path through the souk met a cobblestone road that ran parallel to the bank of the Great River. Flores gestured toward the line of wooden and brick houses that lined the street but did not proceed.

"Come on!" Halvar stepped onto the rammed-earth path that ran along the Great River.

"This is the Yehudit quarter," Flores said. "By agreement with the Yehudit leaders, the Town Guards don't patrol here. They take care of their own, have since they came. Islim don't mix with Yehudit. They keep their own laws, they don't subscribe to Sharia."

"The Yehudit are part of Manatas, just as Green Village is," Halvar stated. "One law applies to all. And if Rav Shimon Layzar thinks he's going to shelter a murderer, I'll persuade him not to."

66

"And if you can't?" Flores was skeptical.

"Then we will have to take Master LaPierre back to the Rabat by force. But I hope it won't come to that. Tenente Flores, you and your men will accompany me to the Yehudit study-house, and that's an order!" He squared his shoulders and prepared for battle. One way or another, he would get his man!

He braced himself against the wind and forged onward. He sent one more quick request to the Redeemer, Mother Mara and Thor: *Please, let Albrecht LaPierre be sane—just long enough to tell me what he knows. After that, he's all yours!*

Chapter 10

HALVAR HAD BEEN IN TOWNS IN THE DANE-MARCH where the Yehudit were confined to certain streets, sometimes separated from the rest of the place by a chain or even a wall. In Al-Andalus, Yehudit mingled with Islim on terms of relative equality during the day but tended to live near their study-houses and baths, for convenience.

In Manatas, as in Al-Andalus, there were no legal restrictions, but the Yehudit still clustered around their own study-house, butcher, and bath-house, making the best of the most windswept district of Manatas.

The houses were built of both brick and wood in the Oropan style, with two rooms on the ground floor and an attic or loft under a peaked roof that was not quite a second story. Squawks, bellows, and bleats came from a pen at the far southern end of the street where chickens, geese, and sheep awaited their fate in the butcher's abattoir.

Halvar glanced up and down the street. All seemed peaceful. A Local woman with a dog-pull stood at one door, bargaining with an unseen housewife within for the maiz and yellow escouash in her baskets. The man with the donkey-cart emerged from the souk and bellowed, "Wood! Fine cut logs!" as he led his animal northward towards the steaming bath-house that marked the end of the Yehudit quarter.

One solemn goose waddled down the middle of the road, daring anyone to stop him.

At the north end of the road were two larger buildings, one on the side of the road next to the river, the other facing it. Plumes of smoke and steam from the river-side building indicated a bath-house, drawing its water from the river. A brawny Yehudit woman was overseeing a squad of Afrikans pegging out freshly-laundered clothes that flapped in the rising wind; the man with the wood now negotiated with another woman while more Afrikans unloaded the fuel from the cart.

Facing the bath-house was the most imposing structure in the row—a two-story brick building with a stepped roof that reminded Halvar of the ones he'd seen in Koben-Haven. The unspoken rule was that no building in Islim territory should be taller than the nearest muskat, so this one circumvented the rule by being wider than it was tall, with two windows on either side of the door, indicating more than two rooms on the ground floor. Halvar suspected the building extended backwards as well, taking up the entire space allotted to it, with one lot to spare on either side.

"That's the study-house," Selim said unnecessarily.

Halvar assessed the place as they approached. There was nothing, apart from its size, to distinguish it from any of the other houses on the street. There was no tower for bells, like a Kristo chapel, or a minaret for the muezzin to announce the times for prayers, like an Islim muskat. There was no signboard or placard, in either Ivrit or Arabi, on the wall announcing its function. Only a carving of a branched candlestick on the door indicated this was anything but an ordinary residence, albeit somewhat grander than any other on the street.

Flores hung back. "What do we do now?"

"We go in." Halvar strode up to the door and rapped.

He could hear muttered voices within. Then Benyamin ben Mendel opened the door and greeted him.

"I wondered when you would show up. I knew you would come here to talk with Master LaPierre once the sultan released him into Yehudit hands. Rav Shimon Layzar insists I should be present, as advocate for Master LaPierre, since I am familiar with both Sharia and Yehudit law." He spotted Flores and the two guards lurking behind Selim. "Did you have to bring the Guards with you? They're not welcome in the Yehudit quarter."

"So I've been told, but all quarters are part of Manatas Town, from the Rabat to the waterfront to the Street of the Afrikans to Green Village," Halvar declared. "As for why I'm here, you're quite right. I want a word or two with Master Albrecht LaPierre.

"I've no objection to anyone speaking up for him. I have all the proof I need to show he is a cold-blooded murderer, and I'm here to take him back to the Rabat, where he can freeze his arse off in a cell until Sultan Petrus comes to a decision as to his time and place of execution. Tenente Flores and his men are here to make sure that happens. Are you going to make us use these halberds, or will you let us inside, where we can discuss this quietly?"

Benyamin stood aside to let Halvar and Selim into the house. Flores hesitated.

"Your men may enter, but only as far as the hallway," Benyamin warned. "Master La Pierre is under Yehudit protection."

"That's what I want to discuss," Halvar said. "Come on in, Tenente. It's better than standing outside in that wind."

Flores and the two guardsmen edged into the house, positioning themselves near the door for a fast retreat.

Benyamin led Halvar and Selim down the hall past the large front room, furnished with benches and a cabinet covered by an embroidered cloth, to a small book-lined study. As Halvar had suspected, the hallway went on through the house to what sounded and smelled like an active kitchen at the rear of the building.

He entered the tiny room, whose walls were shelves filled with bound books, pages sewn together with twine, loose pages, and scrolls. Most of the room was taken up by a tile-covered stove that exuded enough heat to warm not only this room but most of the house.

Huddled next to the stove in an armchair was the ancient leader of the Yehudit, Rav Shimon Layzar, a wrinkled, withered man in a shapeless black coat. A knitted cap covered his bald head. His beard was white and wispy, his mouth nearly toothless; but his dark eyes were sharp under heavy gray brows, and he looked up at Halvar with an air of amused tolerance.

Beside him, on a backless bench, was the errant alchemist, Albrecht LaPierre, his hair wilder than usual, his knitted tunic unraveling at the ends of the sleeves and hem, his mustache straggling over his upper lip. He started to rise when he saw Halvar. Rav Shimon Layzar stopped him with one liver-spotted hand.

Halvar stood in the middle of the room, towering over the rav and the seated alchemist. Selim squeezed next to him, trying to avoid the stove, her pen-case and notebook ready to record the proceedings..

"Salaam, Capitán Halvar Danske," the rav greeted his unwanted visitors in Arabi. "I assume you come here because you want to take this man back to his prison."

"I do." Halvar wasted no time getting to the point. "He's a murderer and belongs in a cell, not in a comfortable house like this one."

"So you say." Rav Shimon Layzar beckoned to Benyamin. "Master LaPierre, what do you say to this charge?"

"I didn't mean to kill him!" Albrecht blurted. "It was all a mistake!"

"You admit that you gave Master Kupernik a cake containing nguba beans?" Halvar said.

"Well...yes...I did do that," Albrecht said. "But I only thought it would make him ill. I didn't know it would kill him!"

Rav Shimon Layzar looked up at Halvar. "A natural error—an unfortunate one, to be sure, but not a deliberate attempt to kill."

Halvar loosened the top frog on his coat. The stove made the room uncomfortably warm.

"I'll get back to that in a bit, for there is another matter I must ask Master LaPierre about. There is a cabin in the woods north of Green Village. What can you tell me about that?"

Albrecht looked startled. "The cabin? What does that have to do with Master Kupernik's death?"

"It's where someone is piling up the makings of gunpowder," Halvar stated. "Selim, what did we find in that cabin?"

Selim consulted her notebook. "Rocks containing sulfur. Jars of urine being turned into saltpeter. Charred wood of the sort used for the binding of the other two into an explosive compound."

"In other words, someone was making gunpowder in that cabin." Halvar pointed at the cringing alchemist. "And since you admit the place was yours, I can only think the someone in question was you. You, Master LaPierre, are making a dangerous substance, one that is forbidden under the laws of Al-Andalus, except under the supervision of the calif and his associates."

"But he *hasn't* actually made it, not yet," Selim pointed out. "Nothing was being used."

"In that case, you may have been scheming to get money for *pretending* to make gunpowder." Halvar's voice was icy. "You are either a fraud or a traitor, Master LaPierre. Which is it?"

Rav Shimon Layzar absorbed this information with a bemused glance at the alchemist.

"This is quite a charge, Albrecht. I didn't think you were so foolish as to try and make gunpowder. It's difficult to control, quite dangerous. Quite profitable, of course, if you can do it, but quite a risky business, nonetheless."

"I have invented a new process," Albrecht whined. "It is much easier and safer, my method of making gunpowder, if it is done correctly.

"I explained it to Rav Nahum at the madrassa. I wanted a workroom, a place to test my theory. He refused me. I told him I could make better gunpowder, cheaper, more efficient. It could be sold, and the profits used to benefit the madrassa.

"He quoted rules, regulations, said my workshop would put the rest of the alchemists in danger. He would not let me do my tests in the workshops owned by the madrassa." Albrecht stopped for breath, red-faced in his indignation.

"And so, when the Bretain came along, this fellow Mac-Alan, and offered you the space, you jumped at the chance to have a place to play with your explosions," Halvar finished for him. "Just when was this? Before or after the Fall Feria?"

"The Bretain came to the madrassa with his son, Owen, just before the Fall Feria opened," Albrecht said. "He wanted to place the boy with someone who would take him on as an apprentice, teach him proper alchemy. I was to be that person. MacAlan had seen gunpowder being made in Bos-Town—he had one keg for sale at the feria—but he could not make it himself. He did not know the procedure.

"He also said he had heard of new muskets being made, muskets that used a flint instead of a match to set the powder alight. These muskets need a particularly pure black powder, much finer than what sparks a matchlock. He wanted to know if I could make it. I told him I had the formula, but—"

"You haven't actually made any gunpowder at all," Selim interrupted him.

"But I have the *technique*," Albrecht insisted. "All I needed was a place to prove my theory and produce the powder."

"And you didn't consider why MacAlan wanted the stuff?" Halvar asked.

"That was his business, not mine. I just wanted to prove my new procedure," Albrecht said earnestly.

"So, MacAlan got the space for the cabin from the Locals and arranged to have it built by one of the Scanians in Green Village," Halvar summed up. "Probably using Samuel Igbo as middle-man in dealing with the Locals, since he didn't know their language, and Igbo did."

"What has this to do with the charges against Master LaPierre?" Benyamin put in. "Whether or not his experiments were legal, where he did them, or the purpose of the final product—this has no bearing on the death of Master Kupernik. The cabin in the woods is totally irrelevant to that case."

"Oh, but it is—very relevant. I'll get to that, you may be sure." Halvar turned back to Albrecht. "Did you oversee the building of this cabin?"

"Of course not. I had other duties, classes to teach," Albrecht said testily. "I told MacAlan what I needed. I assumed he'd do what I told him to do."

"Trusting of you," Halvar jeered. "Didn't you even go there once, just to make sure he'd done what you wanted?"

Albrecht shifted uneasily on his bench.

"I went there once, to make sure he had collected the supplies I asked for," he admitted. "But I had nothing to do with his plans for the gunpowder. If he was going to use it to rebel against Al-Andalus, I knew nothing about it."

74

"He wasn't going to rebel," Selim said thoughtfully. "It may be he was going to sell the stuff. He may even have considered taking the new muskets and gunpowder to the Locals, trading them for land to make his own settlement beyond the mountains, where they say there is nothing but forest."

"Whatever he was going to do, he isn't going to do it now," Halvar said. "As to what all this has to do with the death of Master Kupernik? Master LaPierre, you were seen in Green Village just before the Watch-Night of the Nativity."

"Really?" Rav Shimon Layzar was skeptical. "One man, on a night when Green Village is known for attracting a vast crowd? Are you sure Master LaPierre was seen?"

Halvar grinned. "Master LaPierre is somewhat noticeable. He does not cover his head, and that hair can been recognized across the feria grounds." He turned back to Albrecht. "Is that when you went to the cabin? During the day, after the party at the madrassa had disbanded?"

Albrecht licked suddenly dry lips "Yes, I went to the cabin. I wanted to see if all was in order. I was going to start my experiments, try my new method of making gunpowder after the Festival of Lights, when the days start getting longer."

"And you picked up a chip of wood in the woodpile," Halvar said. "Selim, do you still have that chip?"

"I do." Selim checked her notebook and pen-case. "Here it is." She found it, folded into a page of the notebook.

"A chip?" Rav Shimon Layzar looked puzzled.

"A chip, which Selim will assure you was found jammed under Master Kupernik's door."

"Just a chip of wood,,"Albrecht scoffed. "You can find them anywhere."

"Not this one," Halvar said. "This is aspen, and it's from the woodpile at the cabin. It's quite a walk from the madrassa to the cabin. Even by donkey cart, at least an hour, maybe more. Most of the wood burned in Manatas is pine and birch, brought in by cart from Green Village and the woods beyond, chopped into small logs, ready for the fireplace. No one chops wood here in town, and certainly not at the madrassa.

"So, Master Albrecht LaPierre..." Halvar's voice sharpened. "Tell me how a chip from a woodpile miles from here wound up under the door of a man you hated? Jammed under the door, so that if he was taken ill by something he ate, he could not get out of this room to get help? And to make sure he could not cry out, you poured the water from his jug into the chamber pot."

"That is a very damning accusation." Rav Shimon Layzar turned to the alchemist. "What do you say, Master LaPierre?"

Albrecht sat, gaping at his accuser, silent.

"You were already thinking of killing Master Kupernik," Halvar went on relentlessly. "Even before the party at the madrassa on Watch-Night, you must have already had that chip with you. You had arranged to have the cake with the nguba delivered to you personally at the madrassa. I have the messenger who delivered the cake. He will swear that he placed it into your hands."

"A Waterfront Rat!" Albrecht exploded. "You take the word of a Kristo beggar-boy over mine!"

"When he speaks the truth, and you don't, yes, I do," Halvar said. "If you weren't planning to kill Master Kupernik, why pick up the chip? For luck? As a token?"

"And how did you know the messenger was one of the Waterfront Rats?" Selim put in. "The Scavengers also deliver messages and packages to the madrassa."

Benyamin frowned. "You make a very good case, Don Alvaro. I cannot refute your logic. But whether or not he deliberately gave the poisoned cake to Master Kupernik, Master LaPierre is not involved in any treason to Al-Andalus. Planning on making gunpowder is not the same as making it."

"He still belongs in the Rabat, not here!" Halvar retorted.

Rav Shimon Layzar nodded thoughtfully. "You may be right, Capitán Danske. But Master LaPierre must stay here, with us, until he is brought to trial. The Rabat is not heated, he cannot get proper kosher food—"

"It's Halal!" Selim protested.

"But not kosher," Rav Shimon Layzar chided her. "We will take care Master LaPierre does not escape justice. If he deliberately gave Master Kupernik a cake containing something he knew would kill him, he must pay the penalty for it. If, on the other hand, he did not know it would kill Master Kupernik, it was an act of spite but not deliberate, premeditated murder. We shall think about it."

"Think all you like, Rav, but Master Albrecht LaPierre is a murderer. He has already confessed to giving Master Kupernik the cake that killed him. He may also be involved in a plot to arm Locals against Al-Andalus. He belongs at the Rabat, in custody."

"Under guard, certainly. But not at the Rabat." Rav Shimon Layzar's voice took on a hard edge. "He is Yehudit, he belongs with us."

"It's the custom of Manatas." Benyamin spoke up. "Just as Green Village held to Bretain law and custom, so does the Yehudit Quarter hold to our law and custom."

"It's about time for you people to realize that Manatas is one town, with one law and one Town Guard." Halvar was getting more exasperated by the minute. When would these people understand what the calif wanted to do—to strengthen this unruly settlement?

"We have our own guard. Asher the Butcher and his men will make sure Master LaPierre does not leave Manatas," Benyamin said, matching Halvar's tone. "When you come for him, you will find him. But unless you choose to use force to take him, he remains here."

As if in answer to an unspoken call, two brawny men appeared at the door, their black coats tight over well-muscled arms, their expressions grim above their dark beards.

Halvar clenched his teeth over his natural response. In Corduva, he would have invoked the authority of the calif, summoned armed men to swarm over the house and remove the culprit, with no resistance from the Yehudit within. Here in Manatas, it would seem things were very different. These people were ready to defend one of their own, even an accused murderer.

He weighed his options. He could grab Albrecht, march him out of the room, fight his way past the two Yehudit, and likely set off a riot. Or he could back away from this fight, and choose another time and place to establish the authority of Sultan Petrus and Calif Don Felipe over all the people of Manatas.

"I'll be back," he gritted out, and stamped from the room, past Flores and his guardsmen, with Selim close behind.

The wind slammed the door behind them as they regrouped in the street.

"You should have taken that sniveling Yehudit," Flores sneered as Halvar headed back to the souk. "The Yehudit should be shown who rules in Manatas."

"He'll be under guard," Selim pointed out. "He's not going anywhere."

Halvar said nothing. He held on to his fur cap with one hand, and his dagger with the other. Somehow, he felt he had lost an important skirmish in the battle for control of the island. He marched through the souk, eyes fixed on the towers of the Rabat looming ahead of him.

"What next?" Flores's gruff voice shook him out of his reverie.

"Get the men who are off-duty together. I want to run halberd drill," Halvar ordered. "Selim, do you still have those business papers from Ned Cooper's office?"

"I took them to our office," Selim replied. "I can go over them there."

"Do it. I want to know more about those barrels—who ordered them, what size they were, whether they were meant for fish or gunpowder."

Flores snorted his disgust. "Barrels! You're chasing phantom plotters, and that fellow La Pierre sits in the Yehudit study-house, laughing at us, while you shuffle papers? What kind of capitán are you, Hireling?"

Halvar stopped in mid-stride. "The kind who takes his orders from Sultan Petrus, who takes his from our calif. And you, Tenente, are taking orders from me. And these are my orders—I want Guardsman Zoltan in my office after the afternoon shift is over. I want our men to be proficient in halberd drill. And I want Selim to look over those bills from Ned Cooper's desk, because the business with Captain Girard and the smuggled muskets annoys me, and I want to find out who ordered them and where they were bound. Is that enough for you, Tenente Flores?"

Flores stepped back and salaamed.

"As you will, Capitán."

They proceeded through the souk to the Broad Way, where ramshackle wooden stalls gave way to solid brick buildings. Men in a variety of garb, from the long striped caftans of the Andalusians to the dark cloaks and broad-brimmed hats of Oropans, huddled in the doorways of the mokkashops on the ground floors of the houses.

One of them, his form swathed in a dark-blue cloak and topped with an Oropan-style hat bearing a jaunty feather, called out, "Halloo! Pikeman! Over here!"

"Oh, no, not him!" Halvar groaned. He did not want to have to deal with this man!

Ex-Musket-man Devallon had found him…again.

Chapter 11

"SALAAM ALEIKUM! IS THAT WHAT THEY SAY HERE in Manatas?" Devallon crossed the Broad Way to intercept Halvar and his troop.

"Good day to you, Musket-man," Halvar responded politely in Erse. "What brings you out on such a chilly day?"

"A need for good company," Devallon replied with an expressive grimace. "May I treat you to some of that disgusting beverage they serve in these shops?"

"I'm a little busy..." Halvar started towards the Rabat.

"You wanted to know more about Girard," Selim murmured. "Sieur Devallon was on the ship with him for two voyages. He's got to know more than he's already told you."

"I'll have the men in the courtyard after the muezzin calls prayers," Flores promised.

"I'll look over those papers and have the report ready," Selim added.

"I have to talk to you!" Devallon grabbed his arm, and steered him across the Broad Way toward the nearest mokka-shop. Halvar let himself be led into the Blue Parrot as Selim and Flores proceeded southward.

Like most such establishments, the Blue Parrot was in a low-ceilinged room on the ground floor of one of the brick buildings that lined the Broad Way. The place was filled with men sitting at low tables, their legs folded under them. The air was redolent with tabac—some from water-pipes, some from the clay pipes handed out by the servers—and the enticing aromas of mokka and chai brewing on the rim of the oven on the back wall.

Halvar blinked back sudden sweat at the blast of heat from oven and humanity. It was a pleasant shock after the bone-chilling cold in the street.

Devallon found a table in a corner and awkwardly lowered himself onto the stool next to it. He waved at the nearest server, a halfling lad in a long striped caftan and fez.

"A pot of that mokka stuff, and something to eat," he ordered.

The server set two small bowls, one of salted nut-meats, the other with popped maiz kernels, on the table and threaded his way around the tables to the mokka-pots lined up, ready for serving.

Halvar greedily grabbed a handful of the nuts. "None for you?"

"I don't eat nuts. They gave me a bad cough when I was a boy." Devallon daintily picked through the other bowl to retrieve the maiz-kernels. "These aren't bad. This and tabac are the only good things to come out of Nova Mundum, if you ask me."

"I didn't ask you," Halvar said sourly. "Why aren't you at the cottage, dancing attendance on Milord Summersby?"

"He won't miss me. He's in the goat-shed, arguing with a farmer about his horse." Devallon hitched his seat nearer to Halvar and lowered his voice to a mere shout. "I tell you, Pike-man, I've had all I can take of that one. I don't care how much silver he throws at me."

"Silver, indeed! Where does it come from? Does he have one of those magical purses, like the ones in the old tales?"

"It's bound to run out soon," Devallon agreed. "What with the wine he's been swilling…"

"The stuff he got at the Gardens of Paradise?" Halvar suppressed a laugh. Dani Glick had sold the Bretain the Jerez wine no one else would have. "What does his steward think of that expense?"

"Edgar? He's off doing who-knows-what in the souk. He's picked up some Arabi, enough to get through to the woman who cooks for us. She's off in a temper, too, something about her cooking gear. I can't understand a word of it."

"So he has. He was buying a beginner's glossary in Mendel the Bookseller's stall when he met Master LaPierre, the one who got you lot into that madrassa party yesterday. Ah, mokka!" He grabbed one of the cups the server offered and drank eagerly.

Devallon took the other cup, sipped and grimaced. "How can you stand this muck?"

"You get used to it," Halvar assured him. "It livens you up without fuzzing your wits like wine or ale. It's better with a little sweetener, like honey."

"As far as I can tell, sweetening it only makes it worse. And the food?" Devallon made a noise of disgust. "Fowl and fish, fish and fowl. No pork at all! Not even beef! And the spices are enough to burn your tongue off."

Halvar grinned under his mustache, recalling his own initial reaction to the savory flavors of Andalusian cuisine.

"There must be some other compensations. You're close enough to the waterfront to meet some of the, um, lively ladies who attend the Roumi Rite chapel."

"The whores, you mean? Nice enough, but not really to my taste. And between Milord's whims and Edgar's fine and fancy airs, I'm beginning to think I should have taken the Lad's offer of a post with his new-fangled regiment. I tell you, Pike-man, I'll go mad if I have to stay in this place for the entire winter."

"You've no choice," Halvar said. "The only ships in and out in the winter are the official dhows with dispatches from the other Andalusian sultanates, and the fishing vessels that hug the coast. You can try to book passage on one of them, but it won't be fine quarters like you had on *Belle Fleur*, and you'll stink of fish by the time you get where you're going."

Devallon stared gloomily into his cup."Smelling of fish might be worth it, if I could get away from those two Bretains."

"I still don't understand how 'those two Bretains' wound up in Kibbick. It's Franchen territory, not Bretain. West Caster is where the Bretain ships go."

"I don't know what led them to leave Bretain, but according to Edgar, the captain of the ship that took them across the Storm Sea was a drunken fool who lost his way. Not so hard to do, on the ocean, where there's nothing to go by but the stars and the moon. Even with a compass to tell north from south. As for east and west, that's 'by guess and by golly', as the sailors told me.

"According to them, ships get lost all the time. A superstitious lot, those sailors on the *Belle Fleur*, but they trusted their captain to get them where they were supposed to go. A good seaman was Girard." Devallon sighed mightily in memory of the deceased.

"Ah, yes, Captain Franz Girard." Halvar invoked the man whose violent death had begun his investigations nearly two weeks before. "My learned friend, Frater Leonidas, has translated some of his journals. Apparently, he had made some kind of business arrangement in Bos-town that led to his deciding to put in here in Manatas. Something to do with smuggled muskets. You're sure you know nothing about them?"

"I told you, I had nothing to do with whatever scheme Girard was hatching!" Devallon's voice rose, drawing the attention of the men in dark coats at the table next to them. He lowered his tone again, and the other men turned back to their own affairs. "We talked about other things. Mostly women, and his successes with them."

"That must have been enlightening," Halvar commented. "Especially on the trip from Franchenland to Kibbick, with all those women aboard."

"And all of them meant for the soldiers and farmers of Kibbick," Devallon pointed out.

"Except for your cousin Charlotte. I wouldn't think her the sort to hack a living on a farm in the wilderness. What did she hope to gain by removing herself from a cushy house in Parigi to the wilds of Nova Mundum?"

"Wealth. Position. What she couldn't get in Franchenland after her family's estate got sacked in the wars." Devallon sighed again. "She was supposed to marry some local sprout, but he got killed in a stupid duel, and she got sent off to find her fortune. As did I. She went to Parigi, with one of our trusted servants—"

"Dame Brigitte?

"She came later. I went with the Franchen Musket-Men. You know the rest—you were there. We fought for Imperator Lovis, he paid well. Your Free Danes were on the other side, more fools you.

"It's all over now. Lovis Younger has brought all the free companies under his banner, and that's that. No more work for a soldier, unless he's ready to swear loyalty to Franchenland and Lovis."

"Which you aren't?"

Devallon shrugged expressively. "The pay wasn't worth the groveling I'd have to do. I thought I might marry a merchant's widow who took a shine to me, but the pain of spending the rest of my life with her was more than I could stomach. Then Charlotte introduced me to Girard, Girard made a good offer, and here I am, stranded in Manatas." He took another sip of mokka.

Halvar thought this over. "Charlotte again. You say you two were brought up together. That would make Charlotte at least as old as you."

"Not quite as old," Devallon protested. "She was just a girl when she was sent off to Parigi. And I'm no graybeard!"

Halvar smiled under his mustache. "You're older than me, Musket-man, and I'm thirty-seven. That would make Charlotte…hmmm…at least thirty? Not a maiden by any means!"

"Not a girl, anyway," Devallon admitted.

"I wonder what Milord Henry felt when he saw her without her paints and her fine clothes?" Halvar said with a wry grin. "She didn't look quite so pretty in her Purist gown, with no paint to her face."

"He had a fit!" Devallon snorted. "When I brought her to the cottage last night, to see if there was anything left in the sea-chests for her to wear, he took one look and started to rave that he'd been robbed, that she was no more than an old whore, that he wouldn't have her.

"Then Edgar took over, calmed the fat fool down, said that she came with a land grant, and silver, and that was enough. Then Charlotte had her say, told him what she thought of him and his pretensions, used some Erse I didn't know she had. I'm surprised the neighbors didn't call the Town Guard to stop the brawl!"

"We had other things to worry about," Halvar said. "Dead coopers, for one. I don't suppose you know anything about that?"

"What does a dead cooper have to do with Milord Summersby's marital woes?"

"Maybe nothing, but the cooper seems to have known Summersby back in Bretain; and from what I've heard, Ned

Cooper didn't think Henry Summersby was any kind of milord. He said so yesterday, before witnesses, while Milord was showing off his horsemanship at the lion hunt. Today Ned was found dead in his cooperage in Green Village. Someone stuck a knife in his back. I can't help thinking the two are connected."

"Well, Pike-man, I can tell you for a fact that I was with Milord Henry Summersby from the time we left Green Village after the Watch-night Holy Meal at the fratery chapel until the bells rang for dawn prayers this morning; and whatever else he was doing, he wasn't killing a cooper, with a knife or anything else.

"First, he was arranging the hunt, organizing a pack of students from the madrassa and whatever layabouts he could find on the street to follow him into the woods. Then, he was riding, if you can call it that, into the woods, chasing the beast. It was all he could do to manage his horse. What a mess! I've seen better-managed hunts in the mountains of Hispania.

"Then, he was following the trail of the mountain cat, hallooing and hollering, not even trying to ambush the beast. Any animal within earshot would flee, and that one ran over the rocks to its den."

"Where the Bretain Purist had taken refuge. You weren't with milord all the time. You spent a few minutes with Fru Dani Glick at the Gardens of Paradise."

"To be sure, but Milord Summersby was in full view of the crowd while I tried to arrange better quarters. Ask anyone! He was there when you dispatched the beast, instead of leaving it to him. He was furious about that, said you shouldn't have taken on the beast by yourself."

"He wasn't on that ledge, I was!" Halvar was getting tired of recounting his exploit. "And all I wanted was to get MacAlan to confess, and get him off the ledge and back to the Rabat. Instead, the clumsy fellow tried to knock me over, and wound up going down the hill himself."

Devallon continued his tale. "Then, there was all that foo-faraw in the middle of the settlement, what you call Green Village? With Milord Summersby demanding the skin of the animal as a trophy, and the Mahak insisting you'd earned it, you get it. He came home in a fury, screaming for Edgar, but Edgar wasn't there. Once Edgar came back to the cottage, he taxed him with something or other, and they had a flaming row, all in some barbarous Erse dialect I couldn't fathom."

"Edgar wasn't with him? When he got back to the cottage?" Halvar frowned over his cup.

"He came in later, just after sunset. Milord started slanging at him for not being on hand when needed. Edgar came back at him—all I could tell was something about money. I couldn't understand a word of it. That's when I left the cottage to look for you. I needed someone sane to talk to, even a Danic pike-man."

Halvar took another handful of nut-meats and chewed thoughtfully.

"Ned the Cooper came from the north of Bretain, It's possible he knew Milord there. Although the cooper told anyone who would listen Summersby was no milord, horse or no horse. You say Edgar bought it from some farmer?"

Devallon gave a scornful snort. "Pah! He didn't buy it. Edgar *leased* it from a farmer, some Dane named Bronk who owns land in West Caster, and bought the tack from the pawn-shop on the waterfront. Now Bronk wants to go back to his farm, and he's taking the horse with him; so Edgar is going to have to find another one, which doesn't sit well with Milord Henry, who was arguing with Bronk in the goat-shed when I left the cottage this morning. And that, Pike-man, is where matters stand."

Halvar's frown deepened. "How does this Bronk intend to get off Manatas if there are no ships leaving?"

"He said there's a ferry up the hills where some frater is trying to build a bridge, just past the rocky islet in the middle of the East Channel.. The frater improved the pier, built a proper jetty and a ramp on the Manatas side so the bridge builders can move their supplies across the water. Bronk and his fellow Danes have built a landing on the opposite bank to accommodate the improved ferry service.

"It wouldn't surprise me if those Danes make more use of the bridge than Manatas ever does. According to Bronk, he came across from his farm just before the Watch-Night started, and he wants to get back home to celebrate the Year's Turning before the heavy weather sets in." Devallon smiled winningly. "Any chance of a small loan, Pike-man? Just to tide me over until spring?"

Halvar set down his cup and rose. "I wish you luck, Musket-man, but I can't give you money, because I haven't been paid more than my daily pittance for food."

"What about a place in your guards?" Devallon pleaded. "Anything, just so I can have enough wumpum to keep body and soul together until spring. For the sake of old friendship?"

"Not a chance," Halvar declared. "I'm an outsider, barely tolerated by the Manatas Guards. The Green Village constabulary, the Mahak watchmen, even the *verdammitte* Yehudit—they obey their own laws and customs. I've been here long enough to learn that much. Each little patch has its own leader, just like Bretain, where every milord with two cows and a horse thinks himself the equal of the High King. I have to move carefully, Devallon. I'm not about to bring another outsider in."

"Not even an old comrade-in-arms?" Devallon coaxed.

"Don't try to pull the 'old comrades' stunt with me. We weren't comrades. Your company and mine shared winter quarters one year, and you tried to mash my face into the ground when we played kick-the-bladder. You might as well stay with Milord Henry, Devallon. He's your paymaster, and there's not going to be another until the ships come north in the spring."

Devallon slumped in his seat. "Then it's back to the cottage for me," he said gloomily.

Halvar patted him on the shoulder.

"It's only three months to spring," he consoled his old enemy. He finished the nuts, swallowed the last of the mokka, and set out again for the Rabat. He caught sight of a ragged lad lurking in the doorway of the next shop. "You—you're one of those Waterfront Rats, aren't you? The one they call Foxy?"

The wiry youngster nodded warily. "That's me."

Halvar beckoned the boy closer. "You see that fellow? The big one, with the plume in his hat?" He pointed to Devallon, who had followed him out of the Blue Parrot and was heading toward the Rabat.

"That's the Franchen who's living in the cottage on Pearl Street. What about him?"

"I want you to keep an eye on him for me. I want you to send word to the Rabat if he or any of the other folk in that cottage look as if they're trying to leave Manatas." Halvar slid four white beads off the string of wumpum at his belt.

"I'm not spying for the Guards," Foxy protested.

"I'm not asking you to spy. I'm asking you to send me a message." Halvar pressed the wumpum into the boy's hand. "I think one of the people in that cottage was connected to the one who killed your friend Snake. I want to make sure he doesn't escape before I can prove it. Can you do this for me...and for Snake?"

Foxy nodded. "I'll get Mouse to watch the cottage, and if they try to leave, I'll send word. But I'm not spying!"

Halvar let the boy go. He started again for the Rabat, mulling over what he had learned in his conversation with Devallon. He was certain Milord Henry Summersby was connected with the smuggled muskets somehow. If only he could prove it! Then he could arrest this so-called milord...

He bent forward, trying to ease the effects of the biting wind that blew across the island.

"Capitán! Capitán!"

His head jerked up as a sharp cry brought him out of his thoughts.

"There's trouble in the souk!" Musa, one of the guardsmen who had accompanied him to the Yehudit quarter earlier, grabbed his arm.

"What now?" Halvar grumbled as he followed the man across the Broad Way, past the posts that marked the boundaries of the souk and into the tangled maze of stalls and stands.

A crowd had gathered in front of Yussif the Tailor's shop. Halvar shoved through to the center of the action.

On the ground in front of the tailor's shop lay the body of a Town Guardsman; Halvar guessed at his identity by the size and shape of him. Guardsman Zoltan had not heeded the warnings, and had come to a violent end.

Chapter 12

HALVAR TOOK IN THE SCENE, TRYING TO MAKE sense of what he saw and heard. The body of Guardsman Zoltan lay on its side in the middle of the street, a knife handle protruding from his back, scissors dangling from the front of his coat. His tarboosh had come off as he fell, and was now lying at the feet of the butcher, Asher.

Guardsman Musa now held another bloody knife in one hand, while his comrade Guardsman Isa held the butcher firmly. A slightly-built Yehudit girl shrank back against the Local woman who had been selling in the alley, and whose large dog growled menacingly as Flores lowered the point of his halberd at them.

Yussif the Tailor stood just outside his shop, his newly-hired Yehudit apprentice behind him. Next to him was Edgar Norris, peering over shoulders to see what was happening. Across the road from the tailor's shop were four Andalusian vendors in striped caftans and knitted caps, draped in heavy woolen scarfs. Four argumentative students clustered at the bookseller's stall, the hems of their over-gowns trailing beneath their short capes. Halvar could just make out another man, taller than the students, draped in a dark cloak with a hood, lurking behind them.

The wood-seller had guided his now-empty cart into the souk, apparently trying to make a few extra wumpum by carrying packages and merchandise northward to Green Village. Three burka-clad women shrank back against the wall of the used-clothing shop, protected by large Afrikan servants in knitted tunics and baggy trousers. Everyone in the crowd was yelling in the combination of Erse and Arabi that was the common speech in Manatas.

"Thor's Hammer!" he roared. "Quiet!" The yelling reduced to a mutter "Now…" He turned to Flores. "Tenente Flores. What happened here?"

"Zoltan's dead," Flores declared. "And she did it" He jabbed the point of his halberd at the girl.

"What makes you think so? Did you see her do it?" Halvar looked at the body of the guardsman."How was it done?"

"She's a seamstress. She had a set of scissors," Flores stated. "And she was in that alley with him." He pointed to the gap between Yussif's shop and the wooden shack next to it. "And there are the scissors, right there, in Zoltan's coat!" He ended on a triumphant note. "She did it!"

"And where were you when this happened?"

Flores harumphed. "I was next to the used clothing stall, having a word with Scavenger Rachev," he muttered.

"Emir Achmet's man?" Halvar looked around the crowd for the wily thief. "What about?"

The Scavenger chief's second-in-command was nowhere in sight. Any Scavengers posted to the souk had vanished with him. *No doubt running to tell Emir Achmet what happened,* Halvar thought sourly. He glowered at Flores, whose face was flushed under his scrubby beard.

"I thought we could come to some kind of, um, arrangement,"

"Pay him off, you mean?" Halvar stifled the urge to throttle his underling. This was the way Tenente Gomez had kept order in the souk, but it wasn't Halvar's way, and the sooner the Town Guards and the Scavengers knew it, the better!

"Just giving alms to the poor, like the Prophet says," Flores protested. "And then I saw Zoltan backing out of the alley with the girl in front of him. She had those scissors in her hand, pointed right at him. She jabbed at him, and he stepped away from her, into that knot of students at the bookseller's stall. Then he gave a sort of start, staggered forward, and fell down, right onto those scissors."

"If she had the scissors in front of him, how did she put the knife in his back?" Halvar pointed to the hilt. "And are you telling me that a slip of a girl stuck a knife through a heavy coat and shirt hard enough to reach this guardsman's heart?"

"If it wasn't her, it was that brother of hers, the butcher," Flores insisted. "He's got blood all over him, he carries a knife!"

"Everyone in Manatas carries a knife, especially a butcher.." Halvar turned to Asher. "What do you say, Butcher Asher? Did you kill this man? Not that I'd blame you if you did. He had his eyes on your sister—he as good as told me he'd attack her if he could get her alone."

Asher glared at Halvar. "I was in my shop when I heard that this...this man...was after Raquel again. I came here to protect her, but I was too late. He was already on the ground."

"You had a knife in your hand?"

"I did, but I did not use it."

"Show me this knife," Halvar ordered.

"I don't have it. This...this guardsman took it."

Guardsman Musa displayed a large knife, a serrated blade with a wooden handle.

"I took it off him straightaway when I saw him. He might have used it on someone else."

"I didn't use it on anyone!" Asher roared. "I am a *shochet*! I kill animals, for their meat, in accordance with the laws of *kashrut*. I do not kill men, no matter how much they deserve it."

A loud hee-haw announced the arrival of a donkey cart. The crowd parted to allow it to pass. Dr. Moise and Selim hopped off.

"I sent for the doctor as soon as I saw the...Zoltan," Flores told Halvar. "And I suppose the sultan's brat had to come along, like always."

"Young Selim takes notes for me," Halvar replied. "Good thinking, Tenente." *At least he did one thing according to regulations!*

The lanky Afrikan doctor peered at the knife and the scissors.

"Clear as day," he announced. "Cause of death—stabbing."

"But which one killed him, the knife or the scissors?" Halvar asked.

"That is yet to be determined. I'll examine him at the Rabat." Dr. Moise looked around for assistance. "Someone help me get this guardsman onto the cart."

Halvar looked across the street. Something about one of the men in the crowd of students looked familiar...but he was gone, ducking through the back in Mendel's stall that opened onto the Broad Way.

He recognized Stephane Mercier, the leader of the sporting set at the madrassa, among the students gawking at the scene before them and waved him over.

"Who was that fellow standing with you a moment ago?" he asked as Stephane joined him.

The Franchen shrugged. "No idea. He was at Mendel the Bookseller's."

"Buying books?"

Another shrug. "Couldn't say. He looked familiar., but with his face muffled in that cloak and the brim of his hat pulled down, it's hard to say where I saw him. He did have a fine choice of words for that girl, and he was twitting your guardsman about her."

"Urging him on?" Halvar considered this as two Afrikan servants stepped forward to help lift the body onto the cart. He looked around again."Where is Guardsman Zoltan's partner? Guardsman Fergus?"

The short, wiry Bretain emerged from behind Tenente Flores.

"Guardsman Fergus! What was Zoltan doing in that alley?" Halvar demanded. "You're never far away from him. Where were you when all this was going on?"

Fergus looked to Flores for aid, and found none.

"I was on duty, like you said. But Zoltan…He didn't mean to hurt anyone. He was only funning, Capitán. He just liked to talk to the girls, that's all."

"He'd just been warned off that kind of fun," Halvar said sternly. "Guardsman Fergus, I ask you again, and this time don't try to lie. What happened in that alley?"

"I don't know!" Fergus wailed. "Zoltan was on patrol, like he was supposed to be. He saw the girl with the Bretain…"

"Which Bretain?" Halvar tried to spot trews and a woolen cap in the crowd of striped caftans and black coats, fezzes, turbans and fur-trimmed felt hats.

"Ahem. That would be me." Edgar Norris stepped into the street from behind the tailor's stout assistant. "I took your advice, Capitán Danske. I inquired of this tailor as to which of his sewing-women could alter some of Dame Brigitte's garments for Milady Summersby. They are not the most elegant of gowns, but I thought perhaps more suitable than the one she now wears."

"And I told him Raquel was my best worker for female garments," Yussif said. "She was working in the back of the

95

shop. They came to an agreement—she said she needed her good scissors and needles to do the job properly. I let her go back to her house in the Yehudit quarter to fetch them. She uses the alley, it's the shortest way."

"When was this?" Selim asked, carefully writing down everything in her notebook.

"I heard bells ringing for midday prayers," Edgar said. "And the fellow who cries out the time at the Grand Muskat was calling out."

"That would be noon," Selim said. "About the time we were questioning Master LaPierre in the Yehudit study-house."

"Very well. The girl goes home, gets her sewing gear, comes back. How long would that take?" Halvar asked.

"Not long," Yussif answered. "I gave Master Edgar mokka while he waited."

Edgar nodded. "I wanted to increase my proficiency in Arabi. We conversed for some time."

"And where was Zoltan while Heer Edgar was chatting with the tailor?" Halvar felt anger boiling within him. He already knew the answer.

"Zoltan was waiting for her," Fergus said. "He saw her go through the alley, and he told me he'd meet her when she came back. He wanted to get a smile out of her, that's all! Just a smile, a look, something to show she knew he was there. But she wouldn't look at him, wouldn't talk to him. It got to him, it did. I told him to let it go, there were prettier girls, but he wanted this one."

"I told Raquel, ignore that lout!" Asher sneered. "I told her, don't look at him, don't speak to him."

"And I didn't!" Raquel cried out. "He was always after me, trying to make me notice him, but I wouldn't."

"She was obeying her brother, as a good Yehudit girl should," Halvar said. "And when he came at her, she defended herself. No blame attached to her if she did!"

"Raquel is no taller than Zoltan's shoulder, at best. And if she was in front of him, how could she have stabbed him in the back?" Selim pointed out.

Halvar looked around for more witnesses.

"All you folk...Did any of you see what happened? You, Old Mother." He pointed to the Local woman, whose dog had resumed his protective stance. "Did you see this man go into the alley?"

"Not a good thing, to notice the Town Guards," the woman muttered. "Bad things happen to people who do. Big man is Town Guard. He goes into place between houses. Comes out, backwards. She comes with thing in hand. He goes forward, falls on her, she yells, he is dead."

"Selim! Have you written that? Get this woman's name, have her make her mark." Halvar looked around for more witnesses. "Stephane Mercier!"

The student was half-way down the alley, on his way back to the safety of the madrassa.

"Come back!"

Reluctantly, the Franchen returned to the scene of the crime.

"Tell me exactly what you saw." Halvar said sternly.

"I didn't see much," Stephan demurred. "The guardsman was a tall fellow. I couldn't tell you what he did in the alley. He came out of it backwards, tripped over something in the road, fell against that big fellow in the cloak. The big fellow shoved him forward, and then he fell down, right in the road, with the knife in his back."

"And you didn't call for help?" Halvar glared at the younger man.

"The other guardsmen were here," Stephane protested. "Capitán, it's nearly dark. We have to be back in our lodgings for the evening meal."

Halvar nodded. "You may be called to testify as to what you saw, Stephane Mercier."

"If I must, but I didn't see anything. I don't know who killed your guardsman, but I can assure you, it wasn't me!" Stephane followed his friends down the alley to their lodgings.

Halvar considered his next moves in this increasingly complex situation.

"Tenente Flores!"

"Capitán!" For once, Tenente Flores was ready to obey orders.

"Take this man Asher and the girl Raquel to the Rabat. Heer Edgar, will you accompany us, to make your statement in more congenial surroundings?"

"If you please, I can do so now. Time grows short, and I must return to Milord Summersby," Edgar demurred. "I have little to add to what this Local woman said. I was inside the shop when the girl came back. I did not emerge until I heard the commotion in the street, so I cannot tell you whether the guardsman was going into the alley or coming out of it when he was attacked."

"And you didn't see anyone stab him?"

"By the time I came out of the shop, there was something of a crowd forming," Edgar said. "As seems to be the case in this town. Any small disturbance, any break in the usual routine, and people come out of their shops to see what is doing, and to comment on it. My Arabi is imperfect, but from the tone of the remarks, I gather some of them were ribald, and some were condemning. I could not tell which was which, or who made the remarks." He took a deep breath. "I suppose I must now tell Milady Summersby that the seamstress will not be available to make the alterations to Dame Brigitte's gowns. She will not be pleased. She does not fancy the drab garb forced on her by the Purists of Brook-line."

"I don't envy you that task," Halvar said. He faced Flores. "Tenente, send one of your men to the House of the

Green Crescent. I want Eva Hakim present when we question this girl. I don't want anyone to think that we abused her in any way. As for this butcher…" He regarded Asher sourly. "Just bring him to the Rabat and put him into a cell. Even if he didn't do this himself, he may have seen who did."

"And then…drill?" Flores asked.

Halvar glanced at the sky. The short winter day was already coming to a close.

"Put it off to tomorrow," he said. "This is more important. One of our own has been murdered, in broad daylight, in a crowd. This won't go unavenged, be sure of it!" He stood tall in the middle of the souk and repeated. "No one kills one of the Town Guard and gets away clean. No one! Tenente, get statements from as many of these people as you can before they leave. Then, meet me at the Rabat, and we'll question the butcher and his sister."

Flores scowled. "They're in it together, the two of them and the Yehudit. Who else?"

"Zoltan accosted other women in the souk besides Yehudit," Selim reminded them. "And there were Andalusians and Afrikans in the crowd. Any of them could have put that knife into him."

"Don't forget those students," Halvar added. "They were the ones jeering at Zoltan, and he stumbled against one of them. The question is, which of them did it, and why?"

"We won't get any answers now," Flores said. As if to echo his statement, the wail of the muezzin announced the time for late-afternoon prayers.

Andalusian shopkeepers were hanging lanterns outside their doors, putting up shutters, preparing to close for the night. The students were gone back to their lodgings. The Local woman had packed her brazier and baskets into her dog-pull and was heading towards the Broad Way. Only Halvar and the guards were left in the suddenly empty street.

"Trust these people to come out when there's something doing and leave as soon as it's done," Halvar muttered. "Very well, Tenente. We'll see what Dr. Moise finds out when he examines our guardsman."

"And we'll get the truth out of that Yehudit butcher and his sister," Flores added as they headed back along the path to the Rabat.

Chapter 13

THE PROCESSION WOUND ACROSS THE BROAD Way to the Rabat, where Halvar left Dr. Moise to his gruesome task. Flores dispatched one of his men to fetch Eva Hakim from the House of the Green Crescent, while Selim followed Halvar back to the office, calling for mokka as they went.

The brazier in the corner still glowed with the coals from the morning's fire. Selim blew them into a respectable blaze and added charred wood, while Halvar fell into his chair, took off his fur cap, and scowled at the mass of papers that had accumulated on his desk in the short time he had been away.

"What's all this?" He picked up one paper after another.

"It's Ned Cooper's business papers," Selim explained. "Mostly records of who ordered what, how many, when he took the order, and when it was delivered. Ned wasn't just a cooper, he did other bits of carpentry as well. And that little anvil? If these papers are right, Ned Cooper was something like the Jack-of-all-trades. He could make small copper parts, he was called on for fittings for locks. He was the one who made the hinges for the door of that cabin in the woods and the latch on the door." Selim shifted some of the papers. "All the things Malik the Smith might not be able to make with his iron, Ned the Cooper made of copper."

"A smith as well as a cooper?" Halvar took this in, along with his fresh mug of hot mokka, brought in by one of the sultan's servants.

"So it would seem." Selim turned over several papers. "He wrote everything down, in Ogham characters and Indian numbers. I'm not too certain of the Ogham, but the numbers are clear enough. He kept very good records. Here's one for 'two small hinges, two large ones, in copper' and it's signed with Malik the Smith's mark. And here's one for 'four kegs, of a size to hold a bushel of maiz, well-caulked in and out'. What goes into that? Not grain, certainly."

"To hold gunpowder," Halvar surmised. "Four bushels of it. That's a goodly lot of the stuff."

"Do you think Master LaPierre could make that much gunpowder?" Selim's worried frown deepened, so that her heavy brows nearly met over her snub nose.

"He thinks he can," Halvar said. "Who paid for those four kegs?"

Selim consulted the papers again. "Andrew MacAlan signed his name to the order."

"And that settles that." Halvar set down his mokka with a satisfied smirk.

"Not really," Selim demurred. "All it means is that Andrew MacAlan ordered barrels. It doesn't prove he was going to put gunpowder in them, or that Albrecht LaPierre was going to furnish that gunpowder."

"But it shows that Ned Cooper was up to his eyebrows in whatever MacAlan was planning."

"We already knew that. It doesn't tell us who killed him, or how, or why."

"He didn't owe anyone money," Halvar mused. "He was annoying, but not to the point where someone might want to silence him. He had no wife, no mistress, and as far as anyone can tell, he had no dealings with women except for those two Purists who cook the meals and clean the cottage. What's left?"

Selim said slowly, "Maybe he saw something, or knew something that someone else thought might be a threat to them."

"He knew something about Milord Henry Summersby," Halvar said. "But Milord didn't kill him. He was in plain sight, on that skittish horse."

"Edgar was in Green Village, too," Selim pointed out.

"But Edgar left before dark with everyone else." Halvar shook his head. "It doesn't make sense." Something in the pile on his desk caught his eye. "What's this?"

He shuffled more papers and pulled out a booklet, its edge sewn with thread. He flipped through the pages covered with neat Arabi writing. He wished again he could make sense of those elaborate curls and swirls.

"That's Leon's translation of Captain Girard's private journal. I haven't had time to read all of it, but there are some bits that he marked with red ink as being most important."

Halvar sighed. "What does Leon di Vicenza think I should know?'

Selim picked up the booklet and prepared to read, and Halvar leaned back in his chair, prepared to listen.

"The journal starts with the ship *Belle Fleur* leaving Le-Havre in Franchenland, with what Girard calls "living cargo'. That would be the women bound for Kibbick."

"When did he leave Franchenland?"

"Julian? That's summer, isn't it?"

103

"By the Roumi Rite calendar, it is. We know he left Manatas after the Spring Feria. So, he's in Franchenland for the summer, leaves for Kibbick, arrives there…"

Selim flipped through the pages. "Septem. 'Kibbick with live cargo. Much activity, some distress. No buyer for other cargo.' What other cargo?"

"The muskets." Halvar sat straight, suddenly alert. "He had the muskets when he went to Kibbick. He must have got them in Franchenland, the Redeemer only knows how."

"I don't think the Redeemer had anything to do with this," Selim said. "More likely Shaitan the Deceiver."

"Right again, laddie. What next? What happens when he gets to Kibbick? And when does he meet Milord Henry Summersby and his oh-so-clever servant, Edgar Norris? There's something about that fellow that reminds me of someone else."

"Someone you knew when you were still with the Free Danes?" Selim suggested.

"Not then. In Corduva. It'll come to me."

"Whoever it was, it couldn't be Edgar Norris. He's only now learning Arabi, so he can't have been in Al-Andalus. Everyone learns Arabi if they're in Al-Andalus."

"Even me!" Halvar tugged at his mustache. "I may not have seen him, but I've seen his sort before. Very clever, and they know it. Go on, laddie. What happens when Girard gets to Kibbick?"

Selim scanned the pages. "Here's something, double underlined in red. 'Woman is bought by Bretain milord. Wedding night in Governor's house. Much fun with Dame B.'." Selim's cheeks flushed. "He goes on about what he does with Dame B."

"Skip that bit," Halvar told her. "It just confirms that Girard and Dame Brigitte were a lot friendlier than they should have been. What about Milord Henry?"

"Here. 'Bretain wants to go south, to Powhatan. Much silver in his purse. Why not? Takes Milady C with him, also

Dame B and Musketman. Dame B thinks cargo needs more spice, get it at Bos-Town.' So, he was already planning to sell the muskets, only he needed gunpowder. And Dame Brigitte knew about the muskets."

"For all we know, she's the one who put Girard together with whoever was selling them in Franchenland, but she's at the bottom of the bay, and her secrets with her. So, Girard needs gunpowder, can't get it in Kibbick." Halvar continued the saga. "Which means he has to go to Bos-town, where they make it. Milord and Milady sail with him, with their servants."

"Dame Brigitte and Edgar?"

"And Devallon. Don't forget the Musket-man. Not a congenial company, to be sure, with Dame Brigitte down with the seasickness, and Edgar pestering the captain for information about navigation. But he reaches Bos-Town…When?"

"Septem, end." Selim consulted a chart she had drawn up. "He's got a page about Milady C and her being taken up by the Bos-Town constable. And something about 'silver greases palms. Goods gone to Manatas'. He leaves Bos-Town Septem last, just before the traders returned from the Fall Feria with the news of all that happened from the time you got here and changed everything—the deaths of the Taverniers, the return of Don Felipe, the union of all the different villages into one settlement on Manatas Island under Sultan Petrus and the Town Guard…"

"And he doesn't find out until he reaches Manatas, and by then it's too late," Halvar finished for her. "He goes to the Mermaid Taberna, but the Taverniers are gone, and Hannes Zilberstam is no friend to Franchen. He's had dealings with the Afrikans, he knows Samuel Igbo will work with him, so he sends the message to Samuel that he's looking for someone from Bos-Town who came to Manatas."

"And Snake carries the messages between Girard, Igbo, and MacAlan. And gets killed when he tries to blackmail them." Selim shook her head. "He tried so hard to better himself through learning, but Shaitan must have led him onto the wrong path."

"And Dame Brigitte was led down that same path." Halvar picked up the thread of the story. "And that was on the Longest Night, which was…"

"Ten days ago." Selim marked her chart.

Halvar groaned. "It seems like eternity."

"None of this makes any sense," she decided. "It's all madness! Girard came to Manatas to buy gunpowder to sell with the muskets, but why would the Bretain milord want to sail in winter?"

"He was in a great hurry to get to Terra Mara, that's for certain, even though he didn't know that Sultan Calavera had changed the name of his territory to Terra Mara, and the name of his city to Bel'Mar. No one sails in winter, it's too dangerous. Even the fishermen hate to go out. Storms can blow up at any time, the wind is fierce, even the currents are against shipping." Halvar slapped the table in frustration. "That's what I'm going to ask Milord, as soon as we settle this matter of Ned Cooper. What else does our friend Girard have to say about his passengers?"

Selim consulted the transcription again. "Leon marked this: 'Much fun on deck. Milord and Musketman in mock battle. Both good swordsmen, H is not so foolish as I thought. C looks on with much interest. Musketman is good company, knows new songs and tales. E is at my shoulder when I take bearings. H is no milord'." She looked up from the page. "How would he know what a milord is or isn't?"

"I think that's a judgment of character, not rank," Halvar said. "What's the last entry?"

Selim turned to the last page in the booklet. "'Manatas in sight. A good Franchen meal, a good time with LL, then find spice for cargo.' He was planning to stay with the Taverniers, and we know what he did with that poor woman."

"We also know he didn't eat at the Mermaid Taberna, because he dumped Milord and Milady onto Hannes Zilberstam as soon as he could and headed for Maison Rouge, where he met up with Long Liz…"

"And Zoltan?" Selim's eyes widened as she realized what this meant. "Girard's last meal was with Zoltan and Fergus. Do you think…he might have had too much of that apple cider, the stuff that turns your head?"

"And he talked to them about his adventures," Halvar said slowly. "And…Where's Fergus? I have to talk to him. Right now! He's got the answers we need. Thor's Hammer! Why won't people speak up when they have information?"

"Because they think they can sell it elsewhere," Selim said.

"And that's what got Zoltan killed. Greedy bastard!"

Before he could continue, the guardsman Musa poked his head into the office.

"Tenente Flores said to call you as soon as Eva Hakim got here. She insists on taking the Yehudit girl to the House of the Green Crescent. And Benyamin ben Mendel is here to advise Asher the Butcher. Tenente Flores is sure they're the ones killed Guardsman Zoltan, and he's pushing for a confession."

"He won't get it," Halvar said, jamming his fur cap back onto his head. "Come along, Selim. Flores is on the wrong path. Those two Yehudit didn't kill Zoltan, but they may have seen who did!"

Chapter 14

THE CELLS IN THE FARTHEST TOWER OF THE RA-
bat were small, bare, and cold. Raquel, the Yehudit seamstress, cowered shivering in the corner of the smallest and dankest; Eva Hakim stood guard between the prisoner and anyone who would dare to molest her—particularly, it appeared, Tenente Flores, who followed Halvar into the cell. Selim followed Halavar into the cell and squatted in another corner, notebook and pen in hand.

The tall Sister of Fatima had added a heavy brown wool cloak to her usual attire of brown tunic and trousers and green hijab. She greeted Halvar with a perfunctory "Salaam aleikum" before launching into a tirade.

"Why has this poor young girl been brought here? She is not the one who killed that arrogant guardsman. By what right do you hold her, with lustful men guarding her? She is to be moved at once!"

"Peace, noble Eva Hakim!" Halvar raised a hand in mock surrender. "I know Raquel didn't kill Zoltan. She may have menaced him with the scissors, but she didn't kill him."

"He attacked her!" Eva Hakim declared. "I myself have seen him accost women, first on the waterfront, then in the souk. He was known to take bribes from the women on the waterfront. For their protection, he said. Bah!"

"True," Halvar admitted. "But that was under Tenente Gomez's rule. I am trying to change that. As for this young woman…" His voice softened as he approached the young woman. "Raquel? That is your name?"

Raquel nodded warily, still too shocked to speak.

"Can you tell me, if you please, exactly what happened this afternoon in the souk?"

"You saw him!" Raquel squeaked. "He was big, and he came at me. I had my scissors, I held them, I wanted to stop him."

"You stabbed him!" Flores shouted. "You lured him into that alley, and attacked a Town Guardsman!" He lunged forward, hand raised to strike.

Eva Hakim faced him down. "Do not dare to lay hands on this child!"

"No child—she's old enough to bear children herself!" Flores sneered. "All those Yehudit marry young."

"Yehudit, Islim, or Kristo, you will not strike this girl!" Eva Hakim stood tall, Raquel clutching at her arm for protection.

"Let the girl tell it herself." Halvar stepped between the combatants. Once more, he addressed the seamstress gently. "Raquel, you say you were coming into the souk from the alley when Zoltan came at you."

"That is what he did. He came at me!"

"And you had the scissors in your basket? Do you usually carry scissors with you?"

"I was going to alter gowns for the Bretain Milady," Raquel explained. "Master Edgar Norris came to Yussif the

Tailor's shop. I work there, sewing the fine parts, the buttonholes, the trimmings on coats. The Bretain servant said Milady Summersby's own clothes had been on the ship that went down in the harbor, but her servant's were still on shore, and those could be altered to fit Milady.

"I said perhaps I might have to cut some off the bottom of the dresses to make them fit her, and that I had a finer pair of scissors, which I keep at my own house, where I do fine sewing for the Andalusian and Yehudit women." She glanced at Eva Hakim, who nodded encouragingly.

Halvar nodded as well. "I see. So, you went home and got your good scissors. What then?"

"I got the scissors, and my finest needle and some extra thread. And I went back to the souk through the alley."

"You lured Zoltan into that alley!" Flores pointed an accusing finger at her.

"No!" Raquel cried. "I did not want to meet him at all! It is a lie to say that I made him come to me in the alley. I wanted nothing to do with him. My brother Asher—he told me to stay away from him, but *he* would not stay away from *me.*"

"That's what Guardsman Fergus said, too," Selim murmured. "It seems Zoltan was obsessed with Damozel Raquel."

"He came at me!" Raquel repeated. "I took out the scissors and told him to go away, that I would hurt him if he came closer."

"You see! She admits her guilt!" Flores announced.

"Only that she menaced him," Halvar said. "He came at you, you pointed the scissors. Then what?"

"He went backwards, into the street," Raquel continued. "And there were men in the street, laughing and talking. And then he stopped, and he came back at me! I had the scissors in my hand, and he fell on them! And there was blood on his back…" She burst into tears.

Eva Hakim put her arms around the sobbing girl and turned her wrathful gaze on Halvar.

110

"It is clear to me what happened. That man, enraged by lust, tried to rape this poor girl. She defended herself as best she could."

"That explains the scissors in his front. It doesn't explain the knife in his back," Halvar said.

"If she didn't do it, her brother did," Flores declared. "She waved those scissors at him, and he backed right into her brother's knife."

Halvar considered this possibility.

"He may well have backed onto someone's knife, but I don't think it was the butcher's. Raquel, try to think. When you came out of the alley, what did you see? What did you hear?"

Raquel looked blankly back at him. "I only saw…him! That big man, in the green coat and red tarboosh, so big, so tall, so broad! I could not tell if there was anyone else, all I saw was him, and his smile. That smug, smirking smile! I wanted to cut it out of him!" Her voice sharpened. "I wanted to cut his face! But he was too big, too tall. All I could reach was his chest."

Halvar tugged at his mustache. "You say there were men in the street. Could you tell who they were? Did you recognize any of them?"

Raquel shuddered. "I can't say. They were loud, they laughed, they were making a joke about me, I know they were. They talked in Erse—I don't know what they said, but it sounded lewd."

"Not your brother, then," Halvar said.

"No…I thought…maybe." She stopped crying and wiped her eyes on the sleeve of her jacket. "Asher was not one of them. He came afterward, when the guardsmen laid hands on me."

"Is that enough for you?" Eva Hakim demanded. "This girl did not stab your guardsman in the back, no matter what she did with the scissors."

111

"She wanted to," Flores insisted.

"Intent isn't enough to hang her," Halvar decreed. "Eva Hakim, take this girl to the House of the Green Crescent and keep her safe. Let me know if she remembers something else—anything—about those men who were in the souk when she came out of the alley."

"We already know Edgar was in the souk," Selim said. "He told us he was waiting for Raquel to come back from fetching her sewing tools. And there was a group of students from the madrassa—they were talking in Erse."

"Let's hear what Asher has to say," Flores said with a jerk of his head. "I've got him in the next cell."

"Alone?"

"He's got Benyamin ibn Mendel to advise him," Flores grumbled. "That Yehudit lawyer pokes his nose into everything. Who does he think he is?"

"An advocate for the downtrodden," Halvar said. "Raquel, go with Eva Hakim. The good Sisters of Fatima will keep you safe until this matter is sorted out. If you can recall anything else, please tell Eva Hakim, and she will tell me."

Raquel glanced warily at Eva Hakim.

"She is Islim. She will try to convert me."

Eva Hakim shook her head. "We will not attempt to convince you to follow our path. Yehudit are People of the Book, and the Prophet said we are to respect them, even if they persist in their false beliefs. You will be safe with us, Raquel."

Halvar beckoned to Selim; the youngster scrambled to her feet, and joined him and Flores. The surly guardsman growled and grumbled as they proceeded to the next cell.

"It's clear to me what happened. They were in it together, the butcher and his sister. She makes Zoltan walk backwards, the butcher shoves the knife in."

"That is possible," Halvar said. "Except I saw the butcher myself, coming from the far end of the street *after* Zoltan was dead. How could he have managed to go from one end of the souk to the other and back so fast?"

"He was carrying a bloody knife!" Flores protested.

"But the knife that killed Zoltan was still in his back," Selim pointed out. "Why would Asher carry two knives? So, if the one that killed Zoltan was in his back, the one Asher held couldn't have been the one that killed him."

"He could have had another one. Or there could have been more than one Yehudit ready to get rid of one of our guardsmen."

"He'd have to be a daring man, to do it in broad daylight," Halvar mused. "Or a desperate one. Let's see what Asher the Butcher has to say."

Benyamin stood beside Asher when Halvar and his crew entered the cell.

"This charge is nonsense!" he declared before Halvar could say a word. "Asher the Butcher was not even in the souk when the attack took place!"

"Let him speak for himself," Halvar said as Selim found a spot on the floor . Flores remained by the door, hand on his cudgel. "Asher, you are accused of killing the guardsman Zoltan. What do you say?"

"I didn't do it. I wanted to—the man was a piece of offal, a turd, a—"

"That's a Town Guardsman you're defaming, Yehudit!" Flores stepped forward, cudgel now in hand.

Halvar stepped between them. "Tenente Flores, for the last time, keep your temper! This man has been accused. He has not been convicted of anything more than bad words!"

"Whose side are you on, Capitán?" Flores spat on the floor.

"I am on the side of justice," Halvar told him. "And that will not be served by accusing a man on no evidence other than the tools of his trade."

"Tools of his trade? His knife is wet with the blood of our guardsman!"

"My knife is used to behead chickens and geese!" Asher retorted.

"Enough of this!" Halvar shouted. Once again he deliberately lowered his voice. "Asher the Butcher, tell us what you saw and heard when you came into the souk. Why did you leave your shop?"

"A Scavenger lad came running with the news that my sister Raquel was being attacked by that big guardsman, Zoltan. I grabbed my knife and ran to defend her." Asher's face flamed red with rage. "I was too late. When I got to the souk, the man was already down. I thought she had done it, until I saw the knife in his back. She couldn't have done that, Capitán. She's just not that strong."

"But you could," Flores sneered. "You're strong enough to shove a knife into a man's back."

"I saw Asher myself, and he was nowhere near Zoltan," Halvar repeated, exasperated at the man's blind prejudice.

"Then one of his friends did it," Flores insisted.

Halvar tugged at his mustached. "Asher. Think carefully and tell me—exactly who did you see when you came into the souk?"

The burly butcher shook his head. "I can't remember… I think I saw Mendel the Bookseller, and Yussif the Tailor, and a few of the Islim vendors, the ones who deal in used clothing. Then there was some fellow selling wood from a cart…and a Local woman, with her dog-pull and baskets of maiz and escouash…and you, Capitán."

"No one else?" Halvar prodded gently.

"Asher frowned. "A gang of students. Big fellows, in dark cloaks, talking Erse. I didn't know them. They were making lewd remarks about big fellows and little girls."

"That must have made you angry," Halvar remarked.

"I wanted to shove their smug Oropan faces into the muck on the path," Asher admitted. "But then Zoltan started towards Raquel again, and he fell against her. That's when I ran to help her…but by the time I got there, he was on the ground, and that… that…" He tried to find accurate words to describe Flores.

"Tenente Flores," Halvar offered.

"That guardsman had laid hands on her!" Asher glared at Flores,.

"These students, the ones who spoke Erse," Halvar said. "You say you didn't know them? How did you know they were students, then?"

"Who else could they be? They were big, like those fellows who chase the bladder around the field and play the Peace Game with the Locals. They talked Erse, not Arabi. They weren't Yehudit or Locals. They wore dark cloaks, and hats with feathers in the bands. One had a hood over his head."

"How many of them were there?"

"I don't know…two, three, four? What does it matter?" Asher stepped toward Flores. "My sister's name was defamed! That walking turd had laid hands on her!"

"So, you came to her defense. A most logical thing for a good brother to do," Halvar soothed him. "You say you saw the guardsmen, these students, your sister…no one else?"

Asher shook his head. "I was angry, very angry. I wasn't looking at anyone but my sister, and the guardsman holding her."

Halvar nodded. "Asher, I believe you."

"What!" Flores was outraged.

"You and your sister tell the same story. Zoltan came after her, she showed him the scissors, he backed away, then he came forward again and fell onto the scissors. Is that right?"

"I don't know what happened in the alley, but yes, he fell on her. And the knife was already in his back then. I saw the handle. So, you see, I didn't kill him."

"And that settles that," Benyamin said firmly. "This man is innocent. Let him go back to his shop and the study-house."

Before Halvar could speak, Fergus tapped on the door of the cell.

"Capitán! Dr. Moise wants to talk with you, right now. It's about what killed Guardsman Zoltan. And there's a

Local, one of the Mahak watchmen, says he's got a message from Green Village about Ned the Cooper."

"I'll be right there," Halvar told him. "Tenente Flores, come with me. Selim, hold on to that notebook carefully. Benyamin, your butcher didn't kill Zoltan, but he saw who did. He just doesn't know it yet. I want him to stay here in the Rabat, before that killer can get to him. He can go to the kitchen, where it's warmer than these cells, and the guards can keep an eye on him."

"And what's to stop the *guards* from killing me?" Asher demanded.

"They won't," Halvar assured him. "If you insist, I'll have the sultan's personal guards in keep you company. They don't like the Town Guard, and don't care whether or not you killed one of them. Will that serve?"

"It'll have to," Asher grumbled.

Benyamin followed Halvar and the rest out of the cell, while one of the Town Guards hauled Asher out of the cold cell to the warmth of the barracks kitchen..

"This won't do. I'll stand surety for Asher, to make sure he doesn't leave Manatas." Benyamin's round race creased into a worried frown.

"I meant what I said about a killer on the loose," Halvar said. "There is someone who's gone beyond the limits. He's mad, and getting worse, and we've got to stop him before he kills again."

"You know who it is?" Benyamin asked.

"I think so, but I have to be sure, and there's no real evidence yet to take to the sultan," Halvar admitted. "Let's see what our two medical examiners have to say about our dead men. Two bodies in one day is more than Manatas can deal with!"

"And it's not even feria time," Flores added as they proceeded across the courtyard to the shed where the military physician practiced his craft.

Chapter 15

DR. MOISE GREETED THE VISITORS TO HIS GRIM
shed with his usual disdain. The tall, spare Afrikan had draped
a wool scarf over his usual winter garb caftan and knitted
tunic. His shed was barely heated by the open brazier in one
corner, whose coals added eerie light to that of the lantern that
swung over the table on which the body of Guardsman Zoltan
now rested.

A pair of short-bladed scissors and a long knife lay on
the table where Zoltan's clothing lay neatly folded. The knife
was dull with blood, the scissors pristine.

Halvar regarded the naked body of the tall guardsman
impassively.

"Well, then, Dr. Moise, what killed this man?"

"A very sharp instrument," Dr. Moise shot back. "Insert-
ed into his flesh."

"That I already knew," Halvar retorted. "*Which* sharp instrument, the scissors or the knife?"

"The scissors never came close to killing him." Dr. Moise pointed to a faint scratch on the body's midsection, just over the navel. "He may have fallen on them, but they barely penetrated his skin through the two layers where one side of the coat overlaps the other."

"That clears the girl of the murder charge," Selim said. "Whatever her intention was, she didn't actually kill Zoltan."

"In that case, who did?" Halvar demanded. "Is this the knife that did it?"

"It's what I took out of his back," Dr. Moise said. "It went through the back of his coat and his shirt and penetrated his back, just under the third rib." He turned the body to reveal the wound in the back.

"Not much blood," Halvar observed. "And whoever did it had to have been either very strong or very angry to shove it in hard enough to get through that felted coat. It's almost as tough as leather."

"And Zoltan was no weakling," Fergus added from where he crouched in a corner. "He was strong as an ox! He could take on any sailor on the waterfront. They all knew Zoltan —that's how he kept order in those tabernas and cribs. You shouldn't have taken him away from the waterfront, Capitán. That's where he belonged, not chasing Scavengers in the souk. It was one of them got him."

Halvar picked up the knife and squinted at the length of its blade.

"This is no Scavenger's knife. This is a cook's knife. See those little teeth? This is used to slice meat for the table."

"A cook's knife? Or a butcher's?" Flores growled. "I told you it was the Yehudit!"

"Can't be," Selim objected, annoyed by the guardsman's stubborn refusal to acknowledge plain fact.. "Too many people saw him at the far end of the street from Yussif's shop. And before that, he was with Capitán Danske and me, in the Yehudit study-house."

Halvar eyed the body again. "Dr. Moise, how tall would you judge Zoltan to be?"

"Taller than either you or me."

"And where, on the body, was this wound?"

"As I said, in the upper part of the back."

"If that's so, how tall would you say the killer was?"

Dr. Moise measured the body by eye. "Not a small man," he concluded. "The entry was slightly upward, meaning the killer held the knife at his waist or perhaps a little higher."

"And in daylight," Selim added. "Why didn't anyone see it?"

"Because he hid what he was doing under a cloak," Halvar answered. "According to Asher and Raquel, there were men in long cloaks and broad-brimmed hats across the street from Yussif's, near the path that leads to the madrassa."

"Yehudit!" Flores exploded with wrath. "I knew it! They were after Zoltan for messing with their women. One of them got him!"

"Yehudit wear coats," Halvar reminded him. "More practical, in this wind."

"*Students* wear cloaks," Selim offered. "And Afrikans wear long scarves, like Dr. Moise."

"But there weren't any Afrikans across the street from Yussif's shop," Halvar said. "They were with the Islim women buying food from the vegetable sellers. The only other Andalusians were the man with the donkey cart selling wood and the fellow from the used-clothing stall next to Yussif's shop, and they were well clear of Zoltan."

"So, one of those students?" Selim frowned. "But why? They had no quarrel with Zoltan."

"Not that we know of," Halvar amended. "I don't assume anything any more."

"Zoltan had only been on duty in the souk for a week," Selim said. "Maybe one of the students was involved in something on the waterfront?"

"Something to do with one of those women Zoltan was 'protecting'?" Halvar considered this aspect of the guardsman's former station.

"That's rubbish!" Fergus leaped up to defend his dead partner's reputation. "Sure, some of those young sprouts came to the waterfront for a good time, but Zoltan made sure they got it, and at a reasonable rate, too. And there wasn't any trouble about it, either, unless it came from that mangy Mullah Abadul."

"Zoltan was on duty at the waterfront when the *Belle Fleur* came in," Halvar said thoughtfully, fixing his gaze on Fergus. "He had dinner with Captain Girard just before the Franchen took off with his lady-love."

Fergus shrank back into the corner. "That's...Yes, he did."

"And you were all quite merry, weren't you?" Halvar went on relentlessly.

"Yes."

"And Girard told you all about his voyage, and the Bretains he had brought with him."

"And how he had foisted them onto Hannes Zilberstam at the Mermaid Taberna," Selim added. "Because he thought he'd find Franchen there, but they were gone, and the Dane was there instead."

Fergus nodded. His eyes filled with tears. "He told us all about Milord Henry and his doxy wife and the two servants that weren't really servants at all, and the Franchen musket-man who was worth the whole lot of them."

"And Zoltan decided to make himself a few extra strings of wumpum?" Halvar loomed over the shrinking guardsman.

"Silver pennies!" Fergus protested. "I told him it was a bad idea, trying to get money from those people, but when Long Liz was killed, Zoltan thought he'd make them pay. So he went to the cottage at a time when the Bretain servant was in the souk, and he found the milord drunk. They had a talk, and milord gave Zoltan and me a Bretain penny each, and said there would be more."

"Bretain silver pennies? Not Franchen imperials?" Halvar stepped back to digest this new information.

"That's what he gave us." Fergus fished under his coat and brought out a silver coin. "See? Here's one of them."

Halvar rubbed it with his fingers, then brought it close to the lantern.

"I don't know if this makes things clearer or muddies them more," he said. "This is no silver penny. It's got some silver on it, to be sure, but it's not true silver. It's false coin."

"Counterfeit!" Fergus gasped.

"How can you tell?' Selim squinted at the coin.

"If you look hard at the edge, you can see the base metal under a coating of something else, maybe silver, maybe antimony." Halvar demonstrated. "It's a counterfeit, to be sure. A very good one, but not a true Bretain penny from the High King's mint," Halvar assured him. "And that means that either Milord Summersby is a forger, or a fool."

"He acts like a fool," Selim said. "And he dresses like one, too."

"And they call him one," Halvar agreed. "A fat fool, at that. But I've fought him, and I can tell you that's meat on him, not fat. He's got a good right arm under all that lace and silk. And he may act the fool, but there's a mean temper under the foolery."

"But he never leaves that cottage," Selim pointed out.

"He went to the party at the madrassa. He led the lion hunt. And according to Devallon, this morning he went to the goat-shed where the horse is kept to argue with Farmer Bronk."

"Without Edgar?" Selim sounded dubious. "But Edgar is always by Milord Summersby's side."

"Edgar was at Yussif's shop, so he couldn't have killed Zoltan," Halvar said. "But where was Milord Henry? I think we'd better have a word with Milord...if he is a milord, which I'm beginning to doubt more and more."

"He isn't." Fergus said firmly, finally coming out of the corner. "He's just a soldier, like Devallon. That's what Girard said. He called him Henry, not Milord, and said that Edgar was the one called the tune and Henry danced to his piping."

"A pair of rogues, those two," Halvar said. "And passing bad coin, which gives me a good reason to arrest them in the name of the calif. Guardsman Fergus, Tenente Flores, you're with me. We're going to put those Bretains into cells, and if they freeze, so much the better!"

Chapter 16

THE SULTAN'S AFRIKAN SERVANTS WERE LIGHT-
ing torches and hanging lanterns on the walls that surrounded the central courtyard of the Rabat when Halvar, Selim,
and Flores emerged from Dr. Moise's shed with Fergus close
behind. The voice of the muezzin echoed over the town, followed by the faint sound of the chapel bell from the waterfront. Selim and Flores bowed and prostrated themselves; Fergus went down on one knee.

Halvar remained standing but bowed his head, clutched
his amulet, and sent up a fervent prayer to Whoever was
listening: *Help me, Redeemer! Mother Mara! Thor! Give me the
strength to get through the rest of this day, and the wit to fight
those who go against me!*

Prayers done, Selim scrambled to her feet.

"What do we do now, Capitán?"

"We go to the cottage," Halvar stated as Flores took his
time gaining his feet.

"Without a warrant?" Flores reminded him of the legal niceties demanded by the Bretains when they'd joined forces with Manatas Town.

"We are only making inquiries," Halvar said blandly. "We are answering a complaint that someone is passing bad coin in Manatas. That should satisfy the fusspots in Green Village, for now. Not that I think Dani Glick will argue the point. Passing bad coin is a hanging offense everywhere—in Bretain, in Franchenland, in the Dane-March."

"And in Al-Andalus," Flores said with a grunt of satisfaction. "So, when do we march?"

"As soon as you get a squad together," Halvar ordered. A hubbub at the gate drew his attention. "What's the matter now?"

"A Mahak, says he's got a message," the guardsman on duty called out. "And there's one of those Waterfront Rats with him. *He's* got a message for the Capitán, too."

Halvar tried to remember how many messages he was supposed to be receiving. Events seemed to be moving so rapidly, he wasn't sure who had told him what, or when!

Foxy ducked under the guardsman's arm and dashed across the courtyard. A young Local in wamus and leggings trotted after him. The Mahak did not have the warrior's shaved head and scalp-lock, but wore his hair in two plaits, secured with a leather headband.

"I am Running Deer," he announced. "I bring good cheer. Message from Green Village, from Tenente Donal and my sachem, the one they call the Firebrand."

"He's not a sachem yet," Flores grumbled.

"Give him time, and he will be," Halvar assured him. "What message?"

"Me first!" Foxy implored, fairly dancing with eagerness to impart his message. "I did what you asked, Capitán! I set a watch on the cottages on Pearl Street. Those Bretains–they're on the move!"

Running Deer shoved the youngster aside and handed Halvar a folded paper.

"This is talking leaf is from the frater at Green Village. He said it was important that you see it. It tells what he saw when he looked at the body of Ned the Cooper."

Halvar passed the paper to Selim, who took it to the nearest lantern to read it.

"Anything else?"

Running Deer took a deep breath and recited what he had memorized. "Tenente Donal says that he questioned all who were at the hunt yesterday. Many saw Ned, many heard him talk bad things about the man on the horse. Two men, not the Purists, heard him say that the man on the horse was not a milord, but a man who trapped animals on a milord's land."

"This we already know," Flores interrupted. "You think Ned was killed because he slandered Milord?"

"Milord Henry couldn't have killed Ned," Selim objected. "Everyone saw him on the horse leading the lion hunt. I saw him myself."

Halvar tugged at his mustache. "Henry was in clear sight, Where was Edgar?"

Running Deer took another breath. "Tenente Donal says the same who heard Ned talk bad things about Milord also saw Ned talking to Edgar Norris. They say the two of them went to the cooperage door together. They pressed hands, in the Bretain manner. Edgar patted Ned on the back. Then Edgar left Ned, and Ned went inside alone."

"Alive?" Halvar frowned.

"Tenente Donal says he saw it himself. Ned walked into his house, and Edgar went back to Manatas Town after the hunters left Green Village, just at sundown."

"Ned was alive when he and Edgar parted company," Flores summed up.

Halvar shivered under the blast of wind whirling across the courtyard and stepped back into the shelter of Dr. Moise's shed. Selim and Flores huddled on either side of him, while the Mahak and the Waterfront Rat took what shelter they could under the roof's overhang.

The lanky Afrikan medico shoved Halvar aside so he could hang a lantern on the hook just over the door.

"Is that the report from Green Village? What does that Kristo herbalist have to say?" Dr. Moise sneered.

Selim scanned the report, written in Ogham characters.

"He says that Ned the Cooper was killed with a long, sharp instrument, possibly a dagger, that entered his body just under the fifth rib. It penetrated his liver and kidney…"

"They must have cut him open to find that out," Dr. Moise sniffed scornfully. "I'm surprised the Kristo abbas allowed it."

"I suspect Frater Leonidas had something to do with that," Halvar said with a wry grin. "So, the wound did not kill him immediately?"

"According to Frater Leonidas, it is entirely possible that Ned Cooper did not even know he was dying." Selim looked up from the paper. "Is this true? Can someone be stabbed and not even know it?"

Halvar nodded. "That's what happened in Corduva," he recalled. "The fellow I told you about, the one at court? Turned out, he'd annoyed one of the harem eunuchs, who found someone to slip a knife between his ribs. He went up the stairs to his lodgings, lay on his bed, bled inside, and never woke."

"But you found out who did it," Selim said.

"I did. I asked about, found the knife-man, but it didn't make much difference. The one who hired him was a palace servant, and I couldn't touch him. All I could do was tell Lady Zulaika what I'd found out, and let her deal with it." Halvar grimaced at the memory. Palace intrigue in Corduva was toxic, and he'd tried to stay out of it as much as possible.

Running Deer interrupted the discussion. "I have more. A message from Firebrand, who is also tenente. He says there are lights across the river."

This got Halvar's full attention. "The Great River? Are the Huron on the march?"

"We watch the East Channel, where the Bretains and the Danes of West Caster live. Tenente Firebrand has stationed watchmen at the place where they are making a bridge. There are landing places for boats where canoes can beach, and we watch them to see who comes to Manatas. He says lanterns and torches are lit across the river, as if someone is expected to come there."

"Making sure they can land the ferry," Halvar said. "But who wants to go across the East Channel today?"

Foxy pulled on Halvar's arm. "That's what I'm trying to tell you! The big Bretain milord and the skinny one, the servant, they got the Franchen woman and her musket-man, and they got the Afrikans to load their chests onto a wagon, and they put the horse into harness, and they're trying to leave!"

"Now? It's nearly dark!" Flores exclaimed.

"They've got lanterns on the cart," Foxy said. "But the Franchen woman is making a great fuss, and her Franchen man, he's trying to keep her quiet. If you hurry, you can stop them."

"But...where are they going?" Flores asked.

"To that bridge landing! Thor's Hammer!" Halvar swore. "That's where they're going! Tenente Flores, get your men together! We're going to stop them right now!"

"Without a warrant?" Fergus quavered, behind Flores.

"On my authority as Capitán of the Manatas Town Guard and representative of the Calif of Al-Andalus-in-Exile!" Halvar roared. He turned to Running Deer. "I know you deserve food and drink, but I have to get word back to Tenentes Donal and Firebrand. Run back to Green Village, tell them to set lights along the path to the bridge landing. Tell them to try and stop whoever comes along that path, and if they can't stop them on the path, do it at the bridge landing."

"I go now," Running Deer announced, and headed across the courtyard.

"Foxy, outside the Rabat gate is a fellow called Avaram with a donkey cart. Go now, before he quits for the day. Tell him he's needed," Halvar ordered. "Flores, get your squad together. Never mind drill, this is for real! Fergus, you're with me. We're going to get the *verdammitte* dog-killer who put the knife into your friend."

Halvar strode across the courtyard, Selim right behind, scurrying to keep up with him.

"Edgar could have killed Ned, but he didn't kill Zoltan."

"No, Henry did that." Halvar stopped at the gate.

"Is everyone at that cottage a murderer?" Selim was aghast.

Echoes of a riot in the making drifted over the stone walls and through the gate. The guardsman stepped back to let Halvar and his party through. Before them was a scene of mass confusion, lit by lanterns and torches, fanned by the wind whistling through the gaps between the buildings.

"At least the houses on the Broad Way are of brick. All we need now is a fire," Halvar muttered as he tried to make sense of the chaos before him. This time there would be no delay, no dithering. He was still the Calif's Hireling, with all the authority that gave him, and he would not be deterred, not this time!

Chapter 17

TORCHES FLARED AND FLICKERED OUTSIDE THE
Rabat walls, barely augmented by the lanterns swinging from
hooks over the mokka-shop doors on the Broad Way. By their
light, Halvar could make out at least four men, one woman,
and one very agitated horse, all yelling, screeching, and neighing at the top of their respective considerable lungs.

The racket began to draw a crowd from the mokka-shops.
Students in gowns and cloaks, merchants in coats and caftans, even a few of the women from the waterfront were
drawn by the noise. Avaram's donkey added its bray to the
cacophony, sending the horse into another frenzy of stamping, kicking, and snorting.

The stallion reared and plunged, clearly objecting to being harnessed to a large wagon that held two sea chests and
two small leather valises. A stout man in the leather jacket
and wool breeches worn by Danes tried vainly to calm the
agitated beast, while Milord Henry Summersby yelled at
both of them from the driver's seat on the wagon.

Farther down the street, Devallon dragged Milady Charlotte Summersby up the hill, with Edgar Norris hustling the two of them along.

"I won't go! I tell you, I won't!" Charlotte screeched in Franchen as Devallon hauled her towards the wagon. "No, no, no!"

"You can't stay here all winter," Devallon told her.

"If you please, Milady, you can ride in the wagon," Edgar offered.

"Sirdar! My beauty, my good boy!" the Dane cooed in Danic-accented Arabi as he dodged the agitated steed's front hooves.

Halvar stepped out, into the torchlight.

"What's all this?"

The Dane grabbed for the flailing reins and missed.

"The Bretain milord wishes to leave Manatas Island."

"At this hour? After sunset?" Halvar gazed at the loaded cart. "You could not wait until tomorrow?"

"We're getting off this thrice-damned island, and you can't stop us!" Milord shot back. "Edgar! Get that woman aboard! She's mine, I paid for her!"

"In false coin," Halvar stated. He called out in Erse, "Get down from that wagon, Heer Henry. I charge you with passing counterfeit coins."

"Fake silver!" Charlotte's shrill voice cut through the babble of the rapidly-forming crowd. This much Erse she understood! "You miserable liar, you thief, you…"

"He's a murderer, too," Selim offered. "You don't have to go with him, milady. Even if he is your husband."

"Husband?" Charlotte echoed. "Andres, you told me the marriage could be undone if we got to Manatas. You said they have divorce here…"

"Only for desertion, and for impotence," Selim informed her.

"He's running away from me. He wouldn't come near me, he threw me out of the cottage, and he's no man in bed!"

"Really!" Selim gasped.

"Not relevant now." Edgar ended the discussion. "Milady, get into the wagon."

"I won't!" Charlotte stamped her foot, sending a spray of muck onto Edgar's carefully polished shoes.

"Charlotte, please!" Devallon tried to soothe the agitated woman. "Just...get onto the wagon."

Charlotte turned on her supposed ally. "This is all your fault! You told me to take his offer! You told me he would take care of me!"

"And whose bright idea was it to get a place on that ship with the brides for Kibbick?" Devallon shot back. "And then you talked Girard into taking me with him, all the way south. You said we'd be able to get away from the Bretains once we reached Andalusian territory! So, we end up here, and the only way off this miserable island is with this good farmer, so get into the wagon, Charlotte, and be done with it!"

Halvar watched the byplay, grinning under his mustache. Just as he'd thought! It had been Charlotte's idea for Devallon to join Girard. Now, if he could only make one more move...

At the other end of the wagon, Farmer Bronk was still vainly trying to soothe his recalcitrant steed, murmuring in Arabi.

"What's that gibberish you're saying?" Milord was getting more and more testy.

"Sirdar only knows Arabi," Bronk explained. "If you tell him what you want, he'll do as you say. But he does not like being back in the harness after he's been ridden. It took me nearly a year to get him used to the wagon. He's a war-horse, not a cart-horse, a real Arab Barb!"

"You talk as if he's a person. He's a beast, and he's meant to obey," Milord declared. "Give me the reins, man, and I'll show you how to deal with a horse."

"The way you showed Ned Cooper?" Flores hooted, stepping forward, halberd ready to hook the man off his perch.

"Who?" Milord leaned forward to take up the straps that dangled on the underside of the seat.

"The fellow who recognized you at the lion hunt yesterday," Halvar said. "The one who said you couldn't ride, that, in fact, you never could. He knew who you are, Henry Summersby, and what's more, he knew who you *were!*"

"Stand aside!" Milord Henry grasped the whip lying beside the driver's seat. "Edgar! Get that woman into the wagon!"

Edgar backhanded Charlotte, which sent her spinning against the backboard. With one heave, he picked her up and flung her over the board, leaving her sprawled on the chests.

"Andres!" Charlotte called, pitifully stretching her hand to the one who had always been her savior. Devallon, startled at the sudden show of strength in one who had made no show of it before, stood as if poleaxed.

"Andres! Help me!" Charlotte screamed as the wagon rocked on it wheels.

"Get in, or stay behind!" Edgar ordered, hoisting himself into the wagon.

"Andres! Don't leave me with them!"

With a rueful grimace, Devallon hauled himself over the backboard into the wagon next to his cousin.

Halvar strode forward to grab the shafts of the wagon.

"You're not going anywhere, Henry Summersby. You are under arrest, by order of the Calif of Al-Andalus!"

"Try and stop me! Stand aside, or be trampled!" Milord roared again. He slashed the whip against the horse's back.

Sirdar reared, front legs thrashing, neighing loudly in pain. The wagon rocked, but the wheels held the road. Devallon gripped the sides, and Charlotte held tight to her chosen knight.

"Make way!" Milord yelled.

The crowd parted. Sirdar saw an open space…and took it.

And the chase was on!

Chapter 18

THE BROAD WAY LAY STRAIGHT AHEAD, A FLAT brick-paved road leading through the town from the front gate of the Rabat to the town wall. Sirdar saw this as a means of escape. He stretched his legs, regardless of the impediment strapped on behind.

Halvar fumed as he watched the wagon careen along the road to disappear into the darkness. He leaped into Avaram's donkey cart, clinging to its sides as it rocked under his weight. Selim scrambled up beside him. The Danic farmer, Bronk, followed her.

"Stop them!" Bronk ordered. "That madman's stealing my horse!"

"One more crime to add to his charges," Halvar told him. "Avaram! Get this animal moving!"

Avaram poked the donkey with a long pole. The animal protested, but walked sedately forward.

"Can't this wretched beast go any faster?" Halvar fumed.

"Jacko's a donkey, not an Arab horse," Avaram said, prodding his steed into a more lively trot.

"We could walk," Selim suggested.

"With this hole in my shoulder? I might not get as far as the gate," Halvar admitted.

"You won't catch them, not with this donkey. Sirdar's a Barb," Bronk said proudly.

"I don't care what he is," Halvar groused. "I know he's faster than this donkey, but he'll run out of air soon enough, and when he does, we'll get them."

"Not Sirdar," Bronk insisted. "I've taken him to the races at the New Haven fair, and he's won every time.. He was born to run!"

"He'll have to stop at the wall," Selim reminded them as they followed the wagon past the Grand Muskat and the Manatas Madrassa, through the sector of businesses, past the Street of the Afrikans and its empty villas, boarded up for the winter.

Charlotte's shrill screech echoed through the town, bringing the smokers and the drinkers of mokka out of the comfort of the shops to see what was happening. Students of the madrassa streamed out of their lodgings bearing lanterns. Halvar could hear the babble of male voices behind him.

"Torches!" someone called in Arabi.

"Who is it?"

"Some madman, running a race at this time of night!"

"They're killers, and they're escaping!" Halvar yelled, clinging to the sides of the cart again as the donkey picked up the pace, trotting more briskly northward.

"They're at the wall!" Selim craned her neck to see past the shadows.

"The guard will stop them," Halvar said.

"Not if Sirdar has his way." Bronk spoke as one who knows. "That is a very fierce horse, Capitán. Nothing gets between him and what he wants, and what he wants now is to get away from that madman with the whip. Sirdar doesn't like to be whipped."

"Who does?" Halvar murmured, remembering his punishment for being distracted by a pretty face when he should have been guarding supplies.

The donkey jogged through the dimly-lit street toward the stone wall that marked the boundary between Manatas Town and the rest of the island. They could see the wagon, its passengers still clinging to its sides.

"Hold! Stop!" Halvar called out. "Guardsman! Close that gate!"

Before the terrified guard could obey, Milord slashed down with the whip. Sirdar bolted through the narrow opening. The wagon lurched and banged against the gate but did not tip over. Instead, wagon and riders plunged into the darkness beyond the wall, visible only because of the lantern attached to a pole jammed into a socket on the wagon seat.

"They've taken the east path." Selim pointed at the pinpoint of light careening ahead of them.

"Torches!" Halvar ordered the crowd that remained. "If you must come along, make yourselves useful!"

Another line of lights streamed across the feria grounds. Donal emerged from the darkness carrying a lantern, with Bertram and three more constables behind him. Angry honks and flapping wings accompanied them as the flock of geese on the feria grounds objected to their evening rest being disturbed.

Avaran stopped the donkey cart, partly to let Donal catch up to them, partly to give Jacko a chance to breathe.

"Hold!"

Donal grabbed the side of the cart, panting with exertion.

"The Mahak runner told me the Bretain Milord was making a run for it. Heading for the bridge? At this time of night? The moon's not out, little as it is. What've they done, to take such a risk?"

"Milord knows we're after him and Edgar. One of them killed Ned, the other killed a guardsman," Halvar explained. "And they're passing bad coin as well."

"And they stole my horse!" Bronk wailed. "My lovely Sirdar!"

"Never mind the horse!" Halvar huffed. "That pair of Bretains are murderers, and must not get off this island! Avaram! Get this beast moving!"

Jacko had found a tasty shrub, and was munching happily when Avaram prodded him again. With a mournful bray, the donkey plodded on, responding to Avaram's prodding with an occasional burst of speed.

The path was narrow, meant for feet, not wheels. Scurries under the dried leaves indicated small animals getting out of the way of the donkey's hoofs.

There was a sudden squeal ahead of them, and then a nauseating reek. A wail from Charlotte made Halvar grin. Clearly, Sirdar had run into a sekonk making its rounds. He hoped the smelly creature had saturated the wagon with its odor. It would make them easier to find in the dark.

The chase passed the Algonkin settlement. Nokomis and three more Local women emerged from the round Algonkin wigwams, running alongside the cart with their their burning brands to light the way for the donkey. They continued past the palisade surrounding the Mahak long-houses.

"Where are the watchmen?" Halvar shouted, looking for Firebrand and his men,

"They went ahead to the bridge-head," Donal yelled back. "Firebrand's got them stationed there, to stop anyone using the bridge to get off Manatas."

Halvar held onto the sides of the donkey cart as it careened along the path, dodging the branches that had been placed to stop the runaways. The barriers were not enough to stop an enraged stallion. Sirdar had trampled the branches under his hoofs, whinnying with pain as the twigs pricked his sensitive underparts, slowing his flight just enough for the donkey to catch up with him..

Sirdar and the wagon came to a halt where a space had been cleared for bridge construction. By some miracle, the wagon was still attached, Charlotte hanging on to one side of the cargo space and Devallon to the other. Edgar slid to the ground, ready to grab the reins and lead the snorting, wheezing horse down the ramp to where a large scow lay moored at the jetty.

A lantern was mounted on a pole where a ramp had been constructed to allow bricks and mortar to be carried to the builders. Another shone on the pier below, where whoever commanded the scow that had been summoned to take the fugitives off Manatas Island waited.

Between the wagon and the ramp stood Firebrand and his men, war-clubs in hand, waiting for the order to attack.

Halvar hopped off the donkey cart, taking in the scene.

"Capitán!" Flores struggled to keep up with him. "You're going to need this." He thrust a halberd into Halvar's hand.

Halvar gripped the shaft. Spear, axe, staff in one weapon, one he had used for nearly twenty years. He balanced the shaft in one hand, then stalked forward, eyes on the wagon, hoping Flores and Selim were behind him.

"Watch out for Edgar," he said softly. "He's the one who's got the knife. He's sneaky, he's clever. Don't let him get behind you."

"What are you going to do?" Selim quavered.

"I'm going to take Milord Henry Summersby back to the Rabat to face Sultan Petrus and receive the justice of Al-Andalus. That's the way it should be done, and that's the way it's going to *be* done! I'm going to make things right!"

Chapter 19

HALVAR PACED FORWARD, IGNORING THE GROW-
ing crowd behind him.

"Henry Summersby!" he shouted in Erse. "You are under arrest for the murder of Guardsman Zoltan!"

"And passing bad coin!" Selim added from Avaram's cart.

"And stealing my horse!" Bronk darted forward to comfort his panting steed. "You've half-killed him! And whipped
him into bloody shreds, you butcher!"

Milord Henry regarded the crowd with disdain from his
seat on the wagon.

"You cannot arrest me," he declared. "I am Milord Summersby, and I do not answer to anyone!"

"You can call yourself whatever you like, Henry Summersby. You may even be a milord, no matter what Ned
Cooper said. You're certainly stupid enough to be one."

"Stupid!" Henry's voice resonated with outrage.

"You don't do a thing for yourself. You've got your mus-ket-man to do your fighting for you, and Edgar Norris to do your thinking for you. Maybe Girard did your swiving for you, too."

"No one fights for me!" Henry shouted. "No one thinks for me, and I can take care of my own woman!"

"Then why hire a mercenary? To keep watch on your wife? He's doing that well enough!" Halvar aimed the point of the halberd's axe-blade at the back of the wagon, where the musket-man was carefully easing Charlotte over the side.

"Devallon!" Henry shouted. "To me!"

"Andres!" Charlotte wailed, clinging to his arm. "Don't leave me!"

Devallon hesitated, caught between his mercenary duty to Milord and his attachment to Charlotte.

"Charlotte, go down that ramp," he ordered, shoving her away. He took a step forward, drawing his sword. "Mi-lord! I'm with you."

Charlotte screamed as two men emerged from the dark-ness behind them, knives in hand. Firebrand yelled some-thing in Munsi. His men moved forward to face the party coming up the ramp.

Devallon hesitated, not knowing how to proceed. Who was he to protect—the woman or the man?

Bronk settled the issue. "Gilles! Markus!" he yelled "Get Sirdar to the ferry!"

An Afrikan took the horse's bridle and tried to lead the restive steed to the churning stream. The horse objected loud-ly, stamping and neighing in fear and anger. Firebrand's squad stepped aside, away from the thrashing hooves. Bronk dart-ed forward to unbuckle the harness that connected the horse to the wagon, murmuring endearments in Arabi.

"Andres!" Charlotte's voice echoed over the babble of the crowd.

"Devallon!" Milord roared. "I need you...now! What do I pay you for!"

"Charlotte…go with the farmer," Devallon ordered. "I'll join you as soon as I take care of these savages."

"I won't go without you!" Charlotte quavered.

Bronk took her arm, cajoling as he led her down to the ferry.

"I have a good large house, Milady. My wife is a fine cook. You will be safe there.

"My clothes!" Charlotte howled. "Don't forget my clothes!"

Devallon pointed to the chests. "Take the them down to the ferry. Charlotte, go with the farmer."

He faced Firebrand and the Mahak resolutely. He couldn't get to Milord Henry until he got rid of them.

Back at the wagon, Milord Henry suddenly realized his perch was no longer attached to Sirdar.

"What are you doing? Where are you going?" He called to Bronk, who had turned Sirdar around and was leading him down the ramp.

"This is my horse!" Bronk announced. "He goes with me!"

Sirdar agreed, whinnying loudly. He kicked free of the wagon while Milord fumed.

"I paid you to get me off this accursed island!"

"In false coin!" Halvar announced. "Farmer Bronk, take your horse, if you must. Risk your life on the river, in the darkness. But this man stays here!" With one long stride, he reached the wagon and stretched an arm up to pull the arrogant Bretain down from his perch. "Bretain or not, you are in the territory of Al-Andalus, and you will answer to our laws."

Milord Henry tried to slash the whip across Halvar's face. Halvar grabbed the lash and yanked. Milord fell out of the wagon, cursing loudly in Erse.

Halvar hauled the man to his feet.

"I don't know who you are, but you are no milord. And you have no standing here. You will have a chance to speak

141

for yourself once we get back to the Rabat. For now…Tenente Flores!"

"Here, Capitán!" The Andalusian guardsman stepped forward, halberd at the ready.

"Take this man—"

Before Halvar could finish, Milord Henry jerked away from his captor and grabbed the nearest halberd.

Halvar looked around for assistance from his guardsmen. Beyond the torches, he could see flickers of steel on stone as Devallon held Firebrand and his Mahak away from the ramp. Why was Flores no longer behind him. Where was Avaram and the cart, with Selim? Had that willful girl gone off on her own again?

He couldn't worry about that now. He had an opponent in front of him, armed and dangerous. He took his position, as he had been trained—both hands on the shaft, feet square, ready to move.

Whatever else he might have been, Milord Henry revealed himself to be the equal of Halvar as a halbardier. He ignored the sword at his hip and grasped his halberd with the ease of one who was thoroughly familiar with its use as a weapon of both offense and defense.

"Try and take me!" he jeered.

"I will!" Halvar lowered his halberd. "We've done this before, Milord. There's no snow here to blind me, and no icy deck underfoot. We're equals, you and I, mercenaries. You're no milord!"

"You're a peasant! You're nothing!" Milord sneered. "I am Milord Henry Summersby! I will be ruler in my own country, you will see! One against one, hey? And we'll see who takes who! I'll rule Manatas, if I can't get anything better!"

He circled Halvar, jabbing the point of the halberd at his face, not quite touching, taunting him into making an unwary move.

142

"Rule Manatas? You can't even rule your own household without Edgar to speak for you. You don't have the wit to learn Franchen, let alone Arabi!" Halvar taunted back as they stepped carefully around each other. "You couldn't even deal honestly with my guardsmen.

"Zoltan came to you while Edgar was out at the souk, said he had proof you were no milord, asked for payment to keep his mouth shut. You gave him one of your bad coins, but that wasn't good enough. He had to be stopped, permanently.

"You should have let Edgar do it, the way he took care of Ned the Cooper. But, no, you decided to do it yourself. I'm sure I'll find one of those men from Mendel's book stall, who will testify to the sultan that you were there, that you were the one who made the lewd catcalls that sent Zoltan into that alley after the girl."

"A pack of drunken students? Who'd believe them?" Milord Henry jabbed at Halvar, who deflected the blow easily, and continued to harass his opponent.

"And how do you know they were students?" Halvar shot back. "And they weren't drunk, not that I could tell. You should have left it to Edgar, he's the one with the brains. You're just the muscle, Henry, and not much else!"

"I'll show you who's got brains!" Henry jabbed his halberd, nicking Halvar's ear, then whirled around to face him again.

"You're out of practice with the halberd, Henry. Swords, I'll give you that. You're good with a blade, but you've forgotten what little you ever knew about the halberd. Tenente Flores could give you some good tips—he runs a close drill."

Milord yelled and charged. Halvar nimbly shifted, hooking the other man's blade with the rounded edge of the axe at the end of his halberd.

"Give it up, Henry. You're not going to get away from Manatas. You've killed one of the Town Guard, you've passed

143

bad coin, you stole a horse. Any one of these crimes means death, milord or no milord, and you're no milord!"

Henry gripped his halberd and used it like a quarter-staff, forcing Halvar to retaliate in kind. The two men battled fiercely, equally matched in height and weight, locking shafts, until Halvar surged forward, throwing Henry off-balance.

By this time, a crowd from Green Village had joined the hardy souls from Manatas Town. Their lanterns and torches lit the space at the bridge-head, where the earth had been tamped down and was now firmly frozen underfoot. Voices rang out in Erse, Franchen, and Danic, demanding to know who was fighting whom, betting on the outcome.

Halvar couldn't give any thought to what was going on outside the circle. He could only hope Donal or Flores or Firebrand had the wit and the men to stop the ferry. His attention had to be on Milord Henry. He would deal with anything else later.

He shoved Henry back against the side of the wagon and raised his halberd to deliver a blow with the butt end. Henry ducked away, and Halvar's arms were stunned by the jarring thud of wood against wood. Henry used the blade for one more cut; Halvar ducked that but felt the blade nick his ear again. He winced and whirled around with a thrust of his own.

Once more it was thrust against thrust. Halvar used the point to defend himself, forcing Henry to the edge of the cliff. The Bretain dodged, thrust, and parried Halvar's blow.

There was a pause as both men stood gasping for breath. The onlookers fell quiet, knowing that one or the other of them must give way.

Charlotte's shrill screech broke the silence from somewhere below the cliff edge.

"Stop playing and kill him!"

Something broke in Halvar's brain. He could feel the bubble of rage within him taking over. A red mist seemed to come between him and the rest of the world. He knew this rage—the last time he had felt it was on the battlefield at Pisa when he saw his mentor, Old Sergeant Olaf, fall under the Franchen musket onslaught. That had been his last fight as a Free Dane, and he'd gone bear-shirt, ignoring his own wounds in his passion to kill as many of the enemy as he could reach, even if they killed him.. That screaming voice, that order to kill—that was the one thing that could release him from the bounds of civilized fighting.

With a roar, he attacked, slashing and thrusting, not aware whether he was landing any blows. He forgot he was on the edge of a cliff, barely heard the water gurgling and splashing on the rocks below. He pushed forward, ignoring cuts and blows, deaf to the cries behind him, only thinking of the body before him. It was slash, jab, slash…until one final slash met heavy resistance.

There was a gasp, a groan, a sudden silence. Then there was a faint *plop*, and there was something at his feet.

He looked down as the head of Henry Summersby rolled to his feet. He looked around, propping himself on the shaft of the halberd, not seeing the blood dripping down its blade.

There was a scuffle behind him, someone shouting "Not this time!" He felt a stinging pain in his back. *Not again!* he thought before he succumbed to the blackness.

Chapter 20

HE WOKE IN A NARROW BED, IN A ROOM WITH wooden walls that looked vaguely familiar. He tried to turn his head to see more and was awarded with a swimming head and a heaving stomach. There was something constricting his midsection, his shoulder burned, but most of all, he needed the jakes!

"Where...?" he croaked through dry lips and a rasping throat.

"So, you're awake!" someone at the foot of the bed announced.

He tried to focus on the source of the voice.

"Water?"

Someone bent over him, lifted him high enough to accept a cup of something warm that tasted vile.

"Faugh!" Halvar sputtered.

His vision cleared. He recognized the Afrikan woman who had divested him of his clothing after his encounter with the sekonk.

"Farrah?" He squirmed on the bed, trying to adjust himself. "Gardens of Paradise? How…?" He gulped more of the bitter brew.

"Willow-bark tea. Good for you!" Farrah let him down onto the pillow. "I get Fru Glick."

The willow-bark worked its magic; the headache eased to a mere nagging pain. Halvar hitched himself into a sitting position and tried to remember the last few hours.

He distinctly recalled the fight with Henry Summersby. He had turned around, only to face another enemy. There had been a shout, someone stabbed him…

He tried to remember what happened after he saw the head rolling at his feet. There had been confusion. There were shouts and screams, and then—blackness.

He closed his eyes. He had the image of a tile floor he'd once seen in Al-Andalus. He tried to recall the dream…that tile floor meant something…it was the answer to everything that had happened over the last two weeks…if only he could remember…

"If you keep doing this, I'll have to charge you rent." Dani Glick had appeared in the doorway.

Halvar opened his eyes. "I'm in the Gardens of Paradise. Again."

"You are. Again. And you've been fighting. Again."

"How…?"

"Your faithful follower insisted that, since you were still breathing, we must bring you back from the shores of the Lands of the Dead. She's quite a girl, the sultan's daughter. She started giving orders as soon as she saw you were alive. Sent for Eva Hakim to get her Local women to brew potions for you. Got Frater Iosip in here to bind your wounds with his moldy-bread poultices. Even hauled the medico from the Rabat to sew you up where the Bretain knifed you. You are remarkably hard to kill, Halvar Danske."

"Thanks be to the Redeemer and Mother Mara," Halvar responded piously. *And Thor*, he added silently, just to make sure all deities were properly acknowledged. "As for Selim, she comes by it naturally. Her mama was the Lady Fatima, the one who founded the House of the Green Crescent and the Sisters of Fatima. Now, get me my clothes, and get me out of this bed. There are things that need doing." He tried to sit up, ignoring the swimming sensation between his ears.

"And you are not the one to do them," Dani told him. "That's why you have that girl, and the ugly guardsman. And, I might add, my own man, Donal, who has been very busy on your behalf. Your exploits have lit the lightning under the Town Guard."

"There's one thing no one can do for me," Halvar said. "I need the jakes."

He tried to swing his legs over the side of the bed. Farrah shoved him onto his back with one hand.

"You use chamber pot. I get!"

She reached under the bed for the receptacle.

Halvar focused on the square of light on the wall opposite him. This was wrong. He'd been fighting in torchlight, after sundown.

"How long—"

"Have you been here?" Dani interrupted. "It was well after dark when you arrived. You slept for a day. It's nearly sundown now."

"A whole day lost! I can't stay here!" Halvar tried to lift himself onto one elbow, sending another wave of pain across his back and shoulder. He fell back onto the pillow, cursing his own weakness, closing his eyes again.

Above his head, he heard Dani's voice. "You can't come in here! The man needs his rest!"

"We have to speak to Capitán Don Alvaro!" That was Selim, sharply decisive. "It's important. We sent word to Sultan Petrus about the fight, and he's sent word back."

Halvar groaned. "Sit me up!. What's going on? When did the sultan...?"

148

He looked around the tiny room that suddenly seemed filled with people.

"Firebrand sent his man Running Deer as soon as the fight was over," Selim told him.

"You were overcome by the fatigue of the fight." That was Donal, in Erse.

"And then the Bretain used the knife." Flores added in Arabi.

"And I had to stop him," Selim finished. "And they wanted to put you into the ground, but you were breathing, so I told Tenente Donal to get you to the Gardens of Paradise, and send for Frater Iosip and Frater Leonidas. And the Local woman brewed some kind of potion, and it brought you back from the Shores of the Dead, or wherever Kristo Danes go."

Halvar absorbed this tangled tale as he maneuvered his legs over the side of the bed. Then he realized he was missing a major item of clothing. He had a shirt, but no braies.

"Selim, leave us for a moment. Donal, get me out of this bed and down to the jakes. And then, get me my breeches and a coat, and get me out of this room."

"Not until the medicos have looked you over," Dani decided. "You are in no fit condition to do anything more than lie down, take your potions, and allow yourself to heal!"

"I can't," Halvar responded. "The fighting may be over, but there are things to be done! First, the wagon…Was there anything else in it besides those two big chests? I thought I saw a leather satchel…Where is it? Then, those students from the souk—find them, question them. One of them must have recognized Henry Summersby—they were at the Gardens of Paradise on Watch-night when he threw silver around like white wumpum…" He coughed again, sending waves of pain through his chest.

"Not good!" Farrah warned him. "Lie down! Rest!"

"We've got things in hand, Capitán, just leave it to us." That was Flores who stood just inside the door.

149

"There are messages from across the river." Firebrand stood right behind Flores but outside the room. "As for the wagon, my watchmen are guarding it. They found the leather satchel. I looked into it myself and found coins and some tools. Tenente Donal says they are to make the coins."

Halvar took another breath, waited for the pain to subside. "Selim?"

"Here, Capitán." Selim squeezed past Flores and Firebrand to take a place beside the bed. Her usual padded silk jacket, trousers, and turban had been replaced by the green tunic, brown trousers, and green hijab of the Sisters of Fatima.

"You're..." He waved feebly at her new garments.

Selim sniffled.. "After the fight, when my turban fell off, and everyone saw, Eva Hakim said it would be better for me to dress like the Sisters of Fatima. They go almost everywhere, and no one notices them. It's almost as good as dressing like a boy. Now that everyone in Green Village knows I'm not one."

"That's no matter! Our Selim is quite the heroine!" Donal crowed. "Never saw anything like it! You'd be dead meat if she hadn't tackled that scurvy wretch."

"A mighty warrior, worthy of her father! Like the Prophet's sister, leading the battle against the Infidel!" Flores added.

"A Woman Warrior, indeed," Firebrand agreed.

Selim shrugged. "I did what I had to. I couldn't let you die."

Halvar closed his eyes again. He remembered again the torchlight, and the bloody head at his feet. There had been some kind of scuffle behind him...he had turned, and felt a searing pain across his back...and there was shouting...

And he had a sudden vision of Edgar, with someone on his back.

"Everyone...out! You can tell him the tale when I've finished with him." Frater Iosip shoved through the crowd, with

Frater Leonidas behind him, one short and tubby, the other long and lithe. The guardsmen and Selim muttered rebelliously as they gathered again just outside the door. Farrah shut it firmly in their faces.

"Now, Capitán, if you please, do not move. I must adjust these bandages."

Frater Leonidas lay a hand against Halvar's temple then checked his pulse.

"Not feverish," he pronounced. "Heartbeat is racing, but that's expected, with that lot yammering at him."

Frater Iosip applied more moldy-bread poultices to Halvar's cuts and bruises, and bound them firmly with strips of linen.

"Ow!" Halvar winced. "I need the pot more than those poultices. Get me on my feet! Woman, get out! There are some things that a man must do alone!""

Farrah and Dani Glick sniffed scornfully as they stalked out of the room and pointedly shut the door. The two fraters eased him onto his feet and held him upright as he relieved himself, then lay him back onto the narrow bed. Frater Iosip regarded the contents of the chamber pot with a practiced eye.

"Good color, good odor," he pronounced. "Excellent." He busied himself with the discarded bandages, checking for fresh blood and the odor of putrefaction. "No bones broken, thanks be to Chesu. Cuts, bruises, and that place where the bullet scraped you.

"You are healing nicely, Capitán. You should be able to get about on your own in a week, if you stay put. If you don't, the cuts may open, and you'll have to rely on the Islim bonesetter at the Rabat. Not a bad surgeon, if you need one, but he has no idea of true medication, and he prefers his mineral potions to proper herbal cures."

"I can't sit on my arse while there are murderers on the loose," Halvar grumbled. "Just tie on some bandages, get me my clothes, and get me out of here. I've been out of things for a whole day. Anything can happen in a day!"

Frater Leonidas handed him a linen shirt.

"Nothing would astonish me where you are concerned, my dear Halvar. Your recuperative powers are close to legendary. According to the *Gazetta*, you are nothing short of a Hero of Antiquity, ferreting out dire conspiracies against Al-Andalus, fighting a veritable monster…"

"The cat or Milord Henry?" Halvar hissed as Frater Leonidas slid the shirt over his wounded back.

"Both." Frater Leonidas waved a copy of the printed sheet in front of Halvar. "Illustrated, I might add, by my star pupil. The girl has talent as well as courage."

"Not another ballad?" Halvar grabbed the paper, wishing he could make sense of either the swirls of Arabi or the curves of Ogham. The last time he'd tangled with Manatas wildlife his exploit had been noted by Selim's friends, rendered into verse, set to music, and performed by Willem of Cos and his troupe until Halvar was sick of hearing about it.

"Not at all," Frater Leonidas assured him. "Merely a blow-by-blow account of the most dreadful fight on Manatas. At least, one of the most colorful. And, I fear, the most open secret in Manatas is a secret no more."

"Selim?" Halvar winced and fell back against the bed. Maybe it *was* a good idea to rest, at least until his head cleared. . "Or Salomey?"

"Both, or either. She's much like her forceful mother," Frater Leonidas said, with a wry twist of his lips. "I met that lady, briefly, before I was exiled to Manatas."

"So did I." Halvar dimly recalled the woman who had changed his life by rescuing him on the battlefield and sending him to Al-Andalus instead of to the ruined city behind him. "Frater? Are you finished? I need to talk to my people. Now."

"If you must." Frater Iosip adjusted his lenses. "My medical advice is, stay put for at least another day. Eat small quantities of broth, either of gobbler or goose, with plenty of carrots and turnips, which provide bulk and stimulate the bowels for proper evacuation. I suspect you will not take this advice."

"I'll eat the soup," Halvar said. "But I've got to get back to the Rabat as soon as I can put one foot in front of the other without falling on my face."

"If you do so, I will leave you in the hands of Eva Hakim and her Sisters of Fatima, and the Rabat medico. I suppose they will do as much for you as I will. Most cures are in the hands of the Redeemer and Mother Mara, at the end." Frater Iosip stalked out past Farrah, now at her post inside the door.

Dani Glick waited for the two fraters to leave before ushering one of her many halfling lads into the room, bearing a bowl and a spoon.

"Soup?" Halvar sniffed eagerly. His stomach reminded him it had not been filled with anything more substantial than nut-meats and mokka for more than twenty-four hours. He reached eagerly for the bowl, his hands visibly shaking..

"You'll get more on the sheets than in your mouth," Dani scolded him, batting his hand away. "Greedy-guts! Let someone with steady hands do it."

She sat on the small stool next to the bed and spooned the hearty soup into his mouth, avoiding his mustache as best she could.

"Where were you while I was making a fool of myself?" Halvar asked between sips of soup.

"Not quite a fool. More like one of the gladiators of Old Rouma. I only saw the end of your spectacular exhibition of fighting skill," she said. "When Donal took himself off to arrest the false milord, he took most of the custom of the night with him. I followed with Simon Singer in Padraig's pony cart. Good thing I did, because that was the best and fastest way to get you away from the bridgehead, back to Green Village."

"I didn't want to kill Henry." Halvar took the bowl from her hands and slurped what was left. "I wanted him alive. And you'd better check those coins he was throwing about. The Franchen Imperials were good silver, but he had a store of Bretain pennies that weren't. Firebrand tells me he and Donal found coiners' tools in his satchel."

"More counterfeit?" Dani took the bowl back. "First wumpum, now Bretain pennies. What next—Andalusian dinars?"

"They're still real, as far as I know," Halvar said. He sighed deeply. "That was good, Dani Glick. Now, if you please, send my people back in. I'm wounded, but I will heal. I have to know what's happening to Manatas!"

"The place went on perfectly well before you came to disturb us," she told him. "If anything, you've brought more trouble to Manatas than we ever had. It seems as if the whole island has gone mad."

"The madness was always there," Halvar said. "You just didn't want to see it. Send in my tenentes, Dani Glick, and get me my clothes. I'm not staying here any longer than I have to. My bed at the Mermaid Taberna is bigger and softer than this shelf, and I'll get good, solid Danic meat pies, not gobbler soup and root vegetables. And ale!" he added defiantly.

"You…Dane!" Dani flounced out, allowing Flores, Donal, Firebrand, and Selim to enter.

Halvar hitched himself into a sitting position. "All right, you lot!" He scowled at them "What's been happening while I've been asleep?"

Chapter 21

SELIM TOOK THE STOOL VACATED BY DANI GLICK. Flores stood behind her. Donal found a space at the end of the bed. Firebrand stood in the doorway.

Halvar looked them over. "Speak up!" He glared at Selim. "What's this about you fighting? You were supposed to stay with the donkey cart."

"I know, but I had to see what was going on," the girl said. "And when I saw that evil man draw his dagger—"

"It was the Bretain servant, Edgar." Donal cut in. "He'd been creeping about while you were bandying words with Milord Henry. While everyone was watching you and the milord, the farmer got the horse out of the wagon harness and down the ramp to the ferry.

"His Afrikan servants came up the ramp to help with the chests and put the wagon on the scow, and the Franchen musket-man was there to make sure the Mahak didn't interfere with them."

"The woman insisted that the large boxes be put onto the boat first." Firebrand sneered. "She made a great fuss about it, would not go down the ramp until she saw those boxes stowed."

"She would!" Halvar agreed. "They hold her clothes! Where were your men, Tenente Firebrand? They were supposed to stop Milord from getting away."

"Watching the fight," Donal admitted. "All of us were. No one was watching the ramp, or the scow."

"Not so!" Firebrand objected. "We had our war-clubs and our knives, but that Franchen musket-man had a long knife, and a sword, and we could not get close enough to him to use our war-clubs. He held us away from the ramp until the woman and her boxes were aboard the scow, then he leaped across the water as they broke loose of the pier.

"The scow was full, with the horse, the Afrikans, the musket-man, the woman, the Dane, and the boxes. The spirits of the river must have been with them. They got across without losing any of them."

"They had the towrope," Donal said. "The lanterns were lit on the other side, waiting for them."

Firebrand took up the tale again.

"I saw them land across the river. Then there was noise from over our heads. We went to save you, but you were already fighting, and we did not want to stop a good fight."

"Devallon made his choice, and chose Milady Charlotte. I heard her yelling, something about killing." Halvar closed his eyes, picturing the scene. "I don't know who she wanted killed, me or Milord."

"Either or both," Selim said. "That is a very bad woman, and I'm glad she's off Manatas."

"Where are they now—Milady Charlotte and Sieur Devallon?"

"At Bronk's," Firebrand reported. "I sent Muskrat across the East Channel as soon as it was light. He talked to Bronk's

Algonkin workers. The Franchen woman and her man are living together in one of Bronk's houses, near the road to the ferry, where he sells food and drink and other things."

"Hah!" Halvar laughed, then winced at the stab of pain across his back as the scab pulled. "I knew that musket-man would end up running a tavern! And Milady Charlotte? How long before she finds some women to set up a brothel? Bronk doesn't know what he's getting into, giving that pair house-room."

Donal nodded. "Before long, everyone in West Caster will be going to Bronk's for food and drink and entertain-ment. If he's smart, he'll take a share of it."

"He's a Dane, of course he will!" Flores took over. "Cap-itán, the good news is, we got Edgar Norris—red-handed, as they say in Bretain. He'd come up behind you while you were fighting with Milord Henry. He had his knife out—a wicked long blade it is—and he was ready to take a slice of you when—"

"Young Selim jumped on his back!" Donal interrupted, eager to add his voice to the story. "I never saw anything like it! Screeching, clawing…"

"And then my turban got unwound," Selim confessed. "And my braids came loose. And everyone saw I'm a girl."

"But by that time, I'd got to Edgar and had him at the point of my halberd." Flores took up the tale. "And I would have run him through—"

"But I told him not to." Selim asserted herself. "I said you wanted him alive, to confess and be tried, according to the laws of Manatas and Al-Andalus. So, Tenente Donal and Tenente Flores just gave him a good drubbing."

"How good?" Halvar winced, recalling past beatings.

"He's alive," Flores said. "We even had Frater Iosip look him over. He's got a black eye, and some bruises."

"Where is he? " Halvar looked from one tenente to an-other. "Did you get him to the Rabat?'

"Not exactly," Donal said. "There was snow, and ice—"

"And we knew you'd want to question him yourself," Selim interposed.

"So, we put him here into the cellar lockup," Donal finished. "The one we keep for those who take too much uskebaugh. And he's there now, under guard—Bertram's watching to make sure he doesn't do himself harm. He got food, he got water, he even got to the jakes.

"We took his coat, though. Selim said there might be some unpleasant surprises sewn into it, and the girl was right. He had a small blade in one cuff and a waxed cord sewn onto his belt."

"A garotte, like the one the Franchen assassins use," Selim said.

Halvar tried to unravel the tangled skeins of this recital.

"So, he's safe, for now. Tenente Firebrand, what other news from across the East Channel? Any sign of Huron invasion?"

"Not that I hear," the Mahak said. "The scow landed, the Franchens were housed, that is all I know."

"So, whatever Milord was up to, it wasn't that," Halvar muttered. "I suppose that's one small comfort." He turned to Flores. "What does Edgar have to say for himself?"

"He's not saying a word. Hasn't even asked for an advocate," Flores replied. "And we don't have our own torture expert, not with Gomez gone. He used to handle that sort of thing. Not that we really needed it," he added hurriedly.

"Torture doesn't work," Halvar said. "I'll question Edgar myself, as soon as I get out of this *verdammitte* bed!"

"Capitán, was it Edgar killed Ned Cooper?" Donal asked hesitantly.

"It was."

"For the sake of Milord?"

"More for the sake of their plan," Halvar said. "Or I should say, Edgar's plans for Henry, which weren't exactly

Henry's plans for himself. What a set of rogues! Thieves, bawds, assassins...Manatas is well rid of them."

"But...if Edgar killed Ned...who killed Zoltan?" Flores was baffled.

"Henry did, of course. Selim, get out of here. Flores, Donal, find me some breeches and my coat. I've got to get to the Rabat before Edgar tries to escape again."

"He won't get out of that cellar," Donal assured him.

Halvar hitched up on the bed. Firebrand stepped aside to let Dani Glick and Farrah into the room, the former bearing a green coat and black breeches. Topping the pile were Halvar's battered Danic cap and the araghoun-skin hat he had chosen as additional headgear.

"It seems you are going to leave my establishment, Capitán, with or without your physician's approval," Dani told him. "A messenger just arrived from Manatas Town with an official warrant. You have been summoned into the presence of Sultan Petrus to face the Manatas Town Council. He's called a Divan to settle the matter of the madness that has infested Manatas this holy day season.

"That means I have to go into Manatas, along with our respected Cormack MacCormack, since I've been appointed to said council, along with the Islim woman, to 'lend wisdom to the proceedings', as the Mahak put it when they agreed to join their lands and laws with Manatas Town."

"The Sultan can wait," Halvar decided. "Get me dressed, and I'll have a word with Edgar. I want to be able to present a good case before the Divan. This is one rogue who won't escape the justice of Al-Andalus!"

Chapter 22

THE CHAPEL BELLS WERE RINGING FOR AFTER-
noon prayers when Halvar emerged from his sickroom in
his battered green coat, soiled breeches, and boots. He wore
his old cap but left the araghoun-skin hat off.

His appearance on the stairs leading to the gallery over
the main room of the Gardens of Paradise set off a rousing
response from Flores's Town Guards, Donal's constables, even
Firebrand's watchmen, who had gathered to receive information as to the condition of their leader. Halvar gripped the
banister with one hand and waved with the other.

"If Emir Achmet wanted to take over Manatas Town, now
would be the time to do it," he muttered to Selim, who hovered behind him. "Half the Town Guard is here."

"So are my father's personal guards." Selim noted, spot-
ting the red coats among the green. "I think he wanted to make
sure you go back to the Rabat."

"The sooner I get back to the Rabat, the better." Halvar managed to get down the stairs without a wobble. "Tenente Donal, where is this lockup of yours?"

Donal led the way around the stairs past the back rooms and Dani Glick's private office to a narrow stairway. A lantern hung on a hook, its flickering light sending eerie shadows downward.

"This way. We store food here, and some of the drink that is forbidden to Islim."

"Uskebaugh, rhum, wine. Alcohol." Selim summed it up with a sniff of disapproval.

"It sometimes happens that one of our patrons gets too noisy. We put them here."

Donal headed the procession down the stairs.

"Frater, you can't…"

That was Bertram, at the head of the cellar stairs.

"Of course I can!" Frater Iosip's voice rang out. "There is an injured man down there, a Kristo in need of medical and spiritual attention!"

"Let him through," Halvar ordered. "I want the man whole and sane, to be questioned and testify before the sultan's divan."

Frater Iosip bustled downstairs and through the cellar; Frater Leonidas followed him carrying the leather bag with bandages, medications, and the other tools of the medical profession.

They all assembled in front of the door at the far end of the room; a stout slab of wood with a wooden bar sealed it.

"Donal, you stay here. Flores, find Avaram, and tell him to get his donkey hitched to the cart. Firebrand, you get your men together and be ready to march. As soon as I finish with this rogue, we'll be on our way back to Manatas Town."

"Not until I pronounce him fit to go," Frater Iosip stated. "He is Kristo, and can claim sanctuary in the fratery chapel."

"He's a murderer, caught in the act," Halvar countered. "If he can't stand on his own feet, we'll carry him, but he goes to the Rabat!"

Frater Leonidas ended the argument. "He's had a day to consider his sins. Let us see what he has to say for himself."

Donal banged on the door.

"Edgar Norris! Are you there?"

"And where else would I be?" Edgar's voice was faint, but the tone was sarcastic.

"Step away from the door, Edgar Norris! Capitán Don Alvaro Dánico will speak with you!" Donal raised the bar and flung the door open.

Edgar stood in his breeches and shirt, blinking against the sudden light. The cell was little more than a closet with room enough for a man to stand or sit, not to stretch or lie down. It reeked of urine and vomit left by previous prisoners.

"Get him out," Halvar ordered.

Donal reached into the cell. Edgar tried to evade capture, stumbling out the door into the waiting arms of Bertram, who held him tightly while Donal looked to Halvar for more orders.

Halvar regarded the miserable object before him. The once-dapper servant was filthy, reeking of excrement and vomit. Graying stubble covered his cheeks. He shivered violently in the chilly air of the cellar.

"You say he's had food and drink?" Halvar asked.

"If you call a couple of stale maiz-cakes and a pannikin of foul water food and drink," Edgar spat out. "I am a Bretain citizen. I demand to see someone in authority!"

Halvar sniffed and grimaced. "You'll see someone, to be sure, but you can't appear at the Sultan's divan stinking like the jakes."

"Being kind to this one is a waste of time," Donal warned. "He killed Ned Cooper. String him up and be done."

"Not before he's confessed," Selim insisted.

Frater Iosip ended the argument. "I will attend this man. Frater Leonidas, come with me. We can't do anything until he's been warmed and cleaned."

"Constable Bertram!" Halvar ordered. "Take Heer Edgar to the tubs, clean him, find him clothes. Once he's fit to be seen, bring him to the back room. Fru Glick's gobbler stew will loosen his tongue."

Constable Bertram and the two guardsmen hauled Edgar up the stairs to the bath-house.

"He'll confess," Halvar asserted as he slowly made his way back to the warmth of the stove in the Gardens of Paradise private room.

"He hasn't said anything yet," Donal growled.

"You're coddling him. Medical care for him? Feeding him? He's a killer!" Flores objected. "He should be strung up here and now!"

"He is that, and more," Halvar agreed. "But, like my Old Sergeant Olaf used to say, 'You catch more flies with honey than with vinegar.' He's had a taste of what will happen if he doesn't cooperate with us. And," he added with a sly grin, "didn't the Redeemer tell us to care for the sinner? This man has sinned greatly. Just how much, we will find out." He led the group back up the stairs to the kitchen. "Selim! A word, if you please."

The girl hung back while the others passed.

"You're not happy with me?"

"You could have been killed!" Halvar hissed. "Your father would have had my head for that! He only allows you to follow me because he trusts that I won't put you in danger! You can take notes, you can sort my reports, but you're not supposed to do anything dangerous!"

"I couldn't help it!" Selim protested. "Was I supposed to let that Bretain stick his knife into your back?"

163

"Guarding me isn't your job. That's what Flores and Donal are supposed to do."

"Those two? They were too busy watching the fight. Probably making wagers as to who would win, too." Selim sniffed. "And then, when my turban fell off, all they did was gape, as if they didn't know I was a girl."

"Flores might have known. Donal didn't. When did Eva Hakim decide to make you a Sister of Fatima?"

"I sent for her to look after you, after he and Frater Iosip looked at your cuts and bruises, because I thought she would take care of you better than those bath-house wenches.. She turned up at dawn with a set of the clothes they give the Sisters who are being trained to help in the House of the Green Crescent. She also read me a lecture on proper behavior for a Sister of Fatima. I don't really want to be a Sister. I don't want to tend the sick and minister to the poor."

"Oh? And what *do* you want to do? Other than risk your life chasing criminals?"

Selim gulped. "I want to do what I'm doing now, only better. I want to be your adjutant, and keep Manatas safe."

Halvar looked at the tearstained face within its green hijab. She would never be called pretty—the heavy eyebrows and black hairs on her upper lip made that impossible. But she was intelligent enough to ask the right questions, she had probably saved his life with her prompt action, and she was devoted to him, whether he wanted her to be or not.

"You're my adjutant," he stated. *But for how long?* he wondered as he made his way through the main room of the Gardens of Paradise, receiving the plaudits of the various factions of the Town Guards.

The stove in the back room had been stoked, the table was ready. All that was needed was the prisoner.

Chapter 22

IT WAS A MUCH SUBDUED EDGAR NORRIS WHO was shoved into the back room of the Gardens of Paradise after an hour of intense scrubbing in the bath-house tubs. His black coat had been replaced by one of Bretain tartan, giving him a rakish air, but his breeches were his own. His hair, still damp from the bath, was tied back from his face, which bore evidence of rough handling. One eye was nearly shut, and there was another bruise on his jaw.

Donal prodded the prisoner into the room, while behind him Dani Glick protested against the usurpation of her establishment for official business.

"Here he is," Donal announced. "What do you want us to do with him?"

Halvar regarded Edgar coldly from his place of authority at the head of the long table that filled most of the room.

"Sit down, Heer Norris."

The invitation was enforced by Constable Bertram shoving Edgar down onto the backless stood set at the other end of the table. Selim had found a place between Halvar and Edgar, and spread her notebook and pen-case on the table, ready to record the proceedings. Donal and Flores retreated to the doorway. Firebrand lurked just outside the room, ready to act if the prisoner tried to escape.

Halvar looked Edgar over. "Has this man been fed?"

"We gave him maiz cakes. And some water." Donal said with a sneer.

"Nothing else?"

"He got food and water," Donal re-stated. "As you told us."

"Selim, how long since this man was taken prisoner?"

"More than a day and a half," Selim responded.

"Then he must be hungry," Halvar concluded. "Fru Glick, if you please, another bowl of your delicious soup for this poor fellow, and perhaps, a crust of bread, and some small ale. A whole day in that hole, with nothing more than maiz-cake and water? It makes a man consider, does it not, Heer Edgar?"

Edgar said nothing. Donal retrieved the bowl of soup from the server and set it in front of the prisoner with a wooden spoon and a mug of something dark and foamy. Edgar hesitated, then devoured the soup and bread and drank what was in the pottery mug

The two fraters pushed past the guards at the door. Frater Iosip tut-tutted over the extent of the injuries, applying his salves while Frater Leonidas held the bandages.

Halvar watched while they treated the patient.

"Well enough," he decreed. "Frater Iosip, you've done what the Redeemer said to do. You may leave us. Frater Leonidas, you stay." He leaned back in this chair, easing the pain in his back. "Now that you've been cleaned and fed, Edgar Norris, we can get down to business—to the brass tacks, as the cloth merchants have it. You are accused of murdering Ned the Cooper. How do you answer this charge?"

"Ned who?" Edgar returned Halvar's fierce glare with a bland look.

"The man who announced that Milord Henry Summersby could not ride a horse," Donal growled from his place at the door. "And that he never could. Which, to my mind, means that he knew Milord in the past."

"Or that he knew the man who called himself Milord Henry Summersby was no milord, or that he wasn't Henry Summersby," Halvar amended. "So, Edgar Norris—if that is your name—which is it? Who was Henry Summersby?"

"Who do you think he was?" Edgar answered with another bland smile.

"I don't know *who* he was, but I can guess *what* he was. I think the man who called himself Milord was a soldier, a mercenary. Like me, like Sieur Andres Devallon. Not a great swordsman, but good at pike-work, expert with the halberd."

Edgar sneered, "That's not saying much. You can't arrest a man for knowing how to fight with a halberd."

"That's true," Halvar said. "But a Bretain milord wouldn't lower himself to use a pike or a halberd. Then there was Ned Cooper, and his claim that Henry Summersby was no milord. He jeered that he couldn't ride and never could. In short, Ned knew who Henry *was*, not just who or what he wasn't. What's more, Ned was a Purist, one who insisted on Truth above all else. Did you try to bribe him with silver, Edgar?"

"It would have done no good if I had," Edgar said bitterly. "I know that kind of man. He would have held it over us forever."

"Only one way to deal with a blackmailer," Halvar agreed. "You silenced Ned. Henry did the same for Zoltan. The difference was, you were clever about it; Henry wasn't. You know how to kill silently, so the victim doesn't even know he's dying. Is that not so, Frater Leonidas? Oh, I must introduce you to Frater Leonidas. In a previous life, he was known as the scholar Leon di Vicenza. A man known for his many interests, one of which was anatomy."

Edgar's eyes widened as he stared at the frater in his rough brown robe.

"From Corduva?"

"At one time, I was a lecturer at the Corduva Madrassa," Frater Leonidas responded, with a mock-modest bow. "I am now but a humble frater in the Redeemer's service. As for the method of Ned Cooper's death, that was very clever. To insert the knife so that it does not kill immediately but starts the bleeding within the body. That takes a certain skill."

"The mark of a man who has studied human anatomy," Halvar said slowly. "An educated man. Not a lout like Henry, who shoved the knife in and let the victim die then and there. He must have been a sore trial, that Henry Summersby. For all his fine clothes, he was a boor. He played the arrogant part of being a milord well enough, but he forgot the gentleman part."

Edgar's mouth tightened, either from the pain of Franter Iosip's bandaging or from emotion being held in.

"It wasn't Henry who sought out the scholars at the bookseller's stall and wangled his way into the party at the madrassa on Watch-Night. You were the one who wanted to make contact with your peers, not he. All he cared about was filling his belly with food and wine and making a fine show."

Halvar went on, watching Edgar fidget on the stool.

"You know, Heer Edgar, the more I think about it, the more I have to wonder how you came to link yourself to such a man. You were the one who came up with the plans, the clever one. Henry was the one who did the fighting, the brawn to your brain.

"It's how it goes in this world—the small, clever one teams up with the big, stupid one. The big one protects the clever one, the clever one manages the big one. Until the big one goes off on his own, does something the clever one can't control. Like, for instance, seeing a pretty Franchen woman and deciding to take her for himself."

"Charlotte!" Edgar could control his anger no longer. "He *would* have her! I told him she was trouble, I told him to let her go. He would not listen. He said she came with silver imperials and a land grant. It was his part of the plan, to get land."

"Except that the land she had was forest, and he'd be expected to clear it and farm it himself," Halvar said. "Not what a milord does. So...which of you found the other land grant, the one in Bella Mara?"

"It was Powhatan then," Edgar gritted out. "And I did —of course I did—while Henry was rutting with his Franchen bride. I was the one who found a Franchen soldier who had missed out on the auction. He didn't care whether or not he got one of the women; he just wanted the land. He had a deed for some in Terra Mara, which he couldn't use, since he was stationed in Kibbick. We traded deeds; all I had to do was make a few small alterations in the wording of each.

"Then along came Charlotte, and she persuaded Henry to take ship, to claim the land grant in Powhatan...I mean, Terra Mara. And she talked him into taking that harridan Brigitte, and the musket-man, too."

"And the muskets? What do you know about them?" Halvar leaned forward.

Edgar looked blankly back at him. "Muskets?"

"You didn't know Captain Franz Girard had muskets in the ballast of his ship?"

"Did he? That explains why he was so ready to take us aboard, silver or no silver." Edgar smirked. "A very clever man, Captain Girard. But let me assure you, I had no part in any schemes of his, particularly if they included arming anyone with muskets. That way lies ruin for all concerned."

Halvar nodded. "Your scheme was simpler. Milord Henry would claim his estate and rule it as a Bretain Milord does, with Afrikans doing the work of clearing land and planting crops. The two of you would grow rich, and you would not need to make false coin anymore."

Edgar lost some of his confident air.

"False coin?"

"We found the satchel with your bad pennies and the tools for making them," Donal put in. "Milady Charlotte left it in the wagon. She only wanted the chests with her clothes."

Edgar slumped forward. "That miserable Franchen bitch!"

"What I don't understand, Heer Edgar, is how a reasonable, educated fellow like yourself ever allowed himself to be embroiled with a hothead like Henry Summersby."

Edgar grimaced. "We met in Bristol, waiting for a ship to take us to Nova Mundum. He had run into some difficulties with his former employer, the Baron Oxford. I had my own reasons for leaving Bretain as soon as possible. We decided to throw our resources together.

"He would take service with one of the Afrikans, I would accompany him. He didn't know numbers, had few letters, didn't know any language but Erse—and that mostly in his own Northern dialect. I, on the other hand, know several languages, and can keep accounts."

"And have other talents as well," Halvar mused. "You're a right handyman, Edgar Norris."

"I do my best to give satisfaction." Edgar's smirk returned. "But you have no proof that I killed this Ned Cooper. I admit I heard him declare that Henry Summersby was no milord. He even said he knew Henry from his days as a poacher in Yorvik. And it is quite true I was in Green Village at the time he said these things.

"But you cannot connect me with his death. As I understand it, he died sitting in his own chair, in his own cooperage."

"Quite true," Halvar said. "But Frater Leonidas has compared your knife with the wound in Ned Cooper's back."

"It matches exactly," Frater Leonidas stated. "And no two knives are exactly the same. They develop individual defects with use, which affect the wounds they inflict. I am willing to swear, on the Crux of the Redeemer, that the knife this man, Edgar Norris, wielded at the bridgehead, which he attempted to use on you, Capitán, is the same one that took the life of Ned Cooper."

"So, Edgar Norris, you are not only a forger and a coiner, but a murderer, " Halvar stated. "As has been proven. Do you confess to these crimes?"

"You seem to have made up your mind, whether I confess or not," Edgar said. "Draw up whatever document you like, I'll sign it. I'll appear at your court—this divan—if you like. But I am Bretain, not Andalusian, and you cannot condemn me to death."

"Sultan Petrus can do whatever he thinks best," Halvar said. "Bretain, Franchen, Dane, or Local, all must obey the laws of Al-Andalus in Manatas. And that goes for you, too, Edgar Norris. Tenente Donal, take the prisoner away. He can have his own coat, but look at it carefully again. We've taken a few small things out of it, but he may have some we missed. Assassins hide unpleasant surprises in strange places."

Donal shoved Edgar out the door, leaving Halvar and his crew a little more space.

"What next?" Selim began packing her belongings.

"We go back to Manatas Town before it gets too dark," Halvar said. "Your father's waited long enough. Let's have the divan so we can celebrate the Year's Turning."

Chapter 23

HALVAR EMERGED FROM THE GARDENS OF PAR-
adise to find a crowd waiting for him beyond the iron gates.
The entire population of Green Village had come to acclaim
the hero who had beheaded a vicious killer with one blow of
his halberd only a day after ridding Manatas Island of a fearsome cougar.

Halvar took in the sight and nearly headed back to the
safety of his sickbed.

"Smile!" Selim urged from somewhere behind his right
shoulder.

"Wave!" Dani Glick did the same from his left.

Halvar bared his teeth and and lifted his right hand in
greeting.

Tenentes Flores and Donal parted the gates to allow Halvar to join what was shaping up to be a massive torchlight
parade, complete with musicians. Firebrand's Mahak watch-

men started a chant, punctuated with shell rattles and deer-hide drums.

"What are they singing about" Halvar whispered to Dani.

"It's a praise-song," Selim told him. "They do it for great warriors."

"Like you," Dani added. "You have made quite the impression on the Locals. They call you the Cat-killer, the Slayer of Beasts."

"And cutting off Milord Henry's head with one blow, that's something no one's seen in Manatas before," Selim said.

Halvar smiled weakly and waved again.

The Green Villagers let out a rousing cheer. It turned into a terrifying howl when Bertram pulled Edgar through the door, to be vilified by the crowd. Kevin MacFergus and Angus MacKay were in the front rank, glaring at the accused murderer.

"Is that he? The one who killed our beloved Brother Ned?" Angus stared at Edgar, as if daring him to confess his guilt.

"So it would seem," Halvar said. "Frater Iosip and Frater Leonidas have matched his knife to the wound in Ned Cooper's back. He was seen talking with the cooper. But it is for the sultan to decide his fate. We are taking him back to Manatas Town to face the sultan's divan. Let us pass, good people, and justice will be served. The laws of Al-Andalus forbid private vengeance, vendettas, blood-feuds."

"String him up now!" someone yelled.

"Why wait?" A female voice, from the back of the crowd added to the growing noise of anger.

"Because it's not right!" Halvar roared. "There must be a trial, he must face his accusers, he must be condemned by a court, not by a mob. He has confessed to many crimes, and will pay for them, but not here, not now, not without a trial. Tenente Donal, put the prisoner into one of these carts. Tenente Flores, do not let any of these people kill him…not yet. Tenente Firebrand…" Halvar took a deep breath, and wished he hadn't. "You and your people can resume their watch on the rivers. And I thank you for your song." *I think*, he added si-lently. He'd have to find out exactly what it meant. At least Willem of Cos wouldn't be chanting it in the souk!

The last flickers of daylight vanished, and torches and lanterns lit the path once more. Halvar eyed the assemblage of vehicles lined up in front of the iron fence. Leading the way was Padraig, his mare Molly hitched to the pony cart, which was slightly larger than the ones pulled by the patient donkeys that were the principal beasts of burden in Manatas. Avaram's Jacko followed Molly in the line, with two more donkey carts behind him.

"Get in, Capitán!" Padraig urged. "You deserve more than a mere donkey cart today."

"You can't walk all the way to Manatas Town," Selim warned him. "And more people will be able to see you."

"I don't want people to see me," Halvar muttered. "My coat is stained, I haven't been shaved, and I haven't been to the hammam in three days."

"That doesn't matter," Dani consoled him. "You look like someone who has battled fiercely and won."

"By losing my head in the fight!"

"By making sure your enemy lost his!" Dani shoved him into the pony cart and followed him. Selim hopped on be-hind.

Halvar frowned at Dani. "You're coming along?"

"Sultan Petrus has summoned the entire Manatas Coun-cil to the divan. That includes me," Dani reminded him. "Cormack MacCormack is in one of the other carts behind us. Now, Capitán Halvar Danske, you must act like one of those statues left by the Old Roumi. When we get past the wall, you must stand and wave to the people."

"Daoud the Newscrier and the youngsters who sell the *Gazetta* have been busy on your account," Selim answered his unspoken question. "And the people who watched the fight at the bridgehead have been telling their friends how brave you were."

"And it's the Turning of the Year, so Kristos are ready to celebrate," Dani concluded.

"And not only them." Selim pointed to the line of torches that stretched across the field between the wall and Green Village. The flock of geese, who had been settling for the night, rose up squawking and honking. Once again their rest had been disturbed by two-legged intruders marching across their feeding-grounds.

The oldest gander flapped his wings menacingly at Molly. Molly reacted with a loud whinny, rising on her back legs. Padraic frantically tried to control the skittish mare.

The gander hissed. Molly bolted across the field toward the source of light ahead. Halvar gripped the side of the cart and hoped it was as sturdy as Farmer Brock's wagon.

They reached the wall, and Molly came to a stop, her sides heaving. Behind them, the parade struggled to catch up. Ahead lay the Broad Way, lined with lanterns, torches, and people.

Halvar waited for the line to re-form. He molded his features into what he hoped was an expression suitable for a great hero.

Molly pricked her ears. She was ready to walk sedately forward, acknowledging the applause of the crowd with bobbing head and prancing feet. Just behind them, the drumming started again. The Mahak were not going to be left out of this celebration! Then came Sultan Petrus's personal guard, swaggering in their red coats, halberds shouldered.

Avaram's cart, with the prisoner Edgar Norris, drew jeers and catcalls, and not a few pieces of donkey-dirt. Three more donkey carts ended the procession—one with Angus Mac-Kay and Kevin MacFergus, come to bear witness at the divan; one with Cormack MacCormack, the acknowledged

175

leader of Green Village; and finally, Simon Singer, to record the proceedings for the *Gazetta*.

They proceeded along the Broad Way at a more reasonable pace than the one set by Henry Summersby two days before. By the time they reached the gates of the Rabat, Halvar estimated that at least half the population of Manatas Town must have come into the chill of the night to watch the parade.

The torchlight procession ended at the gates of the Rabat. Dani Glick and Selim scrambled out of the pony-cart, leaving Halvar to face the cheering crowd alone. He nodded sheepishly to the assembled residents of Manatas, hoping he did not look too shabby in his battered coat and fur hat.

He slid out of the cart, noting ragged Scavengers, the slightly neater Waterfront Rats, Yehudit in fur-trimmed broad-brimmed hats, Afrikans in woolen scarves over their caftans, madrassa students in cloaks, even a few of the waterfront women. He turned and waved to the crowd, then squared his shoulders and entered the gates of the Rabat. He would face whatever waited for him at the sultan's divan with his usual stoic calm.

He only hoped Sultan Petrus would not blame *him* for putting his daughter into danger.

A roar went up as Flores and Donal prodded the prisoner forward. Edgar regarded the crowd with a haughty stare, then shrugged as if to say, *I am still more worthy than you!*

"Take him up to the sultan's chamber," Halvar ordered.

Dani Glick patted his shoulder as she slid past him to mount the stairs. Selim followed her, casting a rueful glance behind.

Halvar took a minute to compose himself. He clutched his amulet, murmuring, "Redeemer, Mother Mara, Thor, you know that I only did what I thought had to be done."

176

With the backing of his personal deities, Halvar Danske went up the stone stairs to face whatever waited for him at the sultan's divan.

Chapter 24

SULTAN PETRUS'S CHAMBER HAD BEEN ALTERED to accommodate the harsh weather. Heavy rugs hung over the windows, blocking the wind blowing off the bay. Lanterns on brackets replaced torches, and lamps burned on the large table, which had been moved to the far corner of the room to accommodate the crowd summoned to bear witness to the sultan's justice.

Halvar hesitated for a moment as his eyes adjusted to the light, trying to make out individuals in the mass of people standing around the large chair where the sultan sat. His ivory leg propped on a footstool, he was dressed in his most splendid robe, his turban embellished with a large gold pin.

Mullah Abadul stood to the right of Sultan Petrus, ready to assert the claims of sharia, accompanied by a shorter, slimmer man who also wore the green turban of one who had been trained at the *ulema* in Baghdad. Lurking behind them, in a tatty splendor of mismatched furs and garish turban, was Emir Achmet of the Scavengers, clearly reveling in his new importance, as assured by Mullah Abadul.

A little apart from him, close enough to give their opinions but clearly outside the circle of influence, were the clerics from lesser religious institutions—Prester Nicodemus, the sole Kristo, and and Rav Nahum, representing both the Yehudit and the scholarly community of the Manatas Madrassa.

Tenentes Flores and Donal followed Halvar into the sultan's chamber, jealously asserting their respective positions of authority in Manatas Town and Green Village.

"What's Emir Achmet doing here?" Halvar hissed to Flores.

"I expect Mullah Abadul insisted. The two of them are hand-in-glove," Flores whispered back. "Emir Achmet has his beggars out when the mullah preaches in the street. It makes for a larger crowd, and Islims can practice charity. What's more, he makes sure the Grand Muskat is never touched by thieves, and he makes a great show of giving charity himself."

"And his men are a readymade army, should the mullah need one." Halvar scanned the room again. "Has everyone in Manatas been summoned to this divan?"

"The sultan had his guardsmen rounding up witnesses," Flores groused. "Everyone mentioned in young Selim's reports. Guardsman Fergus, the Widow Tekla, even the gambler Baltasar who's taken charge of the boy from the *Belle Fleur*. He sent his *personal* guardsmen with the message for Fru Glick to attend from Green Village, and the Purist merchant, Angus MacKay as well. Didn't trust my men to do it!" Flores scowled.

"You were in Green Village," Halvar pointed out. "As was I. So, Tenente Flores, we face the sultan's divan. Justice will be served…"

"On a platter!" Flores insisted on having the last word as Halvar limped forward. There was a buzz of chatter as he took his place in the circle of lantern light before the sultan's chair.

A small table was set on the left side of the sultan's chair. There Selim sat, her pen-case and notebook before her. Eva Hakim stood behind her new protégé, her expression daring anyone to question the girl's presence.

Sultan Petrus's voice cut through the chatter, ringing as clearly as it had on many a battlefield.

"Capitán Don Alvaro! You have finally been able to join us."

Halvar salaamed. "As you may know, Excellent Sultan, I've been otherwise occupied. I was wounded, and my physicians would not allow me to leave Green Village for a day and a half. I am here now, to hear your judgment concerning the recent deaths that have occurred in Manatas."

"Recent deaths, indeed!" Sultan Petrus spat out. "First, a Franchen seaman and his doxy; then a poor messenger boy; then an eminent scholar; and finally, one of our own guardsmen! When it it going to end? What have you done to stop these murders? Is that not why our calif, may he live long, appointed you to this post? To keep Manatas safe from danger?"

Halvar waited until the sultan's diatribe ended. Then he said, "Excellent Sultan Petrus, you have summed up the events of the last two weeks admirably. But none of this was the fault of the good people of Manatas. At least, most of it wasn't," he amended.

"There were several events, some of which might have been prevented, some not. We Danes have a tale about the Three Old Women who spin and weave the threads that are our lives, deciding which strand should go where, whose lives will cross and tangle, and where they part. We call it Fate, you call it Kismet.

180

"Many peoples' lives intersected during these recent days here in Manatas. Who is to say whether this was by accident or by design? I leave that to those more qualified than I to know the will of Ilha or the Redeemer." *Or the god Thor*, he added silently as he took a deep breath.

He continued in Arabi. "The strands all came together here in Manatas over the last two weeks. It began when Captain Franz Girard sailed into Manatas Bay on the Longest Day. He brought with him five people, two of whom are dead, two in West Caster, one is here." He pointed to Edgar, standing between the two Green Village constables.

"What's *he* doing here? I didn't send for him." Sultan Petrus looked the Bretain over. Edgar bowed with his usual bland smile.

Halvar announced, "Excellent Sultan, I accuse this man of killing one of the artisans of Green Village. He can also corroborate certain facts regarding the activities of Captain Franz Girard. However, he speaks no Arabi, only Erse and Franchen. I would ask that someone translate for him, so that he may understand what is said here, and answer in his own defense, as is provided by the laws and customs of his own country."

"We're not in Bretain. We're not even in West Caster," Sultan Petrus grumped. "Benyamin Ibn Mendel is here as advocate for the wretch from the madrassa, the one accused of poisoning one of the teachers. He speaks Erse and Arabi, he knows the laws of sharia and Bretain, let him do it."

"If you please?" Baltasar interjected, before Benyamin could speak. "I am quite fluent in both Arabi and Erse. I also know Franchen and Danic. I also have some acquaintance with the law. I am quite impartial, I assure you. I don't know this man, although I have seen him over the last two weeks, going to and from a certain cottage on Pearl Street. I can translate for the court."

Sultan Petrus nodded. "If *he's* willing, I accept the offer."

Baltasar and Edgar had a hurried conversation in muttered Erse. Then Baltasar stated in Arabi, "I've explained his situation to him, This man, Edgar Norris, a citizen of Bretain, allows me, Baltasar of Tours, to be his advocate at the divan."

He turned to Edgar, saying, "Is that not so?" in Erse.

Edgar nodded his assent.

"Now that's settled," Sultan Petrus, retreating to his familiar Arabi, said, "Let's get back to our muttons, as the old story goes. What is all this about Franz Girard, and what does it have to do with all the killings?"

Halvar took over again. "All this, as as I said, started when Captain Franz Girard sailed into Manatas Bay on the Longest Night. He came here with a specific goal—to buy gunpowder for his cargo of muskets, illegally stowed in the ballast of his ship, *Belle Fleur*."

"A goal? I thought he came here on a whim," Sultan Petrus interrupted

"That was what he told his crew," Halvar said. "But he had already decided to make for Manatas, even before he sensed a storm coming."

Baltasar broke in. "How do you know what he intended? The man is dead. Do you have a special contact with the Nether World?"

A nervous titter ran through the crowd. Mullah Abadul scowled. Necromancy was not a cause for levity!

Halvar pointed to the pile of papers in front of Selim.

"Sometimes the dead speak, albeit not from the Lands of the Dead. Captain Franz Girard kept a private journal, which was translated by Frater Leonidas, once known as Leon di Vicenza, a notable scholar of Corduva, now a humble frater. In that journal, Captain Girard makes it plain his aim in coming into Manatas is to contact a source for gunpowder."

"There is no gunpowder in Manatas," the sultan objected over the excited mutterings of the assembled witnesses.

"Not when Girard got here," Halvar agreed. "But there was someone at the Fall Feria who was selling it.

"Angus MacKay!"

The Purist stumbled forward, impelled by the butt end of a halberd.

Halvar switched to Erse. "What merchandise did Andrew MacAlan bring to the Fall Feria?"

Angus licked his lips, looked around the room, and finally said, "He brought kegs of black powder. Small kegs!" he insisted. "And some firearms, to be sold to the Afrikans, the ones who are fighting the Locals for land. He did well, ran out of merchandise before the feria ended."

"Which meant that he needed more," Halvar continued in Arabi. "He could have gone back to West Caster, where they have manufactories that produce the stuff, but he wanted to be able to control the market himself. He had another plan, you see, one he did not want to reveal to any but his closest companions. He needed an alchemist—"

"And he found one at the madrassa." Selim interrupted.

"Did he, indeed!" Sultan Petrus silenced his impetuous offspring with a glance.

"Ask him." Halvar pointed to a far corner, where Albrecht LaPierre cowered next to his advocate, Benyamin ben Mendel, with Guardsman Fergus lurking behind them.

"Albrecht LaPierre!" Sultan Petrus bellowed. "What have you to say for yourself?"

Fergus grabbed the alchemist and threw him into the center of the room. The man landed in a heap at Halvar's feet. Benyamin hurried forward, interposing himself between the sultan and the prisoner. He bowed and salaamed, then announced, "I am here to speak for Master Albrecht LaPierre, who has been accused of murdering his colleague, Master Nikola Kupernik."

"What has that to do with making gunpowder?" Sultan Petrus looked at Halvar, bewildered.

"It doesn't...not directly." Halvar took over, growing more confident with every word. "Master Albrecht was approached by one Andrew MacAlan at the Fall Feria. Is that not so, Master LaPierre?"

Albrecht raised his head to stare at Halvar. "Yes, that is true. He said he wanted to place his son into the madrassa, to study alchemy."

"Did you take the lad on?" Halvar asked.

Albrecht regained some of his former arrogance.

"I thought the boy was more interested in chasing a ball around a field than in serious study. He constantly left his classes to practice the Peace Game with the other Oropans."

"But you accepted him as a student, because his father was ready to finance your tests, what you call experiments, in the making of gunpowder." Halvar loomed over the prisoner.

"Why not? He bargained with the Locals to allow a Scanian to build a small cabin north of the tannery, where I could test my theory as to the origins and manufacture of black powder. In exchange, I allowed his son to attend my classes, when he could spare the time from his athletic labors." Albrecht ended with a scornful sniff.

"But you did not actually make any gunpowder," Selim spoke up. "We were at the cabin. There's no gunpowder there, other than a few grains."

"By the laws of sharia, a merchant may not sell goods he does not actually possess," Mullah Abadul pronounced. "That is theft!" There was a murmur of agreement from the other merchants in the room.

"You were seen on the day before Watch-Night in Green Village," Halvar stated. "You must have gone to the cabin then and picked up the chip of wood you intended to place under the door to Master Kupernik's room, so that he could not leave when he was taken ill by the cake with the nguba beans you fed him.

Albrecht seemed to shrink under the mullah's stony gaze.

"I only went to the cabin when Andrew MacAlan sent word all was ready for me, since he had contracted with the

Afrikan, Samuel Igbo, to procure the materials I needed. We met at the Afrikan's villa, to be sure, but once I gave them a list of what I needed, I left it to them to find the ore and the vessels for the cabin. I had other duties. I had classes. I was going to make gunpowder once the term ended."

"Of course you were," Halvar said, with a sarcastic smile. "But when his son was killed, Andrew MacAlan became more insistent that you start doing it.

"And then along came Franz Girard, who was ready to buy the gunpowder you hadn't made, but that MacAlan was ready to sell with the services of Samuel Igbo, the Afrikan middleman."

"This is getting complicated," Sultan Petrus groused. "Where does the Afrikan come into this plot?"

"Complicated, indeed! But it was in the hands of Kismet, of the Three Old Women, what you might call Fate. Girard came to Manatas because he believed he could call on certain people to help him, not knowing that things had changed since he was last here. Is that not so, Guardsman Fergus?"

Halvar pointed to the red-headed guardsman, who had been stationed behind the prisoners.

"You had dinner with him the night before he died, you and your companion and partner Zoltan. What did Girard tell you at that meal?"

Fergus stepped forward, reddening under the concerted stares of the others in the room.

"That day—it was the one before the Long Night—Girard came into port, his ship was moored in the bay; it was too big for the pier. Girard and his passengers came ashore in the ship's dinghy. Zoltan and I were there on the waterfront—we were stationed there. We'd met Girard, we knew him well, we'd seen him many a time when his ship came into port for the Spring or Fall ferias.

"When he came ashore, he went directly to the Mermaid Taberna, but it was in new hands—the Dane, Hannes Zil-

185

berstam runs it now, not the Franchen Taverniers. He was not happy. He'd thought he'd be safe with the Franchen Taverniers.

"We explained to him things were different, there had been changes at the Fall Feria. He didn't know the calif had come to Nova Mundum, that a new man was in charge of the Town Guards, that Green Village and the Local settlements had come under the laws of Al-Andalus. This was all news to him—he'd left Bos-Town before the traders came back from Manatas. He'd come into port assuming he could arrange things with Tenente Gomez for the usual fee—"

"Bribe him, you mean!" Halvar snorted. "So, learning this, what did Girard do?"

Fergus gulped, glanced at the sultan, and went on. "He left the passengers—the Bretain Milord and his servant, and the Franchen woman and her maid, and the Franchen musket-man—all at the Mermaid Taberna, and he went to the Roumi Rite chapel, where the Waterfront Rats stay, and sent a message to the Afrikan middleman Samuel Igbo. He said he'd dealt with him before, if anyone could get him what he wanted, it was Samuel."

Fergus stopped and looked around for support from his fellow-guardsmen. Flores stared pointedly at the ceiling. Donal studied the floor.

"Samuel Igbo was known to have dealings with both Manatas and Green Village merchants and craftsmen. And he dealt with the fur trappers who go into Local territory, put them together with Oropans who would buy their furs."

"And after Girard sent the message?" Halvar asked.

"Then we had a good dinner at the Maison Rouge, me and Zoltan and Long Liz Lanergan and Girard. And Liz and Girard went off…" Fergus burst into tears. "And now they're both dead! And Zoltan…I told him…."

Sultan Petrus interrupted the recitation. "We know what happened to Girard and his woman. They were killed by

Dame Brigitte, the lady's maid, who wound up at the bottom of the bay when she tried to leave Manatas. Your companion, Zoltan—Is that the guardsman killed in the souk? How does that fit in with this gunpowder plot?"

Fergus sniveled, "I don't know about gunpowder. Zoltan and me, we didn't hear about any gunpowder, it was something else..."

Halvar picked up the story once again. "If you will bear with me, I will show you how all these threads tangle in the web woven by the Three Old Women.

"One thread was Girard's message, which was tied to a fatal course of events even after the writer had met his end. The messenger, Snake, became suspicious, especially after Samuel sent him off to Green Village with a message for the Purist, Andrew MacAlan. He tried to extort money from both Andrew and Samuel, threatening to go to the Excellent Sultan and tell him someone was planning something illegal. He might not even have known exactly what it was the Afrikan and the Purist were doing.

"But Andrew MacAlan would take no chances. He shot the messenger with a pistoia, and left it to Samuel to dispose of the body. Samuel got a Scavenger girl to place it beyond the wall, hoping wild beasts would devour it before anyone found it, or that, even if it was found, no one would care.

"That had been the rule before I arrived, but I am not one to shirk my duty. Even a poor messenger boy is important in the eyes of the Lord God and the Redeemer...and of Ilha."

He bowed towards Mullah Abadul, who bowed back.

"Even as the Prophet says." Sultan Petrus agreed. "You spent your holy day asking questions and demanding answers."

"And Samuel Igbo panicked. Bad enough he moved the body, but he had witnessed the murder and not reported it, as is demanded by the laws of Al-Andalus. He ran for help from Andrew....a bad mistake. Andrew MacAlan was mad —mad with anger at the death of his son, and mad with religion."

"But what purpose was there to selling gunpowder he didn't have?" the sultan asked.

"I'm not sure," Halvar said. "It is possible he planned to use the funds to start another colony somewhere in the interior, away from Andalusian influence. We will never know, because he chose to make his lair in one already inhabited by the mountain cat. I only wish I had gotten there sooner, before the cat did. Andrew died trying to escape the cat, and I killed the cat—"

"Magnificently!" Baltasar cheered. "A stunning performance! I was present when you slew the beast! A feat worthy of the Old Greco heroes Herakles and Achilles!"

"If there had not been a delay in getting to Samuel Igbo, he might not have died." Halvar faced Sultan Petrus. "But Green Villagers demand a warrant—a firman—and the laws of Manatas have been modified to accommodate their demands. Tenente Flores would not disturb you at your rest, Excellent Sultan, and so when he arrived at Samuel Igbo's villa, the man was gone."

Sultan Petrus reddened and coughed. "Hem! That was unfortunate, but Samuel Igbo could have left the safety of his villa for Green Village even before the firman was signed," he huffed. "I regret his death. I have sent alms to his widows and children, and notified his son in Salaamabad to come here and take over his father's business.

"So, this concludes the matter of Andrew MacAlan. He died trying to escape the mountain cat, not by your hand.

"But there is now another charge, this business of the Bretain Milord, Henry Summersby, whose head you removed from his body in front of a multitude. You lead the charge after him for the murder of Guardsman Zoltan. Yet you've got a second prisoner, this Bretain Edgar Norris. What has *he* done to deserve ill-treatment? Did you do this?"

"Not I, but the guardsmen," Halvar said. "They were, perhaps, a little too eager to avenge me when they caught him trying to put a knife in my back. He is present at this divan to answer for his crimes"

"That's good," Sultan Petrus said. "I have begun to think I should employ the services of the Local shaman, who is rumored to be able to connect with the spirits in the Land of the Dead. What does this fellow, Edgar Norris, have to do with the gunpowder plot?"

"Nothing…not directly," Halvar said.

"In that case," Sultan Petrus said, with a glance toward Emir Achmet, "why should I not charge *you* with murder? For you took the life of Milord Henry Summersby without any warrant from me, in full view of half the population of Manatas!"

Chapter 25

HALVAR'S KNEES STARTED TO BUCKLE UNDER him. Where had this accusation come from? He staggered to the table where Selim sat

"If the excellent sultan will excuse me…" he mumbled.

Selim stood up, her face twisted with fury under her green hijab.

"This is outrageous! This man, Capitán Don Alvaro Dánico, has been wounded defending himself against not one but two assassins. I was there, I saw everything!"

Sultan Petrus stared at his impetuous daughter

"You are here only as a recorder," he harrumphed. "And *that* is an indulgence. Sit down, girl, and try to be a modest Islim."

"That she will never be," Eva Hakim murmured, just loud enough for Halvar to hear. "She's too like her mother, the Lady Fatima, may her memory be blessed."

Halvar forced himself to stand straight, bracing his leg against the table.

"I did what I did for the good of Manatas," he asserted. "I admit killing the man who called himself Milord Henry Summersby, but Tenente Flores can testify that Milord struck the first blow, and I defended myself."

"Is that so?" Sultan Petrus beckoned Flores to step forward.

The scarred guardsman glanced around the room, then fixed his eyes on the sultan.

"I was present when Capitán Don Alvaro fought the Bretain," he said. "But I was not there when the fight started. When I arrived with my men, Capitán Don Alvaro and Milord Summersby were already having at each other, armed with halberds. Tenente Donal, Constable of Green Village, he can tell you who started it." Flores smirked at Donal.

"Constable?" Sultan Petrus beckoned again. "What can you tell me of this sorry business?"

Donal bowed towards the sultan. "I met Capitán Danske on the path from Green Village to the bridge and ferry," he stated. "He told me the man called Milord Henry Summersby had stolen a horse and wagon, and was going to the ferry to leave Manatas Island. He sent the Mahak watchmen to stop the wagon."

"You keep saying 'a man calling himself Milord Henry Summersby'," Sultan Petrus complained. "I thought that was his name."

"It is what he called himself," Halvar explained, still leaning against the table. "But what he was named at his birth, perhaps we shall never know. You might ask this man, who was his companion in crime." He pointed to Edgar. "And may I ask that the next part of this divan be conducted in Erse, since he is not familiar with Arabi."

Sultan Petrus focused his gaze on Edgar, who had been listening to Baltasar's whispered translation of the Arabi proceedings.

"And you say he is here because…"

"He is accused of killing the artisan Ned Cooper."

"And why should he do that?" Sultan Petrus frowned over his beard.

"Because Ned Cooper knew who Milord Henry Summersby was," Halvar said. "More particularly, he knew who he was before he came to Manatas, when he was in Bretain."

"What has that to do with Captain Franz Girard and his gunpowder and the smuggled muskets?"

"Nothing, directly," Halvar said. "But when Girard sailed into Manatas Bay, he brought with him his passengers—Henry Summersby and his servants and wife—who had not expected to go to Manatas at all. They were supposed to go to Bella Mara, where, as he informed anyone who would listen, Milord Henry Summersby had a legacy waiting for him, an extensive land grant.

"He hired Girard to take him south, to Sultan Calvera's territory. Girard had his own schemes, and went first to Bos-Town, then here to Manatas, whether Milord wanted to go there or no. Am I right, Heer Edgar?"

"Quite right, Capitán." Edgar had been following both the Arabi and Erse narrations. "Milord Summersby hired Girard to take us to what we thought was Powhatan, what we now know is called Terra Mara. We had no idea there were muskets in the ballast. Whatever Captain Girard was brewing, it was none of our doing."

Halvar had recovered some of his equilibrium.

"Of course not. You were merely passengers on the *Belle Fleur*. Milord Henry Summersby, you, Heer Edgar Norris, the musket-man Sieur Andres Devallon, and Milord's very new wife, Milady Charlotte Besson, together with her servant, Dame Brigitte. Just the five of you on that great round ship. Odd, really, because most ships do not sail in winter, nor will a captain sail without a full cargo or a full complement of passengers. Usually, both."

"There was a certain…inducement," Edgar said dryly.

"Of course. Silver imperials, a lot of them." Halvar nodded sagely. "But Girard had his own reasons for coming south, and for sailing into Manatas Bay. He didn't expect to be murdered by one of his passengers."

"Dame Brigitte was a stupid and greedy woman," Edgar snarled. "She went after Girard when she heard he'd spent the night with a waterfront doxy after leaving her to cope with that miserable cottage. No fire, animals had been nesting in the eaves—it was disgusting! What's worse, he'd given the doxy the money he was supposed to give her!

"She made such a racket going out the Franchen musket-man heard her and followed. She knocked him on the head and took care of Girard, but the half-witted Afrikan saw her, so she had to get rid of *him*. If I hadn't been there...."

"I wondered how she got the Afrikan into the latrine by herself," Halvar commented. "And you were left with the task of finding servants, in a place where you knew no one and could not speak the language.

"I admire you, Heer Edgar. Under the same circumstances, I would have been totally lost.

"But you, Heer Edgar, you followed your nose to the souk, you looked for a place where you might find someone who spoke Erse, and you located the stall of Mendel the Bookseller, in hopes of meeting a Bretain student. And there you were, indeed, fortunate, because you met...him!"

Halvar pointed to Albrecht LaPierre, sitting beside his advocate Benyamin, apparently contemplating the cosmos.

"Master LaPierre, is this so?" Sultan Petrus jolted the alchemist out of his daze. "What do you know if this man Edgar Norris?"

Albrecht blinked at Edgar. "Him? I remember him. He was at the bookseller's. He asked if anyone spoke Erse. I said I did. He said he had been at Oxenbridge, that he had come to Manatas by chance, that he and his companion needed a servant, and that he did not speak the language used here. I did as the Holy Book says, took pity on the stranger. I took him to the back of the Yehudit lodgings at the madrassa. Our cook knew of a respectable widow who needed employment."

"And that explains how you were able to get servants so quickly," Halvar said. "Master LaPierre, when did you invite Heer Edgar to the gathering at the madrassa?"

"Oh, that was a few days later. We met at the bookseller's every day. Master Norris wanted to learn Arabi as quickly as possible, although it is not easy for one used to Erse to master such a different tongue. I found a small book, of a sort given to children learning to read and write, for him to study."

"Very thoughtful," Halvar said. He turned back to Edgar. "Once again, I must admire your determination, Heer Edgar. When I was in a similar situation, in Al-Andalus, I struggled with the language. Of course, I have never mastered the art of reading, whether the letters are Arabi or Ogham.

"So, you were preparing yourself to remain in Manatas until spring. Only something changed. What? Was it Milord Henry? He was getting restless, not willing to stay put in the cottage?"

Edgar grimace. "I should have known better than to get mixed up with his sort! A ruffian, a boor, whether his father was a milord or not. He claimed to be descended from barons, but his mother was simply a woman in the household, and he had been sent as a foot soldier when the Earl of Derby called for men. At least, that was the tale he told me on the ship to Nova Mundum, and I had no reason to doubt him."

"That was when you two met?" Halvar asked. "And then he told you about the legacy, and you, um, assisted him with the document?"

Edgar smirked. "A simple matter of adjusting a few letters on the deed. Only, the idiot steering the ship got caught in some current, and the next thing we knew, the ship was going north instead of south, and we landed thousands of miles from where we wanted to be, in Kibbick, of all places! What's worse, Henry was smitten by Cupid's dart when he saw that Franchen woman and had to buy her!"

"Aha!" Sultan Petrus finally found one fact he could verify. "That was the shameless creature who came with her hair uncovered. Milady Summersby."

"Charlotte." Edgar spat out the name as if to rid himself of something vile. "And her so-called maid. If ever I saw an old bawd, that was one! Nothing I said could make him change his mind. He had to have her. And once he did, he realized what a bad bargain he had made. But by then, we were at sea, and it was too late.

"I thought the Redeemer had heard my prayers when the ship foundered and that woman was stranded across the bay; but no, she had to come back, and demanded that I open the trunk that remained in the cottage, in hopes that some of her dresses had been saved."

"But before Charlotte returned, there was still Henry," Halvar reminded Edgar. "Henry, getting more and more unhappy about the cottage. Devallon told me of Milord Summersby's tantrums, how he was moping about being stuck in the cottage with the gruesome images of Kristos being tortured. You brought him to the party at the madrassa, but he wasn't at home there the way you were, Heer Edgar.

"However, he heard about the celebration in Green Village. He wanted a horse to get there, so you provided one by hiring Farmer Bronk's Arab steed. You went to the Gardens of Paradise, you went to the Holy Meal at the fratery, and on the way back to Manatas Town you saw the mountain cat.

"And that, Heer Edgar, was where the Three Old Women betrayed you. Milord Henry insisted on arranging a hunting party. What's worse, he insisted on leading it…and all your plans were destroyed when, as Kismet or the Three

Old Women would have it, there was one person in Manatas who could identify the man who called himself Henry Summersby as someone else. Not only that, but he was a Purist, one whose word is usually accepted as truth, because they are forbidden by their religion to tell a falsehood. And you silenced him, before he could reveal Milord's secret."

Edgar had listened to this recitation with a bland smile.

"I admit I was in Green village. I was seen there, to be sure. But you have no proof that it was I who stabbed this man in the back."

"You just provided it, by your own words!" Halvar jabbed an accusing finger at the prisoner. "I did not say how Ned Cooper was killed. And, I might add, the fraters who examined the body have matched the wounds to the one in my own back, and declared on oath they were made by the same knife. "

"And I saw him do that!" Selim jumped out of her seat. "He came around behind the capitán, he was ready to stab him, I grabbed his arm—"

"And fought him!" Flores broke in. "That man is stronger than he looks. He fought back, and the girl's turban came undone…"

Selim sank back into her chair.

"And all this happened while Capitán Don Alvaro was fighting Milord Henry." Donal reminded the sultan of the original argument.

"So, Don Alvaro, why *did* you fight this Milord Henry Summersby?" Sultan Petrus demanded.

"I was trying to arrest him, to bring him to the Rabat to answer the charge that he murdered Guardsman Zoltan in the souk two days ago."

"And what proof have you of this?"

"No direct proof," Halvar admitted. "But I saw a large man in the souk slinking away just after we found the guardsman. If I had brought him back here, I could have found other

196

witnesses—the students who were gathered in Mendel the Bookseller's stall across from the alley where Zoltan had tried to accost the Yehudit girl, Raquel. And I could have had confirmation from our own medico, Dr. Moise, concerning the knife left in the fatal wound, matching it to others in Summersby's cottage. As for the charge against the Yehudit woman Raquel, that is totally baseless."

"I identified the knife used in Zoltan's murder as belonging to the Yehudit woman who cooks for the cottage." Dr. Moise spoke up suddenly. "It seems she marks her utensils with a particular sign so she does not mix those used in the preparation of meat dishes with those used for dairy dishes, as is the custom of the Yehudit. She recognized her sign on the knife I removed from Guardsman Zoltan's back."

"And this nonsense about the Yehudit girl and her scissors?" Sultan Petrus frowned over a written document.

"Is exactly that. Those scissors could not penetrate the layers of a guardsman's coat, let alone stab through the flesh." Dr. Moise stepped back, with a smug nod at Halvar.

"So, Henry killed Zoltan. Why?" Sultan Petrus shot out at Halvar.

"For the same reason Edgar killed Ned Cooper. Because Zoltan also knew Henry was not who he claimed to be," Halvar said. "Which brings us back to Captain Girard.

"As Guardsman Fergus told us, the captain was very merry on the night he landed. He had a jolly dinner, he told stories about his passengers. After he died, Zoltan blamed me for the death of his, um, friend, Long Liz Lanergan. He also blamed the folk at the cottage, and wanted to get as much out of them as he could before turning them over to Manatas justice. So, he went to Milord Henry and demanded money from him. Is that not right, Guardsman Fergus?"

The guardsman's eyes filled with tears. "He...He said we would make them pay twice, first in silver, then in blood, for Long Liz. I told him to tell you what he knew, Capitán! I begged him, but he wouldn't listen!"

"And Henry paid you off in bad coin," Halvar said. "And followed you to the souk while Edgar was away, dealing with Milady's dress difficulties. I'm surprised that he did. Usually, Edgar was the one to take care of Henry's messes."

"He should have waited," Edgar broke in. "I could have arranged things. But, no, he had to prove he was the master and I the servant."

"So, he took one of the cook's knives and went to the souk, probably hoping to get Zoltan while he was relieving himself, just as Dame Brigitte had done to Girard.

"In a way, Zoltan made it easy. He was already known for teasing the women in the souk. Henry could assume one or another of the outraged Yehudit or Islim men would be blamed for Zoltan's death. It almost worked, too...except that I saw someone who looked like him.

"And then he tried to run away, a sure sign of his guilt. To do it, he committed one crime that above all others would condemn him—he stole Farmer Bronk's horse, Sindar."

"What a chase!" Flores exclaimed. "That horse is a marvel!"

"It didn't stop until it reached the bridgehead," Halvar said. "And there, Excellent Sultan, I tried to take Milord Henry alive. He would not come...and the rest you know."

"And while they were settling the matter, that man, Edgar, crept up behind Capitán Don Alvaro with his big dagger!" Selim burst out again.

"Got him red-handed," Donal said smugly. "I gave the blade to Frater Leonidas and Frater Iosip, and they matched it to the cut in Ned Cooper's back."

Sultan Petrus turned his attention to Edgar, whose bland smile faded to a blank stare.

"Have you anything to say, Edgar Norris? Gambler Baltasar, does this prisoner understand what has been said?"

"I understand," Edgar said. "Whether I killed the artisan is not for me to say. I fully admit that I attempted to stop this man, this Dane, from attacking my friend Henry Summersby. It was a momentary impulse. I regret it heartily."

"You'll regret it at the end of a rope!" Donal snarled.

Sultan Petrus raised his hand. "Silence!" He directed his attention to Benyamin and Albrecht. "Benyamin ibn Mendel, your client is accused of killing Master Kupernik. You say he did not mean to do it, that he only wished to make him ill."

"So he says." Benyamin glanced at Albrecht, who was back in his daydreams. "Capitán Danske has reason to believe that Master LaPierre wanted the man dead, and made preparations to ensure that he would not get help if the cake made him so ill he would die. It could be argued either way —that the death was not murder, but manslaughter."

Sultan Petrus tugged at his beard. Then he announced, "Both these men are accused of crimes that demand the penalty of hanging. However, we do not have a proper gibbet for such an execution. They will be kept prisoner until one is constructed."

"And where will you hold them?" Rav Nahum spoke for the first time. "The cells of the Rabat are cold stone; they will freeze to death before you can hang them. This is against the laws of both Yehudit and sharia, that speak to mercy for the imprisoned."

"True," Sultan Petrus said. "But there is an empty isolated cabin in the woods north of the tannery, is there not?"

"My cabin?" Albrecht's eyes opened. "My experiments!"

"There is wood there? A latrine? Food can be brought to the prisoners?" Sultan Petrus's smile grew broader. "It is my decision that the two prisoners, Albrecht LaPierre and Edgar Norris, shall be taken to this cabin. There, they will be guarded by the Mahak watchmen and the Green Village constables, in turns.

"They can be let out to use the latrine, there is a stove with wood, food can be brought to them. They will be isolated from the rest of Manatas, so they can harm no one else. They will be confined there until the spring, when a proper gibbet will be constructed, and they will face the calif of Al-Andalus-In-Exile, to receive their proper justified punishment. That is all. Take them away!"

"To the cabin?" Rav Nahum protested. "It's well after nightfall, the cold is worse than in daylight."

"And my men have had a long walk," Halvar said, before Flores and Donal could protest. "They need food and rest and a warm place to lay their heads before they go back to Green Village."

The sultan nodded. "Quite right, Capitán. Your care for your men does you credit." He stroked his beard. "Put the prisoners into one of the storerooms near the barracks kitchen. It's barred against thieves; it's close enough to the ovens they will not freeze to death before they can be properly hanged. They can be guarded so they don't harm themselves or anyone else."

Halvar watched as the sultan's personal guards marched forward and grabbed Albrecht and Edgar to hauled them to their temporary place of confinement.

"And that settles that!" Sultan Petrus clapped his hands to silence the buzz of chatter that followed the prisoners' removal. "This divan is ended. I thank you all for bearing witness to the justice of Al-Andalus and Manatas. You may all return to your own homes, with the blessings of Ilha at the year's turning."

Halvar stepped aside so that Benyamin could follow his client to the cell assigned to him. Eva Hakim hovered over Selim as she sorted her papers and put her pen and ink-jar back into her pen-case.

"Capitán Don Alvaro!" Sultan Petrus voice stopped Halvar before he could turn to leave. "Don Alvaro, if you please, I wish you to remain here, with my...my child Selim. I want to know how you came to your conclusions. And there are a few other matters we must discuss. Eva Hakim, will you be so kind as to visit my wife before you leave?"

Eva Hakim could only nod graciously before she started for the stairs to the upper chamber.

"As you will, Excellent Sultan."

Tenente Flores closed the doors after Dr. Moise and Benyamin followed the prisoners out of the room. Halvar was left alone with the wily old warrior and his daughter.

His thoughts churned wildly. He wished he had the gift of learning, so he could read for himself what the calif had said in those letters on Selim's table. Was he to be turned out, like the old dog in the story whose master set him loose because he would not hunt anymore? Surely not! Had the Emir of the Scavengers managed to unseat him, sensing a rival for power? Had he offended the sultan by exposing his precious daughter to danger?

"Now we can have mokka, and you can tell me how you did it," Sultan Petrus chortled happily as two Afrikans arrived with his favorite beverage. "Sit, sit! You've had a hard time, Capitán! A stool for our brave Dane!"

Halvar sagged onto the seat and took a deep breath, then winced as the scabs from healing cuts and bruises pulled his skin. He only hoped what he had to say would not anger the sultan.

Chapter 26

"MOVE MY CHAIR CLOSER TO THE STOVE," SULTAN
Petrus ordered.

The two Afrikans hauled the massive chair closer to the
source of heat, and added wood to the cheerful blaze within.

"Selim, you sit by me. Don Alvaro, you must sit also.
I've been hearing tales of your ferocious fighting skills. I know
you Danes are the most fierce of fighters, but a pike-man?
Not so much."

Halvar winced as he lowered himself onto the stool offered by one of the Afrikans.

"I didn't mean to lose my temper. I truly wanted to take
Henry Summersby alive, to stand his trial before you."

Two more Afrikans arrived with a tray bearing the sultan's brass mokka-pot and cups. One poured out a serving
for his master, who sipped and sighed blissfully.

"Wonderful stuff, mokka. Delivering justice is thirsty work, Capitán. Now, explain to me how you found out about those two Bretains. The Franchen, that I can understand—he had the muskets. Did he say how he got them in that journal of his?"

Selim shrugged. "He didn't say, only refers to 'loud cargo', which I assume is the muskets. He also refers to 'living cargo', which might be the women he was bringing from Franchenland to Kibbick."

"Or it might be Afrikans, captured and carried by force to work in the large farms in Afrikan territories, growing kutton and tabac," Halvar said. "It takes many hands to grow those crops and prepare them for the feria."

"It takes a lot of land, too," Sultan Petrus mused. "According to what Roderigo says, the Local tribes are not happy with the Afrikan incursions into their territories beyond the mountains. What's worse, it's not just Afrikans but Oropans who are pushing into those lands, and they are bringing their usual plagues with them.

"Worse, they've brought in swine, and the creatures are running wild, eating the Local's crops and anything else they can find. The deer are starving, and so are the Locals who depend on them for meat."

Halvar shivered, partly from his wounds, partly at the thought of the warfare unleashed by Oropan greed for land and position.

"Between the Afrikans and the Oropans, Girard knew he had a market for his muskets," he said. "All he needed was the ammunition—the gunpowder and bullets. Bullets are easy to make, gunpowder isn't. You need a skillful alchemist, one who knows exactly what he's doing."

"Like the ones in Bos-Town, trained at Oxenbridge," Sultan Petrus agreed. "So, he goes to Bos-Town…"

"But the one who sells it has gone to Manatas for the feria," Selim said. "That was Andrew MacAlan?"

"It was," Halvar said. "So, Girard sails south, with the passengers as an excuse for the voyage. It was a mistake slighting his discarded mistress for a waterfront doxy, but I suspect he'd had more than enough of Dame Brigitte and Milady Charlotte and their whims and megrims. He wanted a nice, jolly gal to have a romp with, and that was Long Liz. And it was too good of a joke for Devallon to keep to himself, and he shared it with Milord Henry."

"And Dame Brigitte heard and went after him. She must have been mad," Selim said. "Didn't she think beyond her own anger and greed? How did she think she was going to get off Manatas Island without a skillful captain like Girard to guide the ship out of the harbor?"

Halvar tugged at his mustache. "It's possible that Edgar convinced her *he* could navigate the ship, as long as they had an able steersman. After all, he'd been hovering over Girard while he took his measurements and plotted their course from Kibbick to Bos-Town. I fancy he did the same with the captain of the ship that carried them from Bretain to Kibbick."

"Navigation is a skill that takes years to learn," Sultan Petrus pronounced. "This Edgar Norris—is he so confident of his own powers he thought he could get from Manatas to Bella Mara by himself?"

"He's got a high opinion of his own talents, to be sure. But anyone with a knowledge of mathematics and astronomy can learn to steer by the stars," Halvar reminded him. "When I was a lad, I sailed with my father's kinfolk from the Dane-March to Bretain and from there to Scania, and even I could do that much.

"Learning the ins and outs of the currents, when the tides run and where the hidden reefs are—that's something else. There are charts and maps, but they aren't always correct, and in any case, I couldn't read the letters on them. That was when my father decided I was not cut out to be a seaman." He grinned wryly. "No doubt it made it easier for him to let me go when our thane needed men to fill the ranks of the Danish Free Company."

"But Michel Primero didn't know the currents in Manatas Bay, and the ship foundered, leaving the crew on the Long Island, and the cargo to be plundered. The Algonkin found the muskets, and that was the end of Girard's scheme to sell them to whoever would buy them." Sultan Petrus smiled grimly. "As to the Bretain Andrew MacAlan, how did you light on him as the one who killed the messenger?"

"That was plain enough," Halvar said. " Once I determined that the body of the messenger had been moved, it was a simple matter of asking the right questions and following where they led. Andrew MacAlan owned a pistoia, and had dealings with Samuel Igbo. I wanted to get a full confession from him when I went after him. It was the mountain cat that caused the man's death. I didn't want him dead, Excellent Sultan."

"Don't worry yourself about it," Sultan Petrus assured him. "He was a murderer twice over, and got the punishment he deserved.

"It's this other business, this Milord Henry and the killings in the souk and Green Village, that has me baffled. Why pick on the Bretains, Summersby and Norris? What made you suspect Milord Henry Summersby wasn't what he he claimed to be?"

"It was Constable Donal who gave me the first clue," Halvar admitted. "When we met Henry for the first time, it was Donal who told me he didn't speak Erse with the same accent as a true milord, that he sounded more like a countryman from the north of Bretain. Oh, he acted like a milord —giving orders, throwing money about, but when Edgar turned up, I could sense something not quite right. Devallon thought the two might be, um…"

"Lovers? Like Leon and his Lccal friend?" Selim suggested.

"But that wasn't quite it," Halvar said hurriedly. "More like equals than master and man. Devallon told me they had what he called a 'flaming row' on the day of the two murders. You don't have a row with a servant. You tell him what to do, and he does it, or he gets beaten, or thrown out."

"Devallon. The Franchen musket-man?" Sultan Petrus frowned over his mokka. "Where does he fit into this house of assassins and thieves?"

"Assassins and thieves, to be sure, but Devallon wasn't of their kidney. He was only there because of Charlotte," Halvar said. "I don't know him all that well, but this I can tell you—he's the most honest of that lot. There's no guile in him. He doesn't even know how to dissemble. He is what he is—a mercenary, a fighter. Years ago, he gave his word to look after Charlotte, and that's what he does. When it came to it, he chose her safety over Henry's."

"Even though it was Henry who was paying him?" Selim considered this. "That's a lot like love, isn't it?"

"I couldn't say," Halvar demurred. "To be honest, I don't think Charlotte deserves such loyalty, but she's got it."

Selim giggled. "I wouldn't like to be one of the servants at Bronk's farm this winter. They'll have their hands full, with Milady Charlotte's demands."

Halvar echoed her grin. "If the two survive the winter, it will be one of Mother Mara's great miracles."

Sultan Petrus sipped more mokka. "So much for Milady Charlotte. When you suspected Henry Summersby of being something other than what he said he was, why didn't you charge him with fraud?"

"He hadn't done anything wrong," Halvar pointed out. "You can't arrest a man, a stranger in Manatas, simply for saying he's a milord when he's not. According to the trapper, MacFergus, when someone comes to Nova Mundum, they are accepted for whatever they say they are.

"Of course, if he'd tried to get money from someone, put in a claim for land that wasn't his, that would be different, but he didn't do that, not in Manatas. His land claim was for Terra Mara.

"True, he came at me with a sword when I tried to stop him from leaving, but that was understandable, given that he hadn't wanted to come here at all. Aside from that, he hadn't broken any of the laws of Al-Andalus or Manatas Town.

"Then came the whole business with the dead messenger and the poisoned professor, and that distracted me from the doings at the cottage."

"I don't understand how the Kupernik murder comes into this Summersby business at all," Sultan Petrus complained.

"It doesn't," Halvar said. "Albrecht didn't know anything about Henry other than what Edgar Norris told him. The two met at the bookseller's stall in the souk, where they struck up a friendship, which led to Edgar attending the gathering at the madrassa.

"It was Edgar who wanted to associate with the scholars, not Henry. I could tell Henry was bored—he hated the chatter in languages he didn't understand, he tried the food and didn't like that, either. If anyone was at home with the learned men, it was Edgar...not what you'd expect of a servant, even one from Oxenbridge.

"Henry was far more easy at the Gardens of Paradise later that night, eating Bretain food, drinking the kind of wine that sells to the Bretains. He played the milord very well, throwing silver around, joking with the serving-girls, joining in the songs. He even attended the Watch-Night Holy Meal. If it wasn't for his horsemanship, you'd have thought him a true Bretain milord."

"His horsemanship?" Sultan Petrus echoed. "What was wrong with it?"

Halvar grinned at the memory of Henry Summersby's antics on the Arab Barb.

"He couldn't control the horse. It was a stallion, who had been on a battlefield. Farmer Brork called him Sirdar, and gave him commands in Arabi, a language Milord Henry didn't know and didn't want to learn. Edgar gave in to Henry's insistence on getting mounted, and that was their first mistake."

"How so?" Selim asked, caught up in the narrative.

"One thing I've learned about the Bretain milords, first when I went to Bretain then when I met some who signed onto free companies in Oropa. Even when they were students at the madrassa in Corduva, every one of them was put into the saddle from a young age. They even breed little horses for the children to ride. The only ones more horsemad are the wild men of Tartary who rode out to destroy Baghdad. Yet this fellow, who was supposed to be a Bretain milord, could not control his horse? Impossible!"

"And still you did nothing?" Sultan Petrus frowned.

"He still had *done* nothing," Halvar reminded the sultan. "But he'd aroused the suspicions of Guardsman Zoltan, who had heard enough from the late Captain Girard to think he might be able to get money from the false milord. Fergus tried to dissuade him, but Zoltan was headstrong, went to the cottage, and demanded money to keep quiet about Henry's deception. I don't know why Henry gave them the bad coin…perhaps he'd gone through all the silver from Charlotte's dowry."

"Quite possible," Selim said. "There were only so many silver imperials, and most of them went to pay Girard for their passage. And don't forget the coins Dame Brigitte sewed into her cloak, the ones that weighed her down and led to her drowning in the bay. He must have been running low on silver coins."

"So, he had to find more, and he found them in Edgar's satchel. And he used the false pennies he found in Edgar's satchel to pay off Zoltan and Fergus." Sultan Petrus finished the story.

"Which explains why they had that 'flaming row' that drove Devallon out of the cottage," Halvar said. "Edgar got back from the souk to find out his secret funds had been taken to pay off the very people who would know them for what they were. I doubt that Henry even knew they were false coins. He wasn't the sort to look closely at money;, he just spent it."

Sultan Petrus frowned. "What possessed the man to bring a satchel of false Bretain pennies to Nova Mundum?"

"I suspect Edgar's scheme was to use those coins somewhere in Nova Mundum, probably in Terra Mara, where he would set himself up as a scholar fresh from Oxenbridge," Halvar said. "Edgar and Henry each had his own plot, and neither one told the other all they were planning. Rogues falling in together, and just as easily falling out."

"I still don't understand what brought those two together in the first place," Selim said. "They're so unlike!"

"They needed each others' talents," Halvar said. "Henry needed to make a show to prove that he was truly Milord Henry Summersby. A Bretain milord travels with a servant. Edgar needed someone to protect him from danger on the road, someone large enough and loud enough to deter any other brigands.

"And it probably would have worked well, except the Three Old Women decided to have their fun and sent them here, to Manatas. They were stuck in a tiny cottage looking at horrid images of Kristo holy men being tortured. Edgar escaped on the pretense of shopping for their food, finding servants. Henry stayed indoors until he got bored, and that was when things went very wrong.

"So, Zoltan came to Henry, at a time when Edgar was away from the cottage, and demanded money for his silence. Henry gave him the false coin, but didn't tell Edgar.

"Then, on Watch-Night at Green Village, Ned Cooper saw Henry for the first time. The day after Nativity, when Henry insisted on going a-hunting for the mountain cat, Ned was certain the man he'd seen was the one he'd known back in Bretain...and he wasn't a milord then, oh, no! He was a poacher who had been sentenced to serve as one of milord's private guardsmen. And being a Purist, Ned had to tell the truth to anyone who'd listen."

"And one of those who heard him was Edgar Norris," Selim said smugly. "But what difference would it make to Edgar if Henry were exposed as a fraud?"

"If Henry went down, he'd take Edgar with him," Halvar replied. "And remember, there was a legacy involved, and a forged document. Edgar had to silence Ned as quickly as possible, and he did it just before sundown, with one thrust of his dagger. It was audacious, but he thought he might get away with it.

"And well he might have, except the frater doing the examination of the body was Leon di Vicenza. In most places, the death of so lowly a person as a cooper, a mere artisan who made barrels, would not be carefully investigated by whoever was in charge of such things, because such is the way of the world. But I am not one to ignore a suspicious death just because the victim is a craftsman. What's more, I was looking for anyone who might be in league with Andrew MacAlan and his gunpowder plot.

"So, I insisted on questioning everyone who had anything to do with Ned Cooper, and the one thing that stuck in my mind was that he was seen in company with Edgar Norris. And that, Excellent Sultan, struck me as odd. What business had a cooper with milord's servant? And a very wise man once told me if something strikes you as odd, follow it and see where it leads."

"But you just said Edgar and Henry had no connection with the gunpowder plot at all!" Sultan Petrus burst out.

"They didn't," Halvar said. "But Edgar gave in to a moment of panic and killed Ned. Then he had to get back to the cottage, and Henry, just as Milady Charlotte made her appearance. I would have liked to be the mouse in the corner when she came home, looking for whatever hadn't been taken to the ship!"

Selim giggled. Sultan Petrus guffawed. Halvar grinned, then turned serious again.

"Devallon told me some of what happened. Charlotte was taken in by Fru Marta and her milkmaid daughter. Edgar must have had his hands full, what with Henry being half-shot and Charlotte in a high temper. I don't know when Edgar found out what Henry had done—probably not until he went to fetch some coins to pay for Charlotte's new clothes..."

"And that's when he found out Henry had been filching from his private store of false coins," Sultan Petrus guessed.

"Which explains the row," Halvar agreed. "Henry and Edgar knew the guardsman had to be silenced, and the coin retrieved before it got into the market. Edgar went to the tailor's shop. This time, Henry would do the killing himself.

"I suspect it was Edgar took the knife from the kitchen. Henry followed Zoltan and Fergus to the souk. It's my guess his original intent was to simply knife Zoltan in one of the alleys, and let the Town Guards find the body and accuse either the Yehudit or the Scavengers of the crime. In most towns, that would be that...but not here in Manatas."

"Because we have a capitán who looks beyond the obvious." Selim beamed at Halvar. "You saw right away it was no ordinary murder. You wouldn't accept Tenente Flores's accusations; you insisted on bringing Zoltan's body to Dr. Moise for further examination."

"Once Fergus confessed Zoltan's blackmail scheme, I began to put things together, but I still didn't understand," Halvar admitted. "I was too caught up in the gunpowder plot to see what was under my nose." He tugged on his mustache. "Then, when I saw that Henry and Edgar planned once again to escape, I had to follow them.

211

"The rest you know, Excellent Sultan. I am deeply sorry for my actions. I should not have gone after them without a written warrant, but the madness must have touched me, too."

"A man comes after you with a halberd, and you defend yourself. This is nothing to apologize for." Sultan Petrus waved his hand.

"I didn't really understand how it all fit together until I was half in, half out of a dream, with one of Frater Iosip's potions fuzzing my brain. Then I remembered something I'd seen in Italia—a man trying to piece together one of the tiled floors left by the Old Roumi.

"He couldn't make the picture work, and then he realized there were two images there, not one. That's when I thought to myself, 'There isn't one scheme here, there are two…maybe three, if you count that fool Albrecht LaPierre and his nguba bean cake.'"

"And what does that have to do with Edgar Norris? Or Andrew MacAlan?" Sultan Petrus frowned, struggling to follow Halvar's reasoning.

"Another distraction. Albrecht was connected with Edgar, to be sure. He was Edgar's source of information in the souk, helped him find a Yehudit cook, invited him to the gathering at the madrassa. As far as Albrecht knew, Edgar Norris was a congenial soul—another scholar, down on his luck, forced to become a servant to a rich boor. He was willing to accept Andrew's son Owen as a student if Andrew would back his experiments with gunpowder.

"But his personal spite led him to feed that cake to Master Kupernik, and for that, Excellent Sultan, I agree—he must hang."

"And so he shall," Sultan Petrus chortled. "In the spring. In the meantime, he can play with his rocks and coals all he pleases. He has a companion to assist him. The two of them will be quite safe in the cabin."

Halvar frowned. "I wonder about that. Two murderers together? Is that wise, Excellent Sultan?"

"As you said, Edgar doesn't usually resort to violence, and Albrecht won't be able to poison anyone else with nguba beans. It may be that they actually manage to make gunpowder, which will be very useful for us. If they don't make gunpowder, no loss to anyone. We can build a gibbet when the weather clears, and they will hang on it when Don Felipe returns for the Spring Feria."

"*If* he returns," Halvar muttered.

"Which reminds me." Sultan Petrus ignored Halvar's interjection. "It has come to my attention that your hire is from one Year's Turning to the next, and so, you will be free of your hire to Calif Don Felipe as of midnight tonight. Is that not so?"

"It is." Halvar felt a shiver of chill, in spite of the heat of the stove. *Here it comes*, he thought. *I'm to be let go, turned out to fend for myself.*

"In that case, you will be able to take another hire," Sultan Petrus went on. "I have an offer for you, if you will take it."

"To yourself, Excellent Sultan?"

"Not to me personally. To the Town of Manatas. You will continue to serve as Capitán of the Town Guards, but you would answer to me as the head of the Manatas Town Council instead of directly to the calif, may he rule long. Your pay would be the same—one gold real or its equivalent, twenty silver dinars."

Sultan Petrus clapped his hands. One of the Afrikan servants produced a leather sack that sagged with coins.

"Good silver, I assure you. Selim tells me you owe a sum to the host at the Mermaid Taberna. You must pay your bills. Capitán, as the Holy Books tell us."

Halvar eyed the sack. "And if I don't take this offer?"

"Then you will have no position here in Manatas," Sultan Petrus said. "You will simply be one among many who

213

have washed up on this island without friends or family, seeking their fortune in Nova Mundum.

"It may be that your connections in Green Village will be enough to support you through the winter. You may even find employment with some of the Afrikan or Bretain merchants who come for the Spring Feria. Or, perhaps, you might join one of the trading parties that go into the mountains to deal with the Locals beyond the Great River. There are many possibilities in Nova Mundum for an enterprising fellow with fighting talents."

Halvar smiled wryly. "May I have some time to consider this generous offer? My hire isn't over until midnight."

Sultan Petrus nodded sagely. "Do as you think best, Don Alvaro, but don't be too long in making your decision."

Halvar got to his fee, salaamed, and backed out of the room. His head ached—his very bones ached—and he was caught up in his own thoughts.

Ever since he was a boy he had known nothing but orders. He obeyed them, no matter who give them. Then he'd been put on the transport to Al-Andalus, where he'd been healed by the Sisters of Fatima and turned loose to find his own way. Even then, he'd managed to find someone to take him in, someone whose orders he could follow.

For seven years, Halvar Danske had been the Hireling of the Calif of Al-Andalus.

Suddenly, he could be his own master. Halvar the Hireling...or not?

Chapter 27

HALVAR STUMBLED DOWN THE STAIRS TO THE tower door. He propped himself against the doorjamb, breathing the icy air, a relief after the sultan's overheated chamber.

"Quite a show," Dani Glick said from the shelter of the doorway, where she had waited wrapped in fur against the cold. "I applaud Sultan Petrus for his performance."

Halvar regarded her sourly. "A show, you say?"

"Of course it was. You were trotted out, the hero of the hour, fresh from the field of battle. Master Norris was the villain, deserving of punishment. You didn't have to recite that rigmarole before the entire Town Council; we could have read it in the *Gazetta*."

"Only if you can read," Halvar amended. He checked the courtyard. "Shouldn't you be on your way back to Green Village, Fru Glick? It's well after dark, and cold as Niflheim."

"The seamstress Raquel and her brother Asher the Butcher have offered me house-room for the night," Dani said.

"Cormack is staying with some friends in the Danic sector, and Simon has a standing invitation with some literary scholars at the madrassa. But I thank you for your concern, Capitán. Unless you were considering making me another offer?"

Halvar felt his face burning red. "I thought you might like to join me at the Mermaid Taberna. For dinner," he added hurriedly. "And to come to some kind of arrangement with Hannes Zilberstam regarding Willem of Cos. There seems to be a rivalry between the two establishments—the Gardens of Paradise and the Mermaid Taberna, and Willem is milking both of you, raising his fee accordingly."

"That is no concern of yours!" Dani snapped. "I swore when I came to Manatas I would never spend a night in that place, ever!"

A step on the stairs behind them ended the discussion.

"Don Alvaro!" Selim interrupted. "Are you all right? Do you need a donkey cart to take you to the waterfront?"

Halvar pulled his coat closer and fastened the frogs across his chest.

"I'll do well enough. You should go back to your own quarters."

Selim grimaced. "I'm not welcome at the Rabat anymore. I'm supposed to stay at the House of the Green Crescent, with Eva Hakim and the Sisters of Fatima."

The tall figure of the nizim loomed behind the girl.

"It is far more fitting that you reside with us. Your mother founded our house. You can stop your foolish masquerade and take your proper place as her heiress."

"But I don't want to be a Sister of Fatima!" Selim burst out. "I hate tending the sick and the poor."

Halvar tugged at his mustache. "If I take your father's offer and continue as Capitán of Manatas Town Guards, I'll need an official adjutant. Someone I can trust to read reports and write letters. Someone who will tell me what I need to know, not what they think I want to hear."

Dani Glick and Eva Hakim both looked Selim over and nodded to each other.

"Have you decided to accept the generous offer of the Manatas Town Council?" Eva Hakim said. "I commend you, Capitán. We need an honest man like yourself guarding Manatas."

"This woman and I disagree on many things," Dani pronounced. "But on this we do not. Take the job, Halvar Danske. Manatas needs you."

Halvar gazed around the courtyard for male support. Flores and Donal had likely found shelter in the barracks. He assumed Firebrand had gone to the Mahak longhouse village.

"Sultan Petrus suggested some alternatives if I decided not to continue as capitán. They sounded...tempting."

"Exploring? Trapping? Trading? There's a lot of country beyond the river," Dani admitted. "I know, I've been there. You could see it for yourself if you choose to leave Manatas."

"And wouldn't that please Emir Achmet!" Selim sniffed. "And Mullah Abadul, who is against anyone who isn't Islim. He's all too ready to promote Tenente Flores just because he's Islim and not Kristo."

"Mullah Abadul is, perhaps, somewhat narrow in his views," Eva Hakim agreed. "But I cannot like the idea of Emir Achmet turning his Scavengers loose in Manatas Town, as he surely will, if Tenente Flores is in charge."

"And who will catch the murderers, if you don't?" Dani Glick added with a wry smile. "No one else can sniff out a killer like Capitán Halvar Danske! Murderers, assassins, evildoers of all kinds, beware! Do not come to Manatas, for he will surely find you out!"

Halvar sighed heavily. "So many women, and all telling me what to do."

"And don't forget Widow Tekla," Selim added. "She's got all the Afrikan merchants dancing to her tune, and she was

217

very impressed with how quickly you caught the ones who poisoned her husband."

"We're not telling you what to do," Dani said. "You must decide for yourself what is best."

In the back of his mind, Halvar heard the voice of his mentor, Old Sergeant Olaf. Once, the Free Company had come across a Roumi Rite chapel, and some of the rowdier soldiers had taken the silver crux and the cups used for the Holy Meal. Old Sergeant Olaf had kept Halvar from joining them, and Halvar had been spared the brutal treatment Captain Van Zoon meted out to the thieves.

"Think, laddie," the old soldier had said. "Think about what you want, and how much you want it, and what it's worth to you to get it. Then, and only then, go after it.

"Silver and gold are good, but not worth a beating, or a soiled reputation. Honest dealings may not pay as well, but you'll sleep easier."

"Honest dealings," Halvar murmured.

"And when the Franchen come?" Selim's worried voice broke into his thoughts. "You say they will. Who will guard Manatas then?"

"I'm needed," Halvar concluded. "Go up to the sultan, Selim. Tell him I'll take his coins. I'll get them tomorrow, pay my shot at the taberna, sign whatever contract he draws up. But not tonight."

"What are you going to do now?" Selim asked.

"I'm going to obey all my doctors," Halvar said. "I'm going to do what I started out to do three days ago. I'm going to have a good hot meal and a solid night's sleep. And if anyone else gets murdered, don't wake me. A dead body can wait until morning."

Chapter 28

TWO WEEKS PASSED IN RELATIVE QUIET AFTER the upsets of the Holy Days. Halvar signed the contract the sultan laid before him, vowing to serve the Manatas Town Council for one year for the sum of twenty silver dinars, carefully forming the letters of his name in Rune characters.

Selim was named Adjutant to the Capitán; she now wore the long green coat and red tarboosh of the Town Guards over the drab tunic and trousers and green hijab of the Sisters of Fatima. Her promotion had been noted in the *Gazetta*, where she was listed as Selim ibn Petrus—Selim, son of Petrus.

There were two consecutive days of snowfall followed by a week of intense cold. The East Channel was nearly frozen over. Large blocks of ice floated in the Great River. Most of Manatas's population stayed in whatever shelter they could find, only venturing out of doors for food or religious observance, both considered necessities.

Halvar had spent one day at the Mermaid Taberna, reveling in warmth and companionship, before taking up his duties once again. He then sent Tenentes Flores and Donal out to take statements from as many witnesses as they could find in the souk and Green Village to determine whether there was more evidence that Henry Summersby or Edgar Norris was present of the scene of the murders of Ned Cooper and Guardsman Zoltan.

He had personally questioned Stephane Mercier, the student who had led the lion hunt, and gotten a deposition, signed and sealed, that put the false milord in the souk, just as Edgar had been seen in company with Ned Cooper right after the hunt.

"So, there's no question Henry Summersby killed Guardsman Zoltan," Selim stated after reading Stephane's deposition aloud. "You are completely cleared of any charge of murder. You were only doing your duty when you tried to stop him from leaving Manatas and defended yourself."

"I really never meant to kill him," Halvar repeated. "What news of our other fugitives?"

Selim scanned another paper. "This is from your friend Devallon."

"No friend of mine!" Halvar grunted. "What does the musket-man have to say?"

Selim translated from the Franchen. "He's taken residence at the public house run by Farmer Bronk. Milady Charlotte is with him. They have requested sanctuary under the Kristo rules, and since Bronk's is in West Caster, which is Bretain territory, they are out of Manatas control."

"Just as well," Halvar said. "I hope Bronk's wife…Is he married, do you know?"

Selim shrugged. "No idea."

"If he is, his wife will take care of milady. If he's not I suspect Milady Charlotte will find herself a new husband."

"As long as she does it away from Manatas," Selim said with a sniff.

"What else is there?" Halvar eyed the piles of paper on her desk.

"A petition from Emir Achmet offering his services to Capitán Don Alvaro in regulating what he calls 'minor matters of civic organization'."

"Hmph!" Halvar snorted. "In other words, he wants to run Manatas to suit himself, taking a healthy sum from the town treasury for the privilege. If your father wants to fob some of the more tedious duties of guardianship onto that rogue, that's his lookout, but I don't think he's going to do it."

"Emir Achmet's Scavengers are already in charge of cleaning the streets and removing waste," Selim pointed out.

"Not my concern," Halvar repeated. "As long as he keeps his young rascals in check in the souk and takes care of his beggars, Emir Achmet can do as he likes. I won't stop him. But he's not going to run the Town Guards, and I don't answer to him. What else—"

The conference was interrupted by a loud *boom!*

"What was that!" Halvar jumped out of his chair. He grabbed his fur hat and bolted out the door, through the Rabat and across the courtyard, where his guardsmen joined him. They poured onto the Broad Way, staring northward at a plume of black smoke that hung in the distance.

"That's Green Village!" Flores pointed at the smoke.

"Beyond," Halvar said. "I think our alchemist friend just found out why he wasn't allowed to play with gunpowder within Manatas limits."

"You mean….?" Selim gulped.

"Gunpowder is a very dangerous substance," Halvar said slowly. "I don't know how much will be left of that cabin, or the people inside it. At least, the woods are still damp from the snow, so there won't be a fire."

He turned to go indoors.

"Aren't you going to go and investigate it?" Flores asked.

" I doubt there will be much to find. I'll take a look myself in a while, but I leave it to Constable Donal and Tenente Firebrand to pick through the rubble."

"It won't be easy," Flores said. "I've seen what's left when a cannon explodes. Not pretty!"

"Not pretty at all," Halvar agreed "Of course, if I was a very ruthless and clever man, I'd make sure I was outside when that gunpowder blew up. And I'd also have someone nearby who would take me with him when he went north, into Mahak territory, just to get off Manatas Island."

"Edgar Norris is ruthless and clever," Selim shuddered, likely imagining the horror of what lay under the plume of smoke."Do you think he got away from the cabin?"

"I don't know, but one way or another, he's paid for what he's done. How long do you expect he'll survive out there in the wilderness, with or without help?"

"It's in the hands of Ilha," Selim said. "What a mess! And so many ifs. If Girard hadn't been such a womanizer, if Mac-Alan hadn't been so insistent on secrecy, if Edgar and Henry hadn't been so eager to silence Ned and Zoltan…"

"Don't try to explain the workings of Kismet and the Three Old Women. What is, is, and that's the way of the world, as Old Sergeant Olaf used to say."

"So…what do we do now?" Tenente Flores asked.

Halvar tugged at his mustache, and sighed.

"We go for a stroll along the Broad Way and hear what the people say about the explosion. And then we go and look at what's left of the cabin. Come along, Adjutant Selim, Tenente Flores. We have work to do!"

End….or beginning?

GLOSSARY

AL-ANDALUS	Spain
AL-LARGATO	Alligator
ALGONKIN	Algonquin/Lenape Indians
ARABI	Arabic
ARAGHOUN	Raccoon
BATATAS	Potatoes
BRETAINS	British
CHESU	Jesus
CRUX	Cross
CORDUVA	Cordova
DANE-MARCH	Germany
DANES	Germanic people (includes Denmark)
DANIC	Germanic language (written in Rune characters)
EAST CHANNEL	East River
END-OF-FAST	Eid Al-Fitr; a festival marking the end of ramadan
ERSE	Gaelic language (written in Ogham characters)
ERSE RITE	Celtic Christianity as practiced in Northern Europe

ESCOUASH	Squash
FERIA	Commercial gathering / fair
FESTIVAL OF LIGHTS	Hanukkah
FRANCHEN	The language of Franchenland, written in Roman characters; a native of Franchenland
FRANCHENLAND	France
FRATER	A Kristo cleric
FRATERY	Monastery
GREAT RIVER	Hudson River
HAMMAM	Communal bath
HEMP	Cannabis, Marijuana
HOLY BOOK	The Bible or the Q'ran
HOLY MEAL	Mass
ILHA	Allah
ISLIM	Islam
IVRIT	Hebrew
KICK-THE-BLADDER	Football
KRISTO	Christian
KUTTON	Cotton
KIBBICK	Quebec
LOCALS	Native Americans
MACASSIN	Moccasin
MADRASSA	School / University
MAHAK	Mohawk / Iroquois
MAIZ	Corn

MANATAS	Manhattan Island
MOKKA	Coffee
MOTHER MARA	Virgin Mary
MUNSI	Native trade language
MUSKAT	Mosque
NATIVITY	Christmas
NGUBA	"Goobers," Peanuts
NOVA MUNDUM	"New World," N. America
OLD GRECO	Ancient Greece
OLD ROUMI	Ancient Rome/Romans
OPASSOM	Opossum
OROPA	Europe, excluding Al-Andalus
PARIGI	Paris
PATRI NOSTRI	"Our Father"/Lord's Prayer
PISTOIA	Pistol
POWHATAN	Native name for Terra Mara; Maryland
RABAT	Fortress
RHUM	Rum
ROUMI RITE	Christianity as practiced south of the Alps, centered in Rome
ROUND ISLAND	Staten Island
SALAAMABAD	Philadelphia
SAVANA PORT	Savannah, Ga.
SEKONK	Skunk
SEQUANOK	Pennsylvania

SOUK	Marketplace
STUDY HOUSE	Synagogue
TABAC	Tobacco
"TAKE THE WATER"	Be Baptized
THE PIZZLE	Florida
THE PROPHET	Mohammad
THE REDEEMER	Jesus
THREE OLD WOMEN	Norns, Fates
WAMUS	A deerskin shirt with a fringed yoke and sleeves
WEST CASTER	Westchester/New England
WUMPUM	Wampum; colored shells used as medium of exchange for small purchases
YEHUDIT	Jews/Jewish

About The Author

ROBERTA ROGOW writes historical fiction, although she sometimes twists the history. Her most recent stories take place in a Manhattan Island that was settled by Spanish Moors instead of by Dutch traders: *Last of the Mohegans* meets *Arabian Nights*, with a Spanish Accent. Roberta retired from a 37-year career as a Children's Librarian in 2008. She now lives in New Jersey, and spends her time going to science fiction and mystery conventions when she is not writing mysteries or singing filk (science fiction folk music).

About The Artist

Born in Chicago, WILLIAM NEAGLE graduated from the University of Tennessee with a BFA. Having done work for the US Department of Energy and other companies, his work has been distributed worldwide. He has done book covers for the writing team of Joreid McFate and for his own novel, *Catching the Ghost*. He resides in North Carolina with his wife and two children.